UNDERGROUND

UNDERGROUND

Russell James

LONDON
VICTOR GOLLANCZ LTD
1989

First published in Great Britain 1989
by Victor Gollancz Ltd,
14 Henrietta Street, London WC2E 8QJ

British Library Cataloguing in Publication Data
James, Russell
  Underground
  I. Title
  823'. 914[F]

  ISBN 0-575-04474-8

Typeset at The Spartan Press Ltd,
Lymington, Hants
Printed in Great Britain by St Edmundsbury Press Ltd
Bury St Edmunds, Suffolk

For my wife, Jill

1

You know what I mean? You haven't seen him, but the hairs on your neck tickle against your collar. It makes you shiver. Everything looks normal but it ain't. It's like you got a belly-dancer sucking Turkish delight while she blows hot breath down the back of your neck. You don't mistake that.

Maybe it's an echo to your footsteps. Maybe your subconscious starts to recognize the same pattern of walking: the same guy, in the same shoes, still the same distance behind.

But he's on a loser, because he can't follow you on the underground. Not if you've guessed. Even if you're six foot two, like me, and you stand out in the crowd. You can lose him.

We're at Embankment station. I am leaving the Bakerloo line for the District. But I stay in the train and stand by the door, staring dumbly at the platform. As the doors slide together I jump out and watch from the platform. It's busy. One of the doors hasn't shut, and the guard presses Open and Reclose. A few near-missers on the platform jump in through the gaps. The doors shudder and stay closed and I'm watching who got off. I didn't see him, but like I told you, it's busy. He probably stepped out as I looked the other way. Everyone is moving along the platform while I dawdle by the wall. I'm looking for the guy who doesn't want to go somewhere. I'm looking for the guy who is waiting for me.

In the rush hour it's never easy to pick a guy out. There's people everywhere. I hang about until the next train comes in. I step in and move away from the door. I push through the crowded gangway towards the next door and I pause two paces away. As the doors close I jump outside again. No one follows. There are no false starts on the doors, and the train rumbles away. So he didn't follow me back on. But if he's experienced, he wouldn't. He'd recognize the bluff. He'd be waiting off the

7

platform. Whatever games I get up to, he knows I'm either leaving or I'm changing trains, so he's up there. Waiting.

So I stroll towards the exit and when I get close I spin round and walk the other way. I'm watching all the people. I haven't seen him yet. He is not on this platform. Not any more.

But I can't hang around here.

I slip up the stairs like I was any normal passenger. I take a left and a right, and I ride the up escalator. At the next level I turn right like anyone would and slouch into the grimy concourse. There are six different exits because Embankment is where three lines meet.

As I cross the concourse I turn left and nip anti-clockwise round a pillar and head back the way I came. I ignore the Northern going south, and carry on through to where the stairs lead to the District line heading east. Now I increase my pace. Up the hard steps, sharp right, and I'm on the platform. There's fresh air. I nip ten paces to my right and disappear up the gloomy stairs marked "No Exit".

I'm alone on these stairs and it's what I thought: a bridge across the District, taking you from eastbound to west. West is where I was going. East is where I come from.

When I'm across the bridge I don't spill straight out onto the platform. This is a nice empty pedestrian bridge, semi-retired, as snug a place as you could hope for to lean against a wall till your train comes in.

I hear one draw up and open its doors. I was gonna hang on, chancing my luck for ten seconds, but after five I lurch forward, run down the last few steps, dive across the platform and into the train. Not bad timing. I slam through the doors as they're closing, and turn to watch the platform through the glass.

A woman about twenty-five has dashed onto the platform from an exit, and she stops at the shut door. She's bulky and she isn't pleased. She's as feminine as a bulldog. She's looking for me through the glass and our eyes meet for less than a second. She carries on looking round her — looking anywhere except at me. As the train pulls away I hope to give her a smile. But she's glancing around as if she's lost interest. I see she's wearing Adidas trainers on her feet. She'll be fit. But she's lost me.

When I leave the train at Victoria I'm up the stairs fast and into the main station entrance. I stop by a bunch of phones on stalks and I pick up a receiver. I've got to watch the stairs for another five minutes to see if she guessed where I was going and caught the next train. When someone tails you, you can't be sure how much they know.

But I don't see her in ten minutes and I feel conspicuous standing here clutching the phone, and my feet are cold. So I wander off into the main rail station and start to look for Victor.

In my time I must have read in about twenty-five books that to meet someone at a rail station you stand under the clock. Have you tried it? First you got to find it. Then you discover it's digital and stuck on a big board announcing train departures. If you wait under that, you got a whole crowd of bored commuters standing watching you, waiting for their train to show on the board. And if those twenty-five books ever get read, then you will be standing under the digital with fifteen other guys all holding red roses and all carrying *their* copy of the *Daily Telegraph* too.

So the place to meet a friend on a station is somewhere else. Not the lavatory, because if you hang about in there you'll get arrested. And that's if you're lucky. No, you go into the cafeteria, order a coffee, sit down and go to sleep.

I fetch mine and see Victor while I'm still queuing. He glances at me once and looks away, stirring his coffee. It's cold. No steam is rising.

I take my cup to a table about twenty feet away and sit down. I drink. Mine's hot. It even tastes like coffee. Soon Victor gets up and wanders out, leaving a congealed cup of coffee stuck to his table. I sit and do nothing. That is, I sit and watch who gets up after Victor. There's a couple about thirty years old who look harmless. Tails don't usually come in couples: it's too expensive. And there's this bored-looking plump guy I hadn't noticed. He wanders out looking even dreamier than Victor. He mooches out of the other door, then turns and wanders aimlessly in the same direction as Victor. I gulp some scalding coffee and leg it smartly to Victor's door. I barge out looking anxious as the bored guy crosses my path, and I bump him heavily. We topple in a sprawl on the dirty station floor.

I apologize and hold onto his trousers as he tries to leap up. I'm saying, "Got to catch a train and — hey, look at your jacket — oh, I'm awfully —"

He doesn't let me brush it. He darts off after Victor who of course is not there. Just five seconds and Victor has vanished into thin air. Now my fat guy doesn't look so bored. He whips across the concrete like a rugby-playing bookie and dives straight down the stairs into the smart tenpenny Gents beside where Victor vanished. I nod glumly. The guy is thinking.

Victor meanwhile has nipped up the stairs the other side and hurtled round the Gents to stand out of sight at the top of the same stairs the big lad went down. In two seconds the hulk has also appeared round the first of the two corners and I nod to Victor who slips back down the stairs and up the other side again.

I take the overland route, and am just in time to see Victor pause at the barrier to platform fifteen. There's a train standing waiting, and people looking for empty seats through the windows. Nothing of note bobs up from below, so I assume our large friend is peering under the doors in the catacombs and will shortly find himself the centre of a whole load of attention. Victor has gone for the train.

There's a guard's whistle blowing, so I steam through the barrier, ignoring an angry Asian asking where my ticket is, and I see Victor's head stuck out of a window up the platform where he's waiting for me to see him before he jerks back inside. I take an early door and stand with my own head out the window looking back to the barrier to check our fat guy hasn't made it to the platform. So I'm leaning out like a jilted lover when Victor taps me on the shoulder and says, "We haven't got long, unless you're taking this to Brighton." I ask why he called me.

It seems that Timmy's got himself collected by a carload from the other mob. He has vanished into silence. "They want to discover what we're doing," Victor tells me as we stand cramped close in the corridor. "They'll keep working on him till he talks."

"How'd they find him?"

Victor has a long face at the best of times, so when he shrugs it's like a dray-horse taking a breather from his feed. "Timmy has been rather exposed, darling. We have to gamble sometimes."

10

I say I'm surprised they didn't put a tail on to see where he led them. Then I stop to let the penny drop while Victor nods like a cat. "Thank for standing on my tail," he says.

All the time we are having this chat I am watching down the platform and I ask Victor if he thinks the fat guy will be waiting back on the main station concourse. Victor tells me he doesn't know, but he's going to ride the train to Clapham anyway and get off there. "They won't ask for tickets till East Croydon," he says.

So we stand there in the corridor: me with my head stuck out the window, and Victor making a nuisance of himself by lighting a small cigar. It stinks like a singed carpet. I ask Victor if he paid money for it and he tells me it's Turkish but I say he's got that wrong. "They don't make cigars in Turkey," I say. "Only cigarettes."

"Perhaps it *is* a cigarette," he says. He puffs a lungful of mustard gas in my face and grins at me through the cloud. "There's fireworks like that thing," I say. "The smaller they are the bigger the bang."

He takes the stick of charcoal out of his mouth and squints at it. Then he squeezes it gently along its length with his stubby fingers and says, "I think it's regular. I bought it. They weren't a gift."

"Better chuck it out the window," I say. The train is heading out of Victoria now, and is pulling over Grosvenor Bridge. The Thames is half empty with the tide out, and mud glistens on its banks like wet lead. It's a good place for Victor to throw his cigar.

But he's still rolling it cautiously in his fingers. Then he makes up his mind and cracks it open with his thumbnail and stares at the tobacco inside. "Perfectly good cigar," he sighs, and he frowns at the mess.

"Cup it in your hands and let it smoulder," I tell him. "Then suck in the smoke like it was marijuana. See if it chokes you."

"I'll light another if you don't give up. I'm getting out at Clapham. How about you?"

"Should we been seen together? People will talk. They'll say we're serious about each other."

"This *is* serious, darling. Timmy's been taken. They won't treat him gently. In the end, he'll have to tell them where you live."

"He doesn't know where I live, only where we meet. What's he told them about you? You've just been tailed."

"He doesn't know where I live either."

This doesn't make perfect sense to me, so I ask Victor where he thinks they took Timmy. "I'm not psychic," he says.

"I liked Timmy."

"He was a good man."

Which seems to have developed that conversation about as far as it can go, so we stop talking and stare out into the night. I think about Timmy, trying to remember what he knows. Like I said, Timmy never knew where I live, so he can't tell them that. But he knows it's Deptford. And someone was on my tail too.

Maybe that was because I was meeting Victor. Maybe it wasn't. Maybe they waited around Deptford till they could pick me up. Maybe they staked out the station. Maybe.

Maybe they bugged the phone when Victor phoned. But we didn't say much. We never do. We just used the usual code. He mentioned the letter V, so it's Victoria. He said nineteen, so I knocked one off to make eighteen. Eighteen hundred is six o'clock. And we always meet at twenty to the hour.

OK, so it sounds involved. But it's simple, and it works. You emphasize a letter, and you casually drop a number. The letter tells where to meet you — which one of up to twenty-six favourite spots — and the number tells when. If you want to fix a day, then you say so. Except that again you always knock one day off. Like the hours. Schoolboy stuff, but it's useful.

We creak into Clapham and Victor gets off. He grins at me from the darkness. He turns up his collar and bustles off along the platform. I watch him, and he's not followed. I pull my head inside the window and stand in the corridor, thinking, as the train pulls away.

We're drawing out of East Croydon when I find myself a seat. I look like I just got on. I have to sit in a smoking carriage because the train is busy with office workers going home to the suburbs.

They got tired faces, these people. The men have loosened their ties, and the girls' eyes are drooping. They have that dry hard look that comes from being bright and lively all day. But now they've turned off the juice while they trudge back to their three-up and two-downs in Crawley New Town; back to her parents where she still lives because she can't afford a place of her own; back to her new husband who hasn't made her pregnant because they're saving her wages. Waiting till they can afford something better.

There's some guy playing a personal stereo. It's the same rock tune they all play — squeaky cymbals hissing like a punctured gas-pipe above the rattling of the train. I shut my eyes and try to blot it out. The train noise fades to a rumble, but the scratch is still there. I go through my relaxation drill and start to disassociate.

My eyes open like someone flicked a switch. There's an argument starting across the corridor. A girl has asked this guy if he'll turn the stereo down. She's sitting opposite him and trying to read a paperback. It's been a long day and he's getting to her.

What opened my eyes is the way he swears at her. He is going to play his stereo, and to hell with everyone. A couple of businessmen frown and look away. He looks a bastard and they don't want to know. She asks him again, and he just stares at her. Then he sniffs and gives another mouthful of abuse. I see that she's getting ready to move, and I am annoyed with this guy. I'm getting annoyed with everybody, because they let this kind of scum be a nuisance and they're all too feeble to make him stop. There's a whole carriageful of people here and they could squash him.

I'm the one guy who shouldn't get involved. But I find I've moved across before I really thought about it, and I lean over and I pull the jack on his little plastic tape-player. I am drawing breath to deliver a short lecture, but he's scrambling to his feet and looking pretty mad. He has a problem with the table which slows him up, and since I don't want a fight in public I whack a chop across his Adam's apple which sits him down again fast. He clutches at his throat and his mouth gapes open and he lets out a noise worse than the crap we were hearing from his headphones.

I remove these with my right hand, and use my left to grasp him firmly by the hair and raise his head back. "Don't let me get

13

mad at you, son. Just take your little toy and find another carriage. Somewhere else."

He blinks at me through wet eyes and I hope he's not going to be stupid, but he is. He grabs at my hand with both of his and comes up out of his chair again like a beach ball from under water. So I jab him in his unguarded solar plexus, and he collapses with a gasp like the beach ball got punctured. I hope he ain't carrying a gutful of beer.

Some idiot starts applauding me and I think maybe I should have stayed out of this like all the other guys. But I have this injured lout gulping air like a stranded fish, and I know I can't leave things here. I yank him to his feet and act like I'm helping him down the corridor, but he's still struggling and I have to twist his arm till it nearly breaks while looking like I'm doing nothing. Then he yelps and spoils the effect.

When we're out of the compartment and outside the lavatory he tries to butt me, so I smack him on the jaw and let him slide down to the floor. I'm going to remove him into the lavatory but the train is slowing into a station, and I wonder whether to drop him off or get out myself.

A passenger door opens behind me and I snatch a look to make sure he hasn't got a friend. It's the girl who sat opposite him. "So you don't need a hand," she says, nice and cool. "Is he getting off here?"

Other people are moving into this exit space now, and the train shakes itself and stops. I open the door and drag him, like he's a drop-out from a stag party, over to a damp wooden bench. I see this is Horley station, and a handful of passengers are shuffling up the platform to get home for late tea. No one looks at us. They make a point of it.

The lump is half conscious now, rolling his head and groaning, and I wonder what he's going to do. The girl drops the stereo in his lap. "He didn't have a coat or anything," she says.

"No bag?"

"Nothing."

I try to think of some homily I can leave with this burke so he doesn't lodge a complaint or do anything that might make someone want to ask me some questions.

14

"Are you staying here in Horley?" the girl asks.

I shake my head, and turn back to my patient. He tells me to piss off. "And wet your shirt?" I ask.

I decide he'll put this down to experience and catch another train. He's not the sort to speak to policemen. He's the kind of no-hoper who has to annoy someone just to show he's still alive; one of the millions bored at school who left, couldn't get a job, so decided not to work anyway — just to spite them and to show it was his decision. He probably stole the stereo.

I could almost grow to like the guy. But me and the girl nip back across the platform onto the train as it starts to move off down the line. "Better find another carriage," she says. She's right. We don't want to embarrass no one.

So we move into this compartment nearer the front, with another clutch of tired office workers going home. We get two seats at a table for four, where a woman reads the *Standard* and a fifty-year-old man reads some report out of his briefcase and makes pencil marks in the margin. Every now and then he sucks his pencil and stares out the window. He starts watching the woman's reflection in the glass while she reads what's on TV. Then he gives up and goes back to his report. I can see his eyes glazing and he makes less marks in the margin. Finally he stops reading and falls asleep with his eyes open. She turns the pages of her paper and gets smudges on her fingertips.

The girl and I don't say much. She's quite tall, hungry-looking in an attractive way, and her hair looks like she chopped it with shears. She smiles the kind of smile you owe a guy who opens a door for you, and she goes back to reading her book. It's a fairly highbrow piece of fiction, and I'm trying to invent a smart remark when suddenly there's a guy in a uniform standing over me, saying something. He is talking to the whole table and he's a ticket collector. I relax, and reach into my pocket for a chequebook, but there's something about a blue uniform that always makes me tense.

I hear the girl has a ticket to Brighton, so I tell him I'll have one too. He asks me, "Single or Return?" and I say, "Single." You never can tell. When he's written out the ticket and moved down to the next table, she flashes me a curious glance and asks, "Single?"

"Yeah. You ain't married, are you?"

She shrugs some kind of smile and gets back into her book. I'm left puffing my cheeks and blowing out softly, wondering how to pass the time to Brighton. I wish I had a book. Or even the *Standard*. When it gets dark outside the window you'll read anything. I snatch another glance at the girl. She don't look like a damsel pulled out of distress: she just looks like she had a fight with her hairdresser. She must have cut it herself. In the dark. With blunt scissors. So I look out the window.

I can see the lights of houses scattered through the blackness. Sometimes we pass another train, and I can stare into its windows like watching Fast Forward on the video. But most of the time it's just dark. When I change focus the window works like a mirror, and I watch the girl as she reads her book.

"You want a drink or something?" I ask her, and she says, "Yes, coffee," so I stroll back along the train, glad of something to do. I like the way she asked for coffee. She was natural, hardly looking up from her book, but giving just enough of a smile to make it seem that we knew each other. I guess it's like couples act when they're comfortable together. I wouldn't know.

As I stand in a small queue waiting for our coffee, I muse about the girl's cropped hair and the way she smiled when she said she'd have coffee. The guy behind the counter pulls two plastic mugs off the wall dispenser, and slips behind a partition to pour hot water on the powder. He attaches the lids and balances two little tubs on top, half-full of the stuff that passes for milk. I wonder whether she'd like some chocolate or something, but all there is are Mars bars and Kit-Kat. I take one of each and decide maybe this is better than a box of chocolates anyway. She might have thought I was trying something.

I drop these in front of her by the coffees and sit down. The other two at our table have got out at Gatwick, and the train is thinning out. I wave a hand over the sweets. "It's all they had, except sandwiches."

"This is fine," she says, and snaps the Kit-Kat in half along the join. She offers it. I take a piece. "Makes the coffee bearable," she says.

We eat this chocolate and keep glancing at each other. "You like Mars?" she asks. I say she can have my half. "Everyone likes Mars," she smiles, and she rips the wrapper. Then she licks it, and bites off the end of the bar. You know how that toffee stuff inside never bites cleanly but always comes away with two sticky strings between your teeth, and how if you're not careful they drop down over your bottom lip and make a mess of your chin? Well, this happens to her, and even though she tries to flick them into her mouth she's got two chocolate smudges under her lip. They're close enough for her to lick off but she's got a mouthful of Mars bar and she laughs a little as she chews her way through it. She grins at me from beneath her lashes like she's done something naughty, and hands me the Mars bar while she licks up the smears. I'm watching her tongue move. It's shining and pink under traces of chocolate, and I look down at the rest of the bar in my hand.

On it I can see the marks of her teeth in the toffee, and the edges of the chocolate flaking, and maybe a touch of moistness from her lips. I'm glad she had to bite it in half. I slide it into my mouth slowly and let my tongue lie in the grooves left by her teeth. "Bite it," she says softly. "It's not an ice lolly."

So I'm gazing into her eyes as I bite into the Mars bar, and when I pull it out I don't get mess on my chin. She rips back more of the crackly wrapper and looks at what she's exposed. "I could eat all of this," she says. "In one go." I've got a mouth full of toffee and I'm sucking it slow. "But I won't," she says, and she bites off exactly half of what's there.

She slides the last piece across the table, and when I reach out for it our fingers touch. But I guess we're both too old for that game, and we pull away quickly and act like nothing's happened. I eat the last piece, and it's like a climax has passed. I enjoy it, but in the end it's just a Mars bar.

We don't say much as the train carries on. We've got that evening lethargy — from the regular drumming of the wheels, the fluorescent lights, and the night outside. But we are cosy in the warmth of the train. We exchange names and make the occasional remark, but I don't feel like pushing anything. I decide she has to be going home to someone in Brighton and what's it to me anyway?

"Where do you live?" Rachel asks suddenly.

"Deptford."

She frowns. "Visiting friends?"

I haven't a case or anything, and usually I'd say, Yes, I'm visiting friends, and I'd probably change the subject because it's easier that way, but I say, "No, I just needed to get away."

She raises an eyebrow and I know she has realized about the bag, but I switch and ask her where she's going. "Back to the flat," she says. "I had a day in town."

I wonder if she does a job but I don't want to get into a cross-examination, so I let it drop. We're coming through the Brighton suburbs now, and around the carriage people are rousing themselves, putting away their magazines, reaching up to the luggage racks to fetch down their coats. One or two are drifting off to wait by the doors so they can leap out and get moving the second the train stops. At seven o'clock in the evening it seems pointless. But I guess it's how they wake themselves up.

I think about wives making late supper for their husbands. Somehow, tonight, these humdrum lives don't seem so bad after all. I decide I'd quite like to go home to a warm house and a wife beaming beside my supper.

We're all slouching off the train and I turn my collar up against the cold and I know it's time for goodbye, and I'm sorry. Maybe it's the way Victor dragged me out of an ordinary day and dumped me on this train to nowhere. Maybe it's the nagging feeling I can't go back. Or maybe it's the way I've been talking lightly with Rachel when it's going to be another lonely night ahead.

She's too young for me anyhow. I step off the train knowing it's time to slip out of sight while I work out what to do next.

I fade fast from the train and head off the platform, through the entrance area, on to the street outside. There are two taxis ticking over but I glide past them, across a kind of outer quadrangle, into the top of some road that leads down to the sea. There are cheap boarding houses up here near the station, but tonight I can't face the leftover smell of their cooked lunch nor the groans of trains through the night, so I head down the main road to be nearer the sea.

I'm looking in shop windows wondering who's going to let me in without luggage at this time of night, when for the second time today the hairs on my neck start to tingle. Someone is following. I stop, move on a few paces, and stop again. If the bulky woman in Adidas trainers has made it to Brighton she deserves a medal. And I'm going to pin it on her. So I turn round and catch Rachel, right in the middle of the pavement. We stand looking at each other, then she starts walking on down. She comes close and says, "I knew you'd nowhere to go, so why did you run off?"

"I wasn't running."

"This just leads to the sea."

"That's where I'm going."

For a moment I think she'll turn away, but then she grins and looks up at me like when she ate the Mars bar, and she shakes her head. "Are you running away, or just running?"

"Just running."

"Try some company," she says. "I'll walk you to the sea."

We amble on down the hill and at first I think she's going to take my hand. But she doesn't, though we walk side by side like we've known each other a long time. I remember it felt like this in the train. She's got this quality that makes me feel at ease.

She takes us off the main street, round through some shops with cold bright windows glaring onto empty pavements, and into a big wide thoroughfare running either side of formal gardens that she tells me is called Old Steine. I can smell the sea.

We cross onto the promenade by the entrance to the pier. The lights string out to sea, but it looks like the outside of a party no one wants to go to, so we veer to the left and go down on the beach. It's dark, and the cold night breezes make my jacket feel like it's made of paper, but the sea is slurping across the shingle and the salt smell brings back memories that make me want to weep. I'm breathing in the ozone, and she huddles against me, and I put an arm round her shoulder and pull her to my side.

We stand looking at the chips of light sprinkled on the dark sea, and I feel the bracing air on one side and her warmth on the other. I'm happy to stand here a minute. Then I break away and pick up a stone and throw it far out into the water. It's easy to see it fall, splash, and I feel like I've made contact with something real again.

2

We come off the beach and move into a pub up a lane sheltered from the sea. She drinks wine, and I take a glass of beer. We're talking about a lot of things. Then we move into some pizza-parlour, and eat pizzas with a bottle of wine. Still we keep talking, and we don't say anything about where this is leading. I don't have a suitcase. It's getting late.

Well, shall we drink the coffee here, or do we go to her flat? I pay the bill and we decide to walk. She says there is a bus up to her place, but by this time of night it's one an hour. In the cold night air the sea salt gets mixed up in the smells of fish and chips and people's suppers. We start walking through streets where small front gardens get lost in the dark. Our shoes clatter on quiet pavements.

Her flat is upstairs in a house too small to raise a family. She has two little rooms, a kind of kitchen, and the old family bathroom from the Thirties. I sit on the hard, rented sofa while she goes to make coffee, and I look at her pictures on the wall. They are posters stuck with Blu-tack. They clash with the landlord's wallpaper. Anything would.

When she puts a mug of steaming coffee in my hand she hesitates in front of me. Then she skips trying to think of cute phrases and plays it straight: "You can sleep here, but this is your room, and mine is through there. It's not an invitation."

"Strictly bed and breakfast," I say. "No extras."

She nods, and moves over to sit on the other chair. I realize it's a promise I may wish I had not made.

We have no music playing and the good people round here keep the district pretty quiet. A clock is ticking. I like it. We sit peacefully sipping at our coffee like an old couple with our Horlicks. We don't need words, and no fake expressions tense our faces.

21

When she takes our empty cups away I get up and look at this sofa to see how it shakes into a bed. I'm pulling at the squabs when she wanders back to lend a hand. It folds out into the usual thin mattress, and needs only a duvet and two pillows to make it a bed. "You take the bathroom first," she says, and she disappears into her bedroom. For five seconds I gaze at her closed door with the kind of ache you can imagine. Then I go and splash in the bathroom. There's only one toothbrush, and I think she might not like me to use that, so I swill out with tepid water. Then I hold my face too long in her towel, breathing her scent, and I come back into the main room and call that I'm through. "Tell me when you're in bed," she says.

Since my clothes will have to see me through tomorrow, I fold them carefully onto a chair before I crawl naked under the duvet. I call that I'm in bed now, but my voice croaks.

She doesn't appear immediately. Then she sweeps through in a long dressing-gown. I wonder if it's a man's while I listen to the taps running. I've got no book and the light's on so I can't help watching her when she comes back through. She's clean as an angel. When she pauses in her doorway for a soft goodnight my throat seizes again and I can't reply. I just lie there looking at her.

"You go to sleep now," she says, and she closes the door. It's like all those mothers you read about in kids' books who are bringing up the family bravely because daddy's gone away. I could believe in magic and fairies in the firelight, and I feel so snug under the duvet I could cry.

It was the start of that dream again. A warm old cottage by the sea, with wind outside secure as a second skin. The deep breathing of the sea on the shingle spread ease and tranquillity through my bones. I was curled up in an armchair, watching logs on the fire, listening to plates clink in the kitchen as my mother prepared a meal. Smells of the different courses mingled with sweet smoke from the wood fire. On the table was a white cloth and glistening cutlery, and if I stared hard enough I could create crystal goblets and china plates and that old silver samovar. While I sat there watching, the plates filled with melting dumplings, and the glasses filled, and a bowl of fruit suddenly popped up and overflowed with dark grapes dripping down to the cloth.

My nostrils filled with the burnt-sugar fragrance of roasting lamb, and while I gazed at the waiting table from my chair I felt sad. Today was a celebration. My young arms lay gracefully inside the white sleeves of the kind of fine shirt I never possessed. But in the dream it seemed to have been in the family forever. I think it was brought out only for special occasions, to mark out the person who wore it.

Yet whatever the celebration was, there would be no guests. Only the family had places laid. Around the small table was room for only about four people, but if I tried to focus on their cutlery, the image rippled and grew vague. Whenever I tried to count, it was like crawling through treacle, and there was always one more to count and yet never more than four or five in all. I could feel the dream fading, and I tried to snuggle back into it, because I had to know how many people, and which one was saying goodbye.

I lose the dream without being able to alter its course. When I look up from my bed on the shake-down sofa, it is daylight. I see Rachel fully dressed and standing in front of a chipped mirror on the wall, pecking at her hair with a comb. She sees me watching her, and says, "I made you some tea."

I thank her, and my mouth is sticky. I reach over and take the mug and sit up to sip at it. Normally I drink coffee, but I don't tell her. I let the hot milky tea wash the syrup off my tongue, and I decide maybe this isn't such a rotten drink after all. A guy could get used to it. "What happened to your hair? Or is it meant to look like that?"

"I got fed up with it. I started cutting it off."

"Why'd you stop half-way?"

"I changed my mind."

She goes into the kitchenette while I get dressed. Then I splash around in the bathroom, and finally I stroll into breakfast to see what she's made. There are cereals and some nice-looking breads, and she asks if I want her to cook something but I tell her no. We smile at each other, and nibble at things on the table, and I ask her what her plans are for the day.

She shrugs. I ask her if she hasn't a job to go to, and she pulls a face, as if this was no kind of question at all. As we eat she tells me she makes a living in the summer-time when holidaymakers come down, but when autumn nips the air she is left like a squirrel with only the nuts she has hoarded. When I say I have to go back to London, she nods like it was inevitable and gets up to clear the things.

"You want to come with me?"

She can't afford the fare and tells me not to offer to buy her a ticket. We've started avoiding each other's eyes. I ask if I can come back sometime, and she says, "Sure," casually. But I think she is glad I asked.

I have nothing to get together, so in next to no time I am standing by the door. "Be careful up there," she says.

She has beautiful eyes.

But it's a shame about her hair.

3

I pull into London thinking that things could be hotting up for me in Deptford. Yesterday my tail must have picked me up there, and they won't find it difficult to latch onto me again. They just need to watch Deptford station.

So to go back I don't use the train. I take the tube to Elephant and Castle, cut through the damp understreet walkways, and wait for a bus opposite the Coronet cinema. You probably know that at the Elephant they've improved the amenities. They knocked down all the little buildings and built a jazzy shopping precinct. They scraped up the roads to lay an urban motorway. Then they moved people out of the area so the smart set could move in. Except they didn't come. It's south of the river, moving east. No one wants to know.

I'm waiting for a bus on a dirty windswept road, and sharing the wait with me there are thin old ladies, stunted white men and underpaid blacks. The whites are what tourists call cockneys — wizened little people, London leprechauns, old south-east Londoners who can't afford to move away. Blacks can't afford to move either, but they've settled down to make a patch of ground that's forever Trinidad, ignoring the grimy cold, trying to raise decent families and have a good time.

I get on a 188, and nestle with the people I live among. The whites don't say anything, except when you get two old ladies sniffing over their neighbours, but the blacks are laughing and calling to each other. The sound of black people laughing carries me home.

In this poorest south-east quarter of London they never gave us a tube. Back in Victorian times the rich areas got the tubes, and since then whenever they built an extra line they gave that one to them too. But the rich can afford cars. And for tubes they already had the Circle and Metropolitan, the District, Piccadilly

25

and Northern, with the Bakerloo slicing across for a useful short cut. So the wise city fathers put in the Victoria line in case they'd missed somewhere, then the Jubilee to keep the Queen happy — and what did we get, down in the stews?

Well, it was *nearly* nothing. They did make one little spur line, hanging off the edge of the main system, and this line was even allowed to cross the muddy river to a place called Surrey Docks. A few years back they did up the station. Do you know why? Because they named this dump a Development Area, and painted bright coloured maps and gave cash grants for speculators so they could creep across and build offices and dinky executive houses. And because these houses had a clear view of the river they sold at fine prices.

So then they decided they'd better improve the old station. Because if any of these brave pioneers wanted to invite their rising executive friends to dinner — down across the river into no man's land — and if these friends didn't want to risk their BMWs getting nicked, or if they couldn't find Deptford on the map, there would be a nice new shining tube station for them to aim for. Like a consulate in the jungle.

The bus cruises past Surrey Docks station and it looks very pretty. Though there's no one using it.

I look out the window at the crumbling old houses. They only need a lick of paint and window-boxes for a tasteful façade. But they are safe from gentrification. That's for north of the river, up where there's a chance that property values will improve. No slum is safe up there.

Down here is too depressing for delicate people. We got too much traffic, too much dirt, and we got no money or flash wine bars at all. You can buy a Georgian-looking, Victorian-built house any size you want, but you can't escape the traffic, you can't avoid the high-rise blocks, and you can't get away from *us*. We live here. We're black, yellow, white, and brown, but we got our feet on the pavement and we know we belong.

I'm looking at one of the high-rise blocks as I think this. Washing hangs out on the balconies. But what hits you in the face is a banner about sixty foot long and wafting in the breeze all along the front of the tower about half-way up. It says, "1472

26

Days And Still No Lift". You want to think about that? This is a council-owned block. Those people have a busted lift and have been trudging up the stone stairs for over four years. 1472 days is over four years. I go by on the bus and I see the number on the banner getting bigger and bigger and I ask myself: what the hell is going on here? Don't these people exist?

You can see that by the time I ring the bell and step off the bus in Evelyn Street I'm feeling pretty sore. I am at home down here. I enjoy the vibrancy. I like the fact that these are real people you can talk to and touch. I do not like to see them condemned.

When I stalk into the Black Horse I ask for a pint of Trumans as cross as if I'm cursing. Then I smile at the lady behind the bar and say I'm sorry, and would she like a port for herself? She accepts. I tell her I've just been swearing at the council. So she tells me what *she* thinks of them, and an old boy with yesterday's paper gives me his opinion, and before you know it we're all laughing and I'm glad to be home.

It is one o'clock and the pub is filling nicely when I see Harry walk in. He stops the other side of the wide central bar for a word with two big fellers wearing clean T-shirts under wool jackets. They have not dropped in from the office. Their faces are like blobs of concrete, and they cradle beer mugs in their fists so you can hardly see the glass. By which I mean they have big hands.

I watch to see what they want with Harry, but they are just passing the time of day. He knows a lot of people, and everybody knows him. Two yards along the bar he stops again to chat with a weasely guy out exercising his new winter overcoat. Their heads dip close together and though I can't hear what they're saying I know they have dropped their voices for a spot of trading. They're both shrugging and pretending they've gone as far as they can, but when Harry moves to leave him, the weasel reconsiders and the huddle starts again.

I order another pint for me, and one for Harry. When the landlady places it in front of him he glances across and nods. He looks at the weasel as if to say: I'm a busy man and are you buying or what? I slide away to find a quiet table near the rear, and he joins me in two minutes with the beer half gone. He eases his heavy body into the chair opposite, sighs, and asks what is new.

So we chat about this and that — mainly that — then, because we're both hungry and the Black Horse has the right ideas about food, we order egg, bacon and chips with brown and red sauces, a drop of mustard, and a pile of bread and butter on the side. While we wait for it to cook, he asks if I need something.

He has the kind of mobile face you get if you're born south of the river and you live here all your life. His cheeks and eyebrows dance, but his expression gives nothing away. We discuss the kind of guns he can put his hands on.

His eyes turn sad when you ask for something heavy, but if you were watching from across the bar you would think no more than perhaps the talk had shifted to the disappointments of married life. He'd rather find a case of whisky or a pallet-load of videos, but he has a livelihood to consider, and if he knows you're pukka and you must have something special, he will trade.

He asks if I intend to use these things or just wave them around. I tell him I may have to pull the trigger. While two plates of Black Horse breakfast slide onto the table between us, he blinks at me and takes off his glasses. "Don't want them steamed up," he says, and he puts them away in his breast pocket.

He bursts his fried egg and says, "Most blokes say they're not gonna use them — it's just to scare someone. But they always ask for live ammunition."

We tuck in to the sizzling platefuls and wipe up the egg-yolks with bread. Harry folds a rasher of bacon into his cheek and recommends a couple of well-used Smith & Wessons, ex-Army. "Well-used?" I ask.

"That's right. Police will have them on record. They must have recovered bullets from them both, one time or another."

"How does that help me?"

"Confuses them, doesn't it? Last time they heard of them was up in Newcastle, so if they find one of your spent rounds they'll think you're a northerner. Always assuming you believe all that stuff."

"What stuff?"

"That stuff about what they can do with ballistics."

"Don't you?"

He raises both eyebrows and looks at me solemnly. Then he returns to the remains of his chips. One eyebrow remains stuck up there as he explains. "Put it like this. If you shoot into a barrel of sawdust, like they do, and if you recover your round from the middle of that sawdust, then maybe it'll still have the marks to show which gun it came out of. But if you smack your bullet off the ceiling, or if you crash it through a piece of bone, you'll make such a mess of that little lead slug there won't be any useful marks left on it, will there? The human body's full of bones, you know."

We sip our beers while I consider this. Then he suggests a price and we talk about that. "I don't do any haggling on shooters," he tells me. "Because there's established prices. You take it or you don't." So I take it.

"It'll be a couple of days," he says.

"I need them tomorrow."

"Difficult, son, very difficult."

"Has to be, Harry."

"I won't have checked them over."

"I can do that."

He drains his beer and puts the glass by his empty plate. "Where do you want them?"

"Up to you."

"You do realize it's Sunday tomorrow? You want me to meet you in church?"

"Where better? Except that we might stand out among four old ladies and the vicar."

He recommends Deptford Park. It sounds exposed to me. He says, "Open spaces is how I like it. What time?"

"Morning?"

"Tea-time. But before it gets dark. I won't go in the park at night-time — it's full of undesirables."

He stands up, pats me on the shoulder, and goes back to the bar. A girl asks if he knows where she can get a decent second-hand fridge, and he sits down with her.

"Why not a new one?" he asks. "German, they're the best."

I cut down through the trading estate, under the railway arches, and out into the narrow streets I know so well. In the Rastafarian Community Centre the windows are boarded up, but they still have discos at night. There is graffiti on the walls, rubbish on the ground, and nowhere has the Surrey Docks money made any impact. But there are kids playing in the streets, some well-loved front gardens, and most of the doors are painted bright.

There ain't much grass, and the pavements seem harder than in some places, and I suppose you would say this is a tough area. Maybe it is, but it's straight. These are my kind of people. They may not be straight according to those laws made by dead people, but they are according to something else. Just like you, we're out to do the best for ourselves. We'll fight, we'll bargain, but we ain't looking to kick you in the balls. We don't want you down in the gutter, looking up at us on the clean pavement.

We believe even losers are entitled to something out of life. Like in a boxing match: the winner gets the prize money but the loser gets patched up. He's told he fought well, and he keeps his pride. You could say we know about losing down here. We've been losing all our lives. For most of us, that's why we're still here.

I'm pulling out of Woodpecker Road when a little black kid grabs my arm. He must be about ten years old. He's lived most of his life out on these pavements and he smiles like he's on a Caribbean beach. "Hey! Darius wants to see you. It's urgent, man."

"I'll look in. Is he at home?"

"You got to see him *before* you go home. You got to go to the Robin. I bring him down there."

"He can see me in the flat."

"Don't be a wally, man. If he want to see you in the flat, he knock on the door. There a whole gang of us looking for you, man."

I look down at this boy and I tell him I'll be in the Robin. "Don't let him be too long."

"He never long. Your tea still be warm. You do drink tea, don't you, mister?"

I shake my head. "Coffee. Two sugars." But he has turned and skipped away down the street and vanished round the corner. I hope he knows where to find Darius.

I am fifty yards from the door of the Robin when another little black boy appears, jigging in front of me like the pavement was too hot. "Darius looking for you."

"I'll be waiting inside."

I buy a mug of coffee and a wedge of navvy's wedding cake and I sit at a table in the back. Darius is as good as his word. I am still sipping carefully at the hot coffee and I'm only half-way through the cake when he slips through the door and slides into the seat opposite me. He is twelve years old — sly and laughing and black as a charcoal drawing. He lives next door to me and is the nearest I got to a son. Every time I see him I get a tightness in my throat. I keep this from him, naturally. He laughs at me like I'm just some schoolteacher, but sometimes I think he reads what I'm feeling and he welcomes it. His dad left before I knew him, when Darius was toddling.

"Mum says there's guys in your flat."

"Guys?"

"They came in the night. We didn't hear them go in, but they was there this morning. They still there, and we think they waiting for you."

I nod slowly, and drink some coffee while I think about this. "How many guys?"

He shrugs. "You in some trouble, man?"

I come out with a kind of smile. "I'm glad you warned me, Darius."

"What you gonna do?"

"I don't know yet."

"You want to come round our place? If we use the other stairs they won't know you is there."

He is right. Each side of the building is a flight of stairs. You use the left flight for my place and the right for his. A walkway runs in front, making one long balcony.

So we head round to the flats and slip up the right-hand staircase. He uses his key to let us in, and we stay in the living room because it's furthest away from the dividing wall. I'm perched in the middle of the carpet like a visiting vicar when Jancey comes in from the kitchen. "They still there," she says. She and I sit on her divan, and Darius flops on the floor by our feet.

"How d'you know?"

She fixes me with those deep brown eyes like wax-polished glass. "My bedroom is up against your wall, isn't it? I hear a thing or two."

"I bet. Like what?"

"Like the lavatory flushing. And once or twice, voices, speaking low. I thought it was you, home late."

"How did you know it wasn't?"

"Because when I ring at your door this morning, you not answer. I called through your letter-box, and it was quiet as a grave. I was going to knock on the bedroom wall but I change my mind. Then half an hour after I had come back I heard the toilet flush."

"I didn't know you could hear that."

"You be surprised what I hear. These are thin walls."

"Why did you ring at my door?" I didn't need to ask this question. I just needed to feel good about *something*.

"To invite you to breakfast," she says.

We quite often eat breakfast together. I live on my own, and she only has Darius. We've known each other about three years, and in a way we're family now. Except that we're not. We haven't joined up. We looked at each other a few times — maybe a lot of times — but it soon became too late for just a quick tumble in the sheets. We'd be into marriage or something before we got up. So we skirted round for a year or so until we settled into this.

"What happened when you rang my bell?"

"Nothing. I ring, I rattle your knocker, I call through the slot. So I think maybe you have a hangover. So I go back an hour later."

"And still nothing?"

"Right. But meantime I had heard men talking. Both voices was a man. And I didn't think you was hiding a man from me." Jancey laughs as she says this, but it's kind of a sad laugh, like when she talks of Darius's dad. "Anyway, I know your voice."

We sit in her living room looking thoughtful. Darius is the first to break the silence, with what I didn't want him to ask. "What you going to do about it, man?"

I shrug, and Jancey tells him to shush. "He's thinking, boy. Can't you see that?"

And certainly I am thinking. There's at least two of them in there, waiting for the front door to open. My knowing they are in there is a help, but it doesn't exactly put me on top. It just gives me one card they don't know I've got.

I have several options. I can wait till they come out, and take them then. I can bust in with company, and outnumber them. I can slide in the back while they watch the front door. Yeah, it can be done. And I guess I've been around long enough to make sure I do it right. But I am left with a problem: what do I *do* with these guys? Thumping them over the head is all very well, but where do I put them to recover? And what will two guys with sore heads do when they're back on their feet? I don't see me getting a peaceful night's sleep, knowing they're outside and angry. It'll be like sleeping with a stunned wasp between the sheets.

So what do I do — fix them permanently? The Long Goodbye? Not in the real world, baby! I can't just create two stiffs in my cosy little apartment, carry them out and dump them. It wouldn't look good — a sudden fracas, heavy bumps, then out in the small hours with a dead man round my neck. Twice. People notice that sort of thing in Deptford.

This looks like checkmate, as they used to say in B-movies. These guys have got themselves onto a square which don't allow me to manoeuvre. I'm stuck out here like a tiddlywink that can't hop into its pot.

"I can find you some help if you need it," says little Darius.

"Thanks," I say gravely as I stand up. "But dealing with these two ain't gonna be the end of it. They got friends. Now that they know where I live they can come back."

Jancey looks like she's ill. "How bad is this?" she whispers.

"Bad. I'll have to move away for a while."

She's nearly crying. "You can't let them do this," she sobs. "You can't let them force you out."

"You're not going to just slink away, man, are you?" Darius looks at me like I was a hero who wouldn't fight. I try a reassuring grin, but I guess it looks phoney. He stares up at me with those trusting brown eyes and I think the whole room is going to burst

33

into tears. When I put my hand in his hair he turns away muttering. It breaks Jancey, so I lumber across and take her in my arms.

4

When I'm out in the street again I'm feeling so empty a breeze could lift me off the pavement and blow me over the buildings. It's like I was dumped in a foreign land with nothing in my pockets, and the only memories are places I cannot go.

Since I have nothing better to do I mooch round to the Robin again and sit down with a mug of coffee while Pam cooks me some food. Victor says I eat food for comfort. Whenever I am troubled, he says, I go back to my mother's breast. I tell him he reads too many books.

Pam has this enormous frying pan which could cook a family's breakfast, and she's doing me my very own three sausages, two eggs, bacon, tomatoes and cheap mushrooms. Cheap mushrooms are the stalks. You can have the tops if you want, but that costs more, and like a lot of folk round here I prefer the stalks. They give you something to chew. Pam has thrown in some sautéd potatoes and she asks me if I want a slice of fried bread because I look as if I need feeding, and I say I do.

The noise from the tomatoes sizzling and bubbling in the hot fat is tremendous. It's like she's got a tap splashing into a stone sink. The smell of all that food seems to colour the steam, and my mouth waters so much I gulp down my coffee and call for some more.

An old boy near the window puts down his *Evening Standard* and shakes his head. "I can't read with that smell going on," he says. "It's no use, Pam darling, do me a nice two eggs, with bacon and chips, will you? I'll pass on the tomatoes, 'cos I can pour them out of the bottle."

"Got some money, have you?"

"Don't you trust me?"

"Trust you? I *know* you, don't I?"

"Women, " he says.

She starts piling my fry-up onto a plate, and when she brings it over I can feel the heat come off it like a fire. I reach for pepper and salt. The old man watches my plate with eyes like a blackbird. "You doing my eggs?" he calls.

Pam laughs again. "Let's see the colour of your money."

"The years I've been coming in here," he grumbles.

"Give him a plateful," I say. "I'll pay."

She hesitates a second, then nods and gets on with it. The old man stands up and shambles over. "Bloody good of you," he says.

"I can't eat with you watching me," I tell him.

"You'll be wanting a thank you."

"Just eat it."

"Right," he says. "I will. . . . Here!" he calls to Pam as he marches back to the counter. "That's what I call a gentleman. And while you're cooking my dinner —" He reaches into his pocket and brings out an acceptable little roll of grubby five-pound notes. "You can add a couple of slices of bread and butter. Freshly cut, if you don't mind." We grin at each other. "No one can lose on the dogs all the time," he says, and he swats at an imaginary fly with his paper.

By the time I come out it's starting to get dark. A sulking grey cloud squats over London, too constipated to let go of its rain. First lights have been turned on in shops and houses, but the streetlamps are still cold and dead. I slouch along a pavement that feels like it's had a thousand vacuum cleaners emptied on it, and I hope that when I get to the phonebox the damn thing will work.

A dirty electric glare leaks out of the box through the gloom. I step inside into a reek of urine and stale cigarettes. The phonebook looks like it's been attacked by mice, and a succession of illiterates have practised writing big words on the walls. But the phone works.

I get through to the Big Man, and tell him the bad news. He is so depressed that when he sighs I can feel the force of his breath in my ear. The stink in the phonebox is like he's got halitosis. He says, "You'd better lie low while we sort ourselves out."

36

Wonderful, I think. "They've taken Timmy, they're onto me, and I don't hold out much for Victor. We're like forgotten sappers in a foxhole on the Somme."

"What do you expect me to do?"

"Get me out. This is a write-off."

"You want to hand the game over to them?"

"They got all the aces anyway. Pack it in and deal me another hand."

"I'll try to think of something."

"Do that. Don't take too long."

It isn't the most encouraging conversation I ever had. I stand for a bit feeling as lonely as a tart in a church doorway, then I dial Victor. The sound of the ringing-tone in my left ear is like a little mallet, slowly tapping me deeper into mud. He is not going to be there, and I am not going to know whether they got him or —

"Hello?" It's his voice.

"It's me."

"What's new?"

"I got company in the flat."

"Friends?"

"No."

A pause. Then he asks, "What are you going to do, darling?"

"Hide."

I hear some kind of scratching noise over the receiver and suddenly I am all attention. Victor breathes in sharply, exhales, and I realize he has just lit one of his revolting cigars. "Are you alone?" he asks.

"Totally."

"Do you want to come here?"

"Yeah, but it's not safe."

"My flat is still safe. And if you're alone, so are you. Come over."

"Thanks."

"I'll put the kettle on, darling." He puts the phone down.

I peer out through the condensation on the glass door, and I see they've lit the streetlamps.

What never changes about Victor's bedsitter is that he keeps it nice and warm. I've been there in the summer-time, and he's kept the gas fire on like you'd think he was growing orchids. But when you get a night collapsed into damp introspection like this one, his room is as comforting as a bowl of hot soup.

He sits in cardigan and slippers, curled up in an armchair like a professor of ancient languages. He has found a new packet of cheroots which he's opening very slowly like he's teasing himself with an unexpected birthday present, and he smirks across at me like he's really pleased I'm here. "Just you and I," he says. "And the whole of south London out there against us."

"Only the heavy mob is against us. No one else is interested."

"That's the trouble with people, darling. No one gives a damn."

"I like it like that."

He sucks on that wilting cheroot as if he was really enjoying the thing, he licks his lips all over, then he exudes a grey fog of thoroughly digested smoke. "What shall we do, then?"

I close my eyes and shake my head, because I don't want to talk about it. There's a numbing tiredness up my spine and across my shoulders, as if the air had suddenly got too heavy to bear. My eyes want to stay closed, and I need the whole world to go away and leave me alone. Perhaps Victor sees this. He says, "You know what I'm going to do? I am going to make you some tea — the way you really like it."

I smile, and sit with my eyes closed while he fusses in the room. Making the tea is a distraction for him, and I can hide behind my curtain while the minutes tick by. As I listen to the sounds of tea-making and the underpinning rhythm of his old mantel clock, I am taken back to a kind of childhood memory, in a fairy-tale cottage in the woods, where a benevolent old lady in a rocking chair sings softly to herself as she sits by the fire. But no logs crackle in Victor's room. The gas fire hisses like a breeze in the flue.

By the time he puts the tall glass of sweet black tea in my hands my muscles have relaxed and I am willing to chat. We talk about Timmy, and wonder what has happened to him. "He was so young," sighs Victor. "He was the most vulnerable."

"The younger you are the tougher you're supposed to be. You and me are over the hill."

38

"You and I," Victor corrects me. "You and I have experience. That's precious. Learning from experience is how cavemen developed above animals."

"Today we're dinosaurs."

We finish our glasses of tea, and Victor shuffles over to the gas fire to pour us some more. In the dim light from the fire and one small lamp I watch him pad across the carpet. I shiver for a second, even though it's not cold. "I thought they might have caught you too," I tell him. "That guy at Victoria."

He returns with hot tea. "They got on my tail at Timmy's. No one's traced me here."

"Yet."

He smiles, with eyes that have seen a hundred years of sorrow. "When the fox goes to ground, it stays there till the hounds lose interest. Foxes are caught in open fields. Hounds haven't the patience to lay siege."

"The heavy mob may have."

"I doubt it, darling. Who will pay their wages while they lurk about getting nowhere? After two weeks they will be called off."

"You mean we're not worth a month's wages?"

"It all comes down to money in the end."

"I can't stay here a month, Victor."

"My dear boy!" He waves a hand generously, and a pellet of cigar ash arcs to the carpet. "The problem is," he continues, "I don't think we have a month to spare. I think we'll be in action before then."

"I still can't stay cooped up in here."

Victor's bedsitter is just that: a good-sized comfortable room with the kind of old furniture that suits him perfectly. He has the gas-ring by the fire, and he shares a bathroom across the hall. There is only one bed, so I'll have to create a makeshift out of two armchairs.

"Stay a few days. I don't want you to get caught — I'd get lonely."

The tea is cold now, and the gaps in our conversation are lengthening. I am warm and content, like a cat on a hearthrug. The scent of old cheroots mingles with the fainter smell of gas fire. There's a trace of fragrant tea and a memory of fried onions.

Victor is reminiscing of old times, and his words conjure strong pictures in my mind behind closed eyes.

His words fade.

The dream may have joined seamlessly to the memories he stirred. I was on a hillside, picking berries from a tree and dropping them into an old bucket. The sun stroked my back, and a pair of larks sang at each other so insistently you'd think they were trying out new beaks. I had climbed a low stone wall to reach for higher berries, and in the warm sunlight an old couple wheeled their bicycles along the lane towards me. They stopped, and we began one of those conversations you only get in dreams where a lifetime of things you want to say is spoken in a handful of sentences that probably contain no recognizable day-time words at all. They were interested in my berries. The old lady recalled country recipes, and the man spoke of his youth. All their lives they had lived here, in a village near ours. Now they were retired. They had bought bicycles to let them travel easily in the countryside together. When they mounted their bikes and rode away, I found that, as it often is in dreams, the bucket was overflowing with berries and twice its original size.

When I carried it — full of luscious fruit, yet so light I could swing it carefree in the air — I thought of how the old couple had spent their lives honestly working in our valley, and I imagined the years of gentle exploration that lay ahead of them, and I entered our cottage smiling, in the calm certainty that when my working days were over, I too would buy a bicycle and glide effortlessly across the hills.

But there was a chill in the cottage. My mother looked up from the table, surprised from secret thoughts. She had red eyes as if she'd been crying, and I wondered why she sat at an empty table instead of singing in the kitchen, why the light was fading and a draught blew beneath the door.

I tried to ask her what was the matter but my mouth was full of berries. As I spluttered the words out, pieces of husk and red juice spattered onto the table, and she looked up at me sadly, while specks of red fruit splashed across her face.

I tried to move towards her to wipe it away, but I tripped against the bucket and watched red lizards spill onto the floor and scurry around my feet. I was kicking my way through the slimy lizards, and some were showing teeth, and my mouth was still crammed with berries, and I knew that if I bit into them my mouth would fill with blood . . .

It stays so clear in my mind it's more real than any memory could be. It's like a still-frame stuck on the video, blanking out anything else that struggles to get through. I force myself to stare through the darkness at the features of Victor's room, and I focus on the glow of the distant streetlamp oozing through the curtain. It's enough to pick out broad shapes in the fabric pattern, and I know that if I stare any longer those patterns are going to form themselves into recognizable shapes and they will continue the dream.

I move my deadened legs, and send pins and needles darting through my veins. My ankles have stiffened, and I can't get the circulation going. When I bend forward in the armchair to rub my legs, I hear small bones creaking in my spine.

"Move the armchairs together," mutters Victor from the bed. "It'll be more comfortable."

I stand in the middle of the room with splinters of dream intruding in the gloom. Then I grunt at Victor and move one of the armchairs. I glare around the room as if I'm angry with it.

"The bathroom's across the hall," says Victor. "Down to the left."

Over breakfast I agree to stay for a while. I don't say how long that will be. Victor surprises me by producing a packet of cornflakes and some croissants. "Breakfast is the most important meal of the day," he says.

He has some matching china he bought in a sale. The sugar's in a bowl and the milk's in a jug. We eat off an occasional table that's set too low, and I wonder if he ever lays it with a cloth. I can imagine him dining alone, using paper doilies.

When he goes out about ten o'clock I look around this room and wonder how long I'm supposed to tolerate being cooped up here. He has some books, and one or two of them might be worth reading, but I can't face the thought of that now. It would be like lying in bed in hospital, killing time till the surgeon arrives with his knife.

I leave the television off and spend a few minutes staring out the window like an old lady in a council flat, till I decide to waste some time in a bath. Finding the towels is something I don't like to do because I have to open up all his drawers. I find them in the wardrobe. Then I trek across his corridor and lock myself in the bathroom.

At least there's plenty of hot water. I don't care the bath has brown streaks and stains, at least the hot water didn't give out. So I fill the tub, take off my clothes, and sink in.

You can waste half an hour doing that. You can top up the water when it cools, but when you find yourself stroking your only friend in the water you know it's time to get out. I stand in a cold bathroom, hearing every sound the scummy water makes as it plunges three floors, and I dry myself thoroughly with a towel that's too small. Then I ease back into the clothes I wore yesterday, and slink back across the hall.

His room looks dirty in daylight. I hunt around, but all he has is a duster, brush and dustpan. So I do some dusting, because I can face that, and then I slump down in an armchair and stare at my fingernails. I'm finishing a cup of coffee when Victor comes back. "I can't stand much of this," I say.

"Pretend you have a cold," he says. He has bought a blow-up airbed, so I can sleep more comfortably. Also he has some filled rolls from a takeaway sandwich bar, and two cans of beer. He throws me a paper to read while he lays lunch on the occasional table. "We have to talk about this," I say.

"Plenty of time, darling."

That's the trouble.

I stagger through to nearly tea-time by folding into an armchair and reading some book Victor recommended. It's *The Secret Agent* by Joseph Conrad, and is his idea of a joke. He says it will improve my mind. I don't need to improve it. I need to put it to sleep.

Spectator sports start when Victor shows me how he cooks

spaghetti bolognaise on a single gas-ring. He has a non-stick frying pan in which he fries some onions, chucks in paprika and a bayleaf, then slops in half a pound of minced beef. As this stuff changes colour and fills the room with a smell like boiled rancid cat, he hovers over it, sprinkling in pinches of spice and herbs. He stirs in a can of Italian tomatoes. Then he fits the pan lid and turns down the gas so it's hardly stewing at all. I hope he doesn't start bustling around the room, because he'll blow out the gas.

He settles himself in the armchair opposite me and announces we have an hour and a half to wait. "Suits me," I say. "I'm going out."

He looks alarmed, so I tell him this is a matter I have previously arranged. But he doesn't approve of my explanation: "I got to see a man about some guns."

5

On a chilly day like this it's inevitable I get to Deptford Park early. On the 199 bus I sit upstairs where it's smokier than at Victor's but at least I get a good view of the streets below. I am sad to see that one of my favourite landmarks, R. Soles the shoe shop, has closed down. He didn't sell a lot of shoes.

The trouble with arriving early at a park is you don't look convincing pretending to take an interest in the roses. There are kids near the railings playing Piss On The Most Petunias, and I'm lurking about like I want one of those little boys with chipolatas for my tea. I sit on a bench and re-read the morning paper, and try to do the crossword in my head. Wet air blows in from the river, and the light is fading fast.

I see Harry sauntering through the gates wearing a warm coat and carrying a plastic bag. So I give him a wave from the far end of the park. He takes his time strolling over, and when he gets here he sits at the far end of the bench like he doesn't know me. "Harry," I say. He grunts.

"We're the only two adults in here," I tell him. "Come where I don't have to shout at you." I reach inside my jacket and take out an envelope. As he takes it he asks what I have in my own carrier bag. I tell him it's another shooter, and he gives so little reaction I think he believes it. But I've stopped off at a street market on the way over for socks and shirts and thin garish underpants. All my stuff is trapped in my flat. What Harry doesn't know is he's seeing me with everything I possess.

He doesn't count my money. When you deal in guns no one breaks a bargain. He rummages deep in his plastic bag, below a loaf of white bread and the fruit from a Chinese greengrocer. He brings out my package wrapped in brown paper, and I slip it into my carrier with my clean linen. "Hope you enjoy your supper, Harry."

"A man's got to live," he says.

That's right, Harry.

As I sit on the bus going westward I realize this could be the last I see of this manor. The bus is trundling round the railway arches near Bermondsey when this hits me, and I gaze out the upstairs window with a lot of fondness. God knows why.

There's not a pretty building this side of the Elephant. They're all covered with smoke and grime left over from before they passed the Clean Air Bill, and the only place that might once have looked good is the Methodist Chapel at Southwark that's been taken over by Fundamentalists. Yet when I step off the bus at the Coronet cinema I get the same lurch as when I first left home.

In the back streets that lead towards Victor's place I carry the dead weight in my carrier bag, and I feel rootless. I don't belong here. I'll stay one more night with Victor, because he's got the spaghetti going and he's bought an airbed, but I'll be gone tomorrow. I can keep my head down, but I can't stay cramped in a hole in the ground.

The thought of these two Smith & Wessons brings back an old tingle. Just knowing they are there in the bag is as comforting as Victor finds his cheroots. I can already feel the shape of one resting in my palm. I could believe my first finger has threaded through the trigger-guard.

It's been a long wait. For three years I've been biding my time, digging in at Deptford. For three years I've fiddled around, doing small things, waiting for the Big Man to say the word. For three years I haven't known what the big job will be. Meanwhile I've found my way around, made contact with some useful guys, bought some merchandise, and settled in.

All that time I've kept myself in trim. At first I had the same impatience I'm feeling now. I'm not a guy for hanging around. I'm built for action, and it seemed a raw deal being dumped in a desolate corner of London with the kind of instructions you'd give an old man on retirement. I felt I was wasted. For a decade till then I'd had the adrenalin flowing. I'd been active and motivated. This wasn't for me.

45

But you know how it is. You get used to it. You're not in prison — you don't have to stare at the walls. After a while your pulse rate slows and you come to think maybe these ordinary law-abiding folks ain't zombies after all. It happened to me.

I picture Victor cooking spaghetti in his bedsitter, and I realize it's happened to him too. It's been too easy. We're getting soft. The Big Man is just a voice on the phone: he's left us too long. For a moment I wonder if he's set all this up to sharpen our reactions and test us out, but I know it's not that. This is real, all right. Something has begun. It usually starts sudden, like this. And it's not before time. We've been on Hold too long.

Victor fusses over his gas-ring like I'm his long-lost son. He lifts off the frying pan and replaces it with a saucepan of water. The pan is left at the side with its lid on to keep the sauce warm while he stands over the heating water, muttering incantations to make it boil. "I brought a bottle of wine," I say. "Since it's spaghetti."

"Ah," he says, not taking his eyes off the ring, "I opened some Valpolicella already."

I say it should be a nice evening, and I think to myself I may need all that wine.

"Everything all right outside?" he asks, and I tell him I checked before coming in. I scanned the street for lurking strangers as I came near, and no one was there. They haven't found his place yet.

"Just as long as no one's taken a room opposite," I say.

It does make a difference — red wine and an airbed. Victor surprised me with his spaghetti. As the pasta drained, he gave the sauce a quick blast on the ring, and we ate in the middle of his room as enjoyably as in a trattoria.

Now I'm lying on his airbed, under a spare blanket and his overcoat. My stomach feels contented and the back of my mouth retains the taste of the wine. There are plans to make for tomorrow, but for now I want a dreamless sleep.

Over breakfast I break it to him. He nods morosely, as if he always knew I would leave him, and he tries to impress on me that I have to disappear out of sight. I make reassuring noises, and accept another mug of coffee to clear the silt that's in my brain. No dreams last night, and I bless the wine.

There's a lingering smell of machine oil in the room, and I see that Victor got up early to strip and clean his gun. He handles it with the familiarity of a mother with her baby, yet he has a look in his eyes as if he was removing specks of vomit. The old sadness has returned, and I feel like I've brought contagion into the house. "We gotta have protection," I say, but he still looks glum.

"While I didn't have a gun I didn't feel threatened," he says. "Having a gun just means the other fellow feels he has to shoot you first. You're a threat to him, so he wants to remove you. And you, once you feel that weight in your pocket, you're changed. You respond differently under pressure. The pistol acts like a magnet to your hand. Once you've touched it there's no going back."

I've lost interest in breakfast, and the half-eaten slice of toast grows cold on the plate. I remember the last time I saw Victor with a gun in his hand. He stood ice-cool in the confusion as if practising on the range; feet apart and gun at arm's length, squinting through the sight so he didn't waste a round. There was blood and people dying and Victor solid as a signpost at a crossroad, picking off those who had a gun, eliminating threats.

I raise the delicate question he's been avoiding. With Timmy taken and me on the run, what happens if the heavy mob find out where he is? "I've spoken to the Big Man," he says.

"What did he say?"

"Lie low. Keep your head down. That sort of thing."

"Very helpful. Are you supposed to wait here till they find you?"

"They won't, if I lie low, darling. Timmy never knew how to reach me."

"He led them to my place. What if they catch me?"

"You wouldn't tell them where I live. You're a tough guy."

"No one's that tough. You'll need a bolt-hole, just in case."

He smiles, because that's what the Big Man said. He gives me the address of a boarding house he could stay at in Earls Court. "I hope I don't have to use it," he says.

Apparently the place is straight, with nothing connecting it to us. It's random choice. If he can't get in there, he'll try the one on the left, and if that's full, he'll try the next one, and so on. He mentions a café where he would eat once a day.

"It won't happen," he says. "It's just a precaution."

As the little piggy said, when he built his house made out of bricks. I collect my things and pack, and it takes less than a minute.

6

I'm not too sure of the reception I'll get. I ring her bell and stand looking pitiful, clutching my possessions in a Marks & Spencer bag. She opens the door.

She's been hacking at her hair again. It's like a little girl has been playing with her mother's scissors, and she sat in front of the mirror wondering what her mother's going to say, and whether if she snips a little more it'll be OK. I want to reach out and touch her, like she's just been bereaved. Then she smiles, nods me in, and leads the way upstairs. When we're in the flat she says she'll make some coffee, and I sit down on a chair with my carrier by my side.

Her place is bigger than Victor's but it wasn't built by someone who appreciated rooms. The ceiling is too low and the windows were stuck in the middle of each wall only because you've got to have windows to satisfy the regulations. This is the sort of place would satisfy regulations. It might even satisfy the drab clerk who wrote the regulations. Perhaps he lived in a cage like this.

She brings two mugs of hot coffee, places one in my hands, and prods the carrier bag with her foot. She says, "I doubt if that's a present. Were you thinking of staying the night?"

"It *is* a present," I say, and I fish in the bag for a bottle of Marks & Spencer Chablis.

"Thanks." she says. "My mother warned me about men who turn up late carrying wine."

I feel like a schoolboy caught by Matron with a *Playboy* in his desk. After about five seconds silent embarrassment like only that schoolkid knows, we both break it by saying, "Sorry," together. It allows us both to smile.

"I haven't spoken to anyone all day," she says. "I can give you soup and bread and cheese."

"It goes well with Chablis."

*

It is not until we're sitting on the floor dropping cheese on the carpet she tells me she is moving on.

"Where will you go?"

She shrugs. "There are other flats. Or a room, more likely."

"In Brighton?"

"Maybe. But it gets cold in winter."

"Can't you afford to keep this place on?"

"They want me out. The landlord was here again this morning."

He has been pressing her to move for some time. Downstairs is now vacant, and she should have quit last weekend.

"How much notice do you have left?"

"Minus eight days."

I'd like to suggest we find some place together, but I realize it's stupid. It's just I get the feeling we could live alongside each other very well. I don't mean . . . Hell, I didn't even bring her chocolates or flowers or whatever a man brings a girl nowadays. I brought the wine because I like it, which is no way to treat a lady, but I also liked the thought of sitting down with her, talking about interesting things, in the way you do with wine. I even looked forward to her sofa-bed and duvet, because it beats the hell out of Victor's rubber lilo. I suppose if you put all this together you would say I'm not exactly the archetypal Mills & Boon tall dark stranger when it comes to courting girls.

This is a thought that has occurred to me before.

Anyway, we've finished all we can eat of this Cambozola, and the wine bottle is only good for sticking candles in, and we are still sitting on the carpet lit by one small lamp somewhere over in the corner, and she keeps filling in the pauses by staring into my eyes as if she's checking I don't wear false eyelashes, and I start to think it's about time I got up off the floor.

"Listen," I say as I creak to my feet, "can I help with the washing up or something?"

"We'll just pile it in the kitchen."

I help her to do this, and it takes no time at all. "Well," I begin.

"Yes, well," she says.

"That seems to be that," I say.

She's smiling softly as she stands in the dim glow, and she asks, "Do you want to go to bed?"

I stretch slowly. "Yeah, I'm kinda tired after the journey. You pop along, and I'll shake out the sofa-bed."

The smile she gives me is really sweet. It's like she flashed a bright light in my eyes, and I have to look away. She says, "I'll bring your duvet in a minute," and she slips into her bedroom and shuts the door.

It's as if that bright warm light has left the room, but the air is still full of her presence and I'm smiling to myself while I fiddle with the bed. It clunks into position and I sit on it to take off my shoes. Two new Marks & Spencer socks wink up at me.

I reach into my carrier. There isn't much to find: shirts and underwear, a new toothbrush that's fallen to the bottom, and a brown paper parcel for the gun.

Then the bedroom door opens and Rachel steps out clutching the big duvet. She is already in her nightdress, and I stand up holding my toothbrush like I've found the present I forgot to give her.

"Not undressed yet?" she asks.

I say, "You go ahead and use the bathroom because I'm not quite ready." She laughs and throws the duvet at me, and I sit back on the sofa-bed as she slips out into the hall.

It's dark. For several seconds I don't know what made me wake up. Then I hear the guy laugh downstairs and what really woke me was the dog. It sounds big and I decide there's two men with an Alsatian down there, so I slip out of bed and grab some clothes. As the racket comes nearer I climb into my trousers. Rachel comes out of her room looking as frightened as you'd expect, but I say nothing and concentrate on easing into my shoes. Suddenly there's a crash at our upstairs door because the Alsatian has hit it, and his claws scratch the paint with a sound like he's skinning a rabbit. One of the men starts thumping.

Rachel signals for me to stay quiet, and she asks through the door what these guys want. I'm standing behind her feeling nice and cold and angry, but I let her ask the questions so I can see how this game is played. As they answer she leans back, and her nightdress brushes against my bare chest and tickles my hair.

It's the usual crap. Bangs on the door and laughter, explicit threats as the dog whines. I put my hands on her arms and try to move her aside. Two punks and a snarling alsatian are just what I need. I've been waiting to smash something ever since I left Jancey and said goodbye to my flat.

But Rachel spins round and mimes furiously that I'm not to get involved. Then she tries to reason with the frighteners through the door. They make as if they're gonna break into the room, and one of these guys is enjoying himself saying how he's decided to rape her and then hand her to the dog. But it's clear his orders are to stay outside and keep it verbal, and soon he comes on heavy with the landlord's message. Rachel doesn't seem too scared. She can tell this is just harassment, and she lets him spill his speech. Because they're the sort of brainless beefoes who don't know when a job is finished we get a re-run of their fantasies, and Rachel shrugs and walks away from the door. I'm left staring at it with my adrenalin draining into the floorboards, and though I wish she'd let me take them I find I'm getting bored.

The heavies clump downstairs laughing, and they jeer all the way down the garden path.

Reaction after a scene like that is never easy. You were tense, and straining on the balls of your feet with your arms hanging loose and ready, and you have passed a kind of barrier that's hard to come back across. It's as if you were leaning forward and you overbalanced. I am prowling around the room flexing my fingers, while the hard men fade away with Rover. When I see Rachel's trembling face it makes me gasp like I've been hit.

Grabbing hold of that girl and pulling her into my chest is like a thousand dreams exploding, and her fragrance rocks me on my heels. We stand holding each other, and she shivers like a butterfly and her tears trickle down my skin. My hand gets lost in the spikes of her hair, and it is soft like I cannot believe.

Her face lifts towards me and she sniffs and I touch her cheek. It's like caressing something sacred. We are gazing at each other, and it never occurs to us to kiss. In that trance-like state we drift apart, still staring, but when I turn aside it's as if we snapped a silken cord.

Oh, I suppose you've been in love, probably several times, so you know how it feels to hold someone, and perhaps what I'm feeling is what anybody feels when their life is startled and transformed. But it's new for me. Perhaps it's something about the way I live, but love hasn't made any mark before. I've had sex — I'm not some kind of celibate — but sex isn't love, is it?

Anyway, love it is that seems to have smacked me one now, and I'm standing there hugging her in that thin nightdress and the thought of those bastards with the dog makes me squeeze her till it hurts.

Their taunts must have sickened her, so this ain't the time to start mauling — even though I've got a bulge in my pants like a bunch of bananas and I want to rip that nightdress of her and throw her on the bed.

But she has eased away and stands right in front of me, as close as you can get without touching, and her teeth are clenched and she almost glares into my face and her fist punches against my stomach as she says, "Listen, you," like it really hurts her. Then she grabs the waistband of my trousers and tugs, and a button pops across the room, and she yanks on that zip like it ain't gonna be needed any more and she slips her hand inside my pants.

Well, what did you expect? That I was gonna tell you every detail? You wanted to hear all that stuff about nipples and erections and squeezing and pushing — how we fell onto the bed and nearly crashed it through the floor? Well, I'm sorry, that's our secret. It's like I leapt up and pulled the curtains, and you were left across the street, peering from your darkened upstairs window at the moonlight on our wall. These are *our* moments, and you can spend the rest of this trembling night dreaming on your own.

7

I am sitting eating cornflakes in the benign haze you are left with from making love before breakfast. Rachel has started packing up to leave, and I try to divert her with more coffee. I can separately feel every single cornflake in my mouth — which ones are melting, which are still hard — and a creamy coat of milk lies sweetly on my tongue. Rachel fidgets round the room like it's a hotel we got to leave by ten.

Since she doesn't respond to my telling her to relax I ask who is this landlord anyway and has she got a rent book? She hasn't, of course, but she gives me the landlord's name. I carry on munching through my toast, and since there's no point carrying the last dregs of marmalade to wherever it is we're going, I scrape an inch-thick layer out of the jar and ask through a mouthful of carbon where the landlord lives. She looks suspicious. "Why do you want to know?"

Innocently I point out that we'd better return the key to him, since if we leave the flat unattended he could say we stole his best furniture. Though she sees the sense in this she is reluctant to spill his address. I drop the subject.

Packing does not take long. There's a large suitcase her father gave her which holds all her clothes, there are two carriers full of food and cooking things, and that's that. "What about the duvets?" I ask.

It seems they belong in the flat. I was fond of that duvet because I thought it was hers. I liked to hug the cuddly soft bulk of it. Now I know it's the landlord's it's as tainted as an unfaithful lover. The duvet symbolizes the whole wretchedness of leaving, so I slump at the table, pulling a long face and blowing ripples in the surface of my coffee which has grown cold anyway. Just before we leave, I go into the kitchen and turn on the tap so his hot water can run down the drain.

*

This is a day that's growing bleaker, and I feel my face has aged ten years. A taxi brought us to a boarding house she knew, and we're shown into an apology for a bedroom. The landlady looks like she's just been told she'll stay ugly for the rest of her life. When she clumps out I sit on the bed and ask Rachel, "What the hell are we doing here?" and she shrugs.

This room is off a narrow corridor on the first floor. It ought to be a single, but it's filled with an old double bed they must have folded in half to squeeze in here, and the internal walls are cheap partitions from where they gutted the Edwardian interior and crammed in as many cubicles as they could. A thin radiator huddles under the window. There's an oil stain beneath it, but I bet it hasn't been on since last February. Through the grease on the window you see only the house next door. Nothing else.

When I ask Rachel again to let me pay for somewhere decent she says, no, this place is recognized by the DHSS. Because she is now out of work they'll pay for it, and she'll have a few pounds left to see her through. It is either pride or obstinacy, but she is determined to pay her way and I'm not allowed to help her out. If dumps like this are what she has to put up with, then up with this she'll put.

We can both feel the strain plucking at the atmosphere, so when I say I'll return the keys to the landlord she gives me his address to get me out of the way.

It ain't a palace the guy lives in, though it would suit some people. You walk through a low wrought-iron gate, up a drive all of ten feet long, and you're touching a house where everything is fake. It aspires to Mock Tudor. It has a white painted top-half with black lines where beams should be, red brick cladding for the ground floor, and a thick wooden door studded with medieval wheel-nuts. The iron knocker is shaped like a lion's head.

I ring at a plastic bell and hear an electronic chime. There is a tiny glass bead in the door, one of those squint-through devices where you check the daily rapist, but since the landlord has never seen me before I am content to stand there looking serious, like an estate agent with news.

He opens the door no wider than an old lady would, and I notice he has one foot firmly behind it just in case. A cautious habit, well ingrained. "Mr Hatchard," I smile at him, "I believe you have a house for sale?"

"Several," he says without returning my pleasant smile. "The agent has the details."

"I have an offer that could interest you," is enough to relax his guard. My smile stays really charming as I stop forward and kick, flat-footed, against the edge of the door. He flinches for only half a second, but it's enough to take me inside the hall. As I calmly shut the door he cringes back against the wall. These are the five leisurely seconds while I see what he will do. He can swing a punch, which would give me pleasure, or he can call for help, which will give me warning, or, as he is doing, he can cower against the wall.

After you leave junior school you grow out of smacking guys who are scared of you, but I look on this as a job to do — like polishing your shoes. I mention Rachel's old address, and ask him about our nocturnal visitors. He has hardly started his denial before he realizes this is unwise. "All right, listen," he says, and I cock my head. "I have to sell the place. I can't have sitting tenants. No one will buy."

Perhaps my face looks like the message is not getting through.

"Listen, I asked her to go. The others went. What was I to do? That place was costing me a fortune. Listen, in the end you can't get rid of tenants. Whatever they say about the law being on the landlord's side, if they won't go, the law won't make them. What are you supposed to do?"

"These guys you sent round, what were their names?"

"Come on, mister. Listen, be reasonable. I didn't realize what they would do. I'm sorry."

"That's nice."

"Oh, Jesus! I'm sorry. It won't happen again."

"That's nice."

"What do you want me to say?"

"I want you to say ouch. I want you to say sorry like you really meant it."

"Listen, I do, mister, come on. It was wrong. OK. I'm sorry. I didn't know what they'd do."

You mustn't let these conversations go on too long. You get trapped into arguing a point.

So I bring this one to an end with a nasty short jab to his belly. As he crumples I grab hold of his hair. I hold him up like he was an old coat at a jumble sale, and his eyes are like a frightened rabbit. "Don't hit me in the face." He covers it with both hands. So instead I crunch in a low right-hook that will end his sex life for a month. His head falls forward, his hands drop, and before he can vomit I jab the right again to split his nose and cover his face with blood. I drop the puking mess on the carpet and walk to the front door. The sight of that blood has made me feel a whole lot better.

By the time I get back to this dump we're staying in I've decided to say nothing to Rachel. Did I do it for her or to release the frustration that's been eating me since I left Deptford? Ever since then it keeps stabbing me — this feeling I gotta smash something, that I can't just do nothing, drumming my fingers while others make the game. Three years I took it easy, stayed out of sight, made contacts, laid pathways. You can stay a long time in neutral, ticking over — provided nothing happens. But once the adrenalin spurts back into your system it will not gently leak away. You can feel it bursting the shell. Maybe it's like driving an expensive sports car: you ease through city traffic, choking on fumes and endless queueing, and then you finally edge out onto a motorway, you drop down into a stronger gear, and you press the accelerator. The roar of the engine is what I've waited to hear.

But I shouldn't have let myself get near that cringing landlord. I have to stay below the surface, under control. What if he'd had back-up? Didn't I almost want there to be someone — to make the fight worthwhile? You will know this already, I suppose, but the point of a good fight, the way you relieve the tension, is not just in hitting someone: you got to get hit yourself. You gotta feel a smack on the cheek, to make you draw back your teeth and react. You gotta have something to react *against*, otherwise you might as well hit punchbags in the gym.

And as I walk back through the streets the other thing fuelling this self-criticism is that I turned up there with the gun. No, I wasn't gonna use it, I just couldn't leave it in that boarding house for Rachel to unpack. But I shouldn't have taken it there. There are rules about these things. Carrying a gun when you don't need it is a risk you do not take. I can hear Victor asking what I'd do if I started losing the fight; let them kick me about while all the time I could stop them; let them find the gun? It would be a magnet, like Victor said, pulling at my fingers and the palm of my hand.

You're better off without the thing. You're freer, and can act as you please — like you travel freer without possessions. But possessions stick like leeches: you're scared to let go, but they weigh you down. Everyone knows it. Everyone fails. It isn't greed that causes this, it's fear. We hold onto stuff because we're afraid someday the money will run out. Fat people can't stop eating because someday there will be no more cream cakes. I keep carrying this gun because if I put it down, then someday I'll meet the man still holding his.

8

"Victor?"

"Yes?"

"This is me."

"Who else. Are you all right?"

"Bored. What you doing — staying in permanent?"

"Permanent*ly*. It's an adverb. Permanently, darling."

"Can you do me a favour?"

"Such as?"

"Check out my flat. Go round to Jancey, next door. You remember Jancey?"

"Of course."

"Use the right-hand staircase. They can't see it from my flat."

"How can Jancey help?"

"She'll know if they're still there. Tell her you're from me. She may not trust you, so ask if she's heard a loo flush in the night. Say I told you to ask that."

"Is this some kind of code?"

"She'll understand. You got it?"

"Of course."

"And use the right-hand staircase."

"I heard you. Tell me, are you behaving yourself down there?"

"What else could I be doing?"

"That's what worries me."

When the landlady opens the door she acts like I'm trying to sell brushes. She stands on the step looking more solid than the door. "Bed and breakfast," she says. "You're not allowed in the rooms in the day." I ask who comes in to sleep while we're out. She tries to slam the door, but I've got my foot there like I really was selling brushes. Though she thumps the door against

59

it, I hold my ground. "Do that again," I smile and tell her, "and I'll squeeze you through the letter-box."

My foot feels like it's trapped in a mangle, and she shouts in my face that I'd better not address a lady in that tone. "Then stand aside and let me in."

She turns and calls down the corridor for a guy named Malcolm and all the time she's leaning hard against the door trying to break my foot. My patience is draining like water from a colander, but the guy called Malcolm appears at her side so fast you'd think he was joined on a spring. Before he can open his mouth he gets a simple instruction from each of us, so he stands switching his gaze from her to me and back again like he's at a tennis match. Since he is smaller than either of us I wonder who frightens him most.

"I'm counting to five," I say. "And then I'm pushing you *both* through the letter-box." This has no immediate effect, so I start counting at "three, four." She recoils in outrage, and I barge through the door.

Malcolm tries to look strong, but I pretend not to notice. I glance round the hall like I've come to change the wallpaper, thirty years late. "Nice place you have here," I say. "I suppose you're gonna tell me there's no one in?" The dragon smoulders and repeats her rule.

"Suppose I want to get hold of a resident?" I say. "Suppose she left a message where she is?"

"She didn't."

"Then I'll stay till she comes back."

Even as I say it I know this is not how I wish to spend the rest of the day. "Call the police, Malcolm," she smirks, and she gleams like she's played an ace.

"Move and I'll squash you," I warn him, and we all stand still and listen to her breathing. I try to think of something smart to say to hide the fact that I'm beaten, and finally come out with a pathetic "I couldn't stay in this stink without puking on the carpet. I'll be back."

I shut the door behind me, because I don't want to hear it crash as I walk down the path.

*

It's a big place, Brighton. Where do you look for a girl who's nothing to do but drift about for the daylight hours? I try the seafront, but it's wet and windswept — the summer attractions shuttered and shivering in the damp off the sea. I buy a cup of tea so thin it could have been made by Rachel's landlady, and I stare out through a steamed-up café window across the cold empty promenade.

In the end, it's on that rainy promenade that I see her. I'm just back from the railway station, where I have deposited in Left Luggage a small brown parcel containing one Smith & Wesson and two dozen rounds, and I have detoured on the way back to buy three more shirts, some underpants and some socks.

She has a greyness under her eyes and a slouch from spending most of the day on her feet. As we sit to yet another cup of greasy coffee in a steamed-up café I suggest it's time we got out of all this. But no: she has hung around the DHSS while clerks forgot her like she was goods in the stockroom, and now she has a chit that says they'll pay her lodging at the boarding house. Bed and breakfast only. I don't mention my chat with the landlady. Nor with her previous landlord.

Outside, the daylight sludge is darkening, and it's nearly time we will be allowed back in that depressing hole. Rachel wants to make sure her DHSS chit is acceptable and her luggage is still there, and I'm wondering where we can go this evening to find something to eat, and to spend as long as possible outside that cubicle.

I'm pensive as we drag back round to the poorhouse. First there's my relationship with the dragon and little Malcolm. What will we all say to each other when we meet in the hall? Second, there is Rachel. She says she's determined to go along with the system, so no one can say she bucked it. And if they tell her to bed down in a flea-pit, that's what she'll do. If the Department of Health are prepared to shell out money to keepers of a vermin-infested tenement then the officials are to blame. I am not to interfere. This is her life.

Approaching the lodging house it looks as if the old harridan has got a gang together to repel unwelcome boarders. A dozen or so desperados lounge round the door. But two are women, and three are kids. They are just queuing at the door, waiting to be let in. We stand with them for the last gloomy minutes till the clock strikes the hour.

Someone starts hammering at the door. It's time to let us in. People who make rules should stick to them. I wait for the door to open, and for the expression on the old dragon's face.

Sarcastic cheers as a bolt slides and the door shudders open. The lodgers shuffle into line as if places were limited, like on a crowded bus. When we shamble inside I see we have a new dragon. This must be the evening shift: a man and a woman, mid-forties, looking wary. They wave most through, leaving Rachel and me, and a teenager with two kids. We let her go first. The doorkeepers study her slip of paper like either it's a forgery or they can't read, then give her a room number and send her upstairs. Rachel bites her lip, and frowns at me as she hands over her chit. The new dragon holds out her meat-cutter's fist to take mine. "I don't have one of those," I say. "I'll pay cash."

"Cash?"

Yeah, I think, remember that? But I smile, because I have Rachel by my side. "How much do you want?"

"This is for people on Social. You got a chit?"

"No."

"UB40?"

"No. I'll pay. OK?"

"We don't do paying guests. There's plenty of other places. Better ones."

"Especially at this time of year, I know. But we're together."

"Oh, yes?" She squints at Rachel. "You asked for a double room."

"That's right. We're together, as he says."

"Your chit's for a single."

I drudge up a smile. "I'll pay the extra. It'll be cash, so how much do you want?" I'm relying on the magic of the word cash: it's that slippy stuff, untraceable and real. It slides into your pocket like rain down the drain.

I produce paper money and straighten a few notes. "What's the extra for a double?" The woman's face twitches like a tramp's to the smell of soup. "That'll do nicely," she says, and snatches some out of my hand. She stares at me hard with a you-ain't-getting-change expression. "You know which room," she says.

I follow Rachel up the stairs, feeling like I just paid money in one of those Soho hotels where you take a girl and hire a room by the hour. That's what the landlady thinks too.

When we get to the room there's a key in the door. Inside, it looks much as we left it. Rachel hadn't unpacked. She wanted to sort out the Social Security first. I smile at her to lighten the atmosphere. It isn't easy when you're in a single room jammed up with a double bed, and the dump is decorated as carelessly as the inside of a rarely used cupboard. I touch the skeletal radiator under the window. It's still cold. The size of this room, the two of us will warm it up anyway.

When I try to use the shared bathroom I am met by the teenage mother — the one with two kids. She has them in the bathroom with her, and she apologizes: "I've just put fifty pence in the meter to get water for our bath."

I chat with her while she waits for the tub to fill. The kids are larking about in the steam-filled room, and the girl seems grateful for adult conversation. She looks permanently worried, and it doesn't take long to find why. She and the kids are on two council-house waiting lists, and each council has found out about the other, so she is suspended by both of them and now has to fend for herself. What this means is she has to find a job fast. If she stays unemployed, relying on DHSS boarding houses, the kids will be taken away. She won't be allowed to bring them up in a series of bed and breakfasts, and they won't give her a council flat or help her pay for somewhere private. Eventually the council will take her children. They'll provide accommodation and three meals a day, at only four times the cost of letting her do it herself. Then the kids will get worse problems and go bad sure as sure, and they'll have to be rehoused and in the end they'll cost ten times as much. But it's better than giving handouts to the real mother in the first place, because with kids round her apron she can't find herself a job. Not like decent people.

So I stand shaking my head, making clucking noises. Then one of the kids yells that the tap has run cold, and they turn it off and start taking off their last few clothes, and the girl slips back in the bathroom and shuts the door, and the kids shriek in the water and I drift slowly back to our bedroom where it's quiet and drab.

I ask Rachel what kind of work there is for a woman alone with two kids. "Teacher," she suggests, "if she's got qualifications. A cleaner if not — in the evenings, maybe."

"She'd have to look after the kids in the evenings."

"Maybe some places need cleaners in the day-time. Or she might get temporary work. There's not much about." Rachel has unpacked into the dressing table, and I like to think of her things and mine sharing the furniture. She has put out ornaments and several books, and has stuck a poster on the wall. It's an attempt. We stand for a few moments in each other's arms, and I ask what we should do this evening.

"Go somewhere," she says. "Anywhere. We can't stay here."

I am pleased to hear this. This is a place that will not grow on me. It will not improve with time. I give it two nights. At most.

Nobody else in this dive has any money, and for them it will be a long cold evening. But I drag Rachel out to a warm comforting Indian restaurant. You can feel good about yourself in a Curry Corner. The skinny little waiters bow and grin the moment you enter, there are dim lights on heavy red wallpaper, white linen tablecloths, candles, and you get poppadums in your hands in no time at all.

I order a bottle of Beaujolais. It may not go with a tableful of curry, but a mug of cold beer is not what I need. Then the beaming dark guy appears with the heated dishwarmer and plates. Each gets a final polish with his cloth, and he grins into them as if they were mirrors. When he slides them in front of us you can feel the heat rising.

This is a guy who speaks little English, but he buzzes round us like a bee on a rosebush. He lays out food for us to admire. We haven't been ambitious, but you'd think every dish was topped with one of those silver-foil slips the rajahs ate. In fact Rachel is taking it easy with a perfumed chicken korma, I'm looking forward to my tandoori biriani, and we share a mixed vegetable bahjee, some chutneys, and a great omelette of nan bread. All this absorbs the Beaujolais like blotting paper soaks ink. It fills us with a deep warmth that will last past midnight.

The coffee's not bad either.

When we finally spill outside, Rachel says she wants to go down to the beach again. "That's what we did the first night we met." I give in to this, since the weather's behaving like it usually does at the seaside: drizzling all day and clearing up at night.

Maybe I've forgotten or maybe I never knew, but just plain walking in night streets with a pretty girl is the happiest thing you can do in this world. It's enchantment, with every street like a glade in the forest. Streetlights and shop windows are like stars drifting by. The draught on street corners is like a tropical breeze.

We float down to the beach by Old Steine, just like that first night. Even the tatty Dolphinarium suggests a forgotten fairground in the dark, and the pier timbers are like the legs of an artificial dinosaur, sturdy and reassuring in the gloom. Sea slurps against them, rattling the pebbles. I'm looking for the magical pleasureboat, to carry us off and lose us in a kingdom out at sea.

A concrete breakwater stretches away to sink slowly in the dark distance. It's about three foot above the water, and maybe a foot wide. I walk along it, pretending to be a tightrope artist. Ten yards out on the sea I turn to yell back to Rachel. She shouts that if I get soaked I needn't expect sympathy, and I call for her to join me. She smiles and shakes her head. In the dark she has to show her teeth for me to know she is smiling. Then she stoops for some pebbles and warns that I'd better come in now. But I stay out there singing some made-up song that goes with the waves crunching on the shingle, so she tosses stones in the water to plop near me in the darkness and I shout like an idiot and run back to the shore.

Without half a bottle of red wine inside me I might have slipped on the slimy breakwater, but I jump onto the stony beach and chase her along the shore. We're laughing and panting as we clamber through the sucking stones. Then we collapse into each other and stand gulping salt air in the night.

Well, you might want to, but at this autumnal time of year you don't sink down onto cold pebbles making love in the starlight, unless you're carrying a groundsheet. So we go back to the house.

The night landlady's better half sits scowling in the hallway. He hands over Rachel's key. As we climb the stairs it sounds like people have brought bottles in. Some of the kids are still up. Television keeps them subdued.

When we close the bedroom door behind us the noise level does not reduce. These thin walls were built only as dividers: they mark out the cells, they don't stop the sound. We smile at each other, but though we're still light and happy the urgency has gone. This is the kind of house where flowers fade overnight.

When we go to see if the bathroom is free, a young guy I ain't seen before starts talking in the corridor. Apparently there's a guest lounge. There has to be a public room to satisfy the local DHSS, and we can all pile in there provided we don't make it obvious we're drinking alcohol. The landlords allow this because it's better than having parties in the bedrooms.

We go down. A lopsided notice on a door says "Guest Lounge". Inside there's no carpet, just old lino, a few vinyl-covered stacking chairs, and two tables that have seen better days. You can smell the lack of money. It reminds me of that make-the-best-of-it jollity in a jumble-sale hall. These fingers holding cups and glasses are the ones you see picking over clothes on the stalls. Rachel touches my arm and leads me into a corner, where we drink our coffees quietly, like strangers at a wake. She is realizing she does not belong here.

When I look at these shabby partygoers waving their coffee-cups and leaning on metal-frame chairs, it's like the plague has settled on them, and they're twitching out the rest of their time. Or it's like the radioactive cloud has drifted down, days after the holocaust, and dusted their skin softly to start the decay.

We slide out of the room and up the stairs. We sleep badly.

I wake to see a scrap of sunlight pushing at the curtains. The room fills with beige light as we lie listening to the house coming to life. We hear water running, inmates talking, footsteps clumping on loose floorboards, street noise, children shouting — and somewhere underneath it all a woman is sobbing in her room. I wonder why she is crying before breakfast, and whether she wakes up weeping many days.

Seeping up the stairs come smells of real cooked breakfast: smoking fat, bacon, burning toast. But first we stand in line to use the bathroom: people popping their heads out of doorways to see how big the queue is, me letting Rachel in by herself. Cleaning up is not an act to share; it's a thing you do alone. I follow her in, sluice around, dry up, come and fetch her. Before we go down to breakfast we make sure we lock the door.

They have to serve a cooked breakfast here to meet some kind of official standard. We get a bowl of cereal, and a plate with sausage, egg and single piece of bacon. Everybody gets the same. The tea tastes like we got it heated up again because no one would drink it yesterday, and there's no coffee at all. We are each issued with two slices of bread.

It lies sullenly in our stomachs as we trudge back up the stairs. I make a crack to some little thin guy in a blazer who is following us up, but we says nothing and stares in front of him like he's forcing himself forward in a hill-climb. So we go to our room, unlock the door, and step inside to find the guy in the blazer has not gone away. He takes out a notebook.

We watch him like you watch a dog crapping on the pavement. He recites Rachel's name and reads out sentences constructed by a constipated computer. The nub of it is that since this is a double room Rachel is therefore cohabiting, and she is not entitled to state help to pay for the rent. I point out that I'm paying for my half, but they both ignore this. They seem to understand each other. Rachel cheers me up by saying she was leaving anyhow, and if he wants her to pay for the night then she will and to hell with it. It don't satisfy him. He drones on about deception and intent to defraud and the imposing of penalties, and I'm watching dumb like a picture on the wall.

He carefully writes out a form and Rachel gets the top copy. He points out that now she is cohabiting the only benefit she will get is the basic dole. She is advised to seek work immediately, preferably today. He turns to me: "Can I have your name, please?"

"No."

"We need your name."

"So do I."

He shrugs, and fits his notebook back in his inside blazer pocket. He has the nonchalance of a guy it never occurs to he could get bust on the nose. Which is extraordinary in his position.

When he goes I tell Rachel I am sorry. I felt as useful as a Latvian dictionary. But she strokes my arm and says, "We're cohabiting now. It's official. Do you mind?"

It gives me an excuse to kiss her.

9

"Hello, Victor."

"Sweet of you to phone, darling."

"Any news?"

"I haven't checked your flat yet. But the Big Man has phoned."

"What did he say?"

"It's time to go for the jackpot."

"When?"

"Saturday nights are the best time. They're at their slackest."

"How does he know that?"

"Timmy told him. He's making the arrangements."

"Who is?"

"The Big Man. He's taken over Timmy's contact. The poor sod doesn't like it, but the boss gave him no choice. This Saturday, in the middle of the night shift, around one in the morning."

"Jesus. I can hardly believe it. It's happening at last. How do we know the other mob ain't onto us?"

"We don't. But according to Timmy's contact, the new consignment is in. So there's no point waiting."

"The same plan as before?"

"You're the one with the details. Look, I don't like talking about this on the telephone. But have you everything you need with Timmy gone?"

"Sure, no problem. We went over there together."

"Inside?"

"No, do me a favour. But we cased the outside."

"So you're all ready to go?"

"I've been ready three years, Victor."

"We both have, darling. You'd better come back up to town. Make sure you're not followed, and slip over to my flat."

"Not again, thank you. We'll stay at that guest house you mentioned."

"We?"

"What?"

"You said 'we'. Have you got company?"

"Ah. Yes. Don't worry about it."

"This is no time to get involved with women."

"It never is."

"You can't possibly bring a woman along. Leave her in Brighton."

"I'll lose her on Saturday. I ain't spending the next three nights on an airbed at your place."

"You don't have to stay here. You can stay in the guest house. But you stay alone."

"Don't worry, we'll keep out of sight. We'll spend most of the time in bed."

"Phone me tonight when you get here. Give me a nineteenth nervous breakdown."

Nineteen. Minus one is eighteen. Eighteen means six o'clock. Twenty to six.

Rachel doesn't argue about coming to London. She doesn't complain when I scrap all those carrier bags and buy two soft holdalls. Even so, with her suitcase as well, we look like holidaymakers returning from a wet week away.

I think she accepts whatever comes now. Yesterday it was the authorities, today it is me. She is grass on the wind, floating where it takes her. I don't like this. It makes me uneasy. She has switched off from any responsibility for her own life.

At the station I pick up my other parcel from Left Luggage, and toss it in a holdall. I wonder if Victor has cleaned his again. Rachel and I wait at the little barrier in the station terminus, and again I think what an ordinary pair of holidaymakers we must look — too tatty to be honeymooners, but the same kind of contentment together. Must be lovers, they'd say. Or adulterers. Something wicked like that.

"Hello, Victor. We've arrived."

70

"I don't like this 'we', darling."

"Don't worry about it."

"I worry about everything."

"Did you go to the flat?"

"Yes. Nice girl, Jancey. We had a long chat."

"Really? Did you tell her anything?"

"Interesting fiction. She asked more questions than I did."

"But what about the flat?"

"She seemed genuinely fond of you. Can't think why."

"The flat?"

"It's clean. They've gone. But you can't go back."

"I know. Are we meeting?"

"Twenty times I tell you."

"So soon?"

"Yes."

So at twenty to seven I come out of the Earls Court hotel into the street and look around for him. Nothing. I turn right and stroll down the pavement. He's probably watching, to see I'm alone. I cross the road, slip into an alley, and wait. No one follows, so I come out the other end and nip round the small block. If I was on my own I'd turn round now, to walk straight into anyone on my tail. But Victor will be watching, so I leave it to him.

I turn another corner, and slow down. Victor walks towards me grinning and stripping cellophane off a new pack of cheroots. He sticks one between his teeth but doesn't light it — just holds it there like a storeman's pencil. I suggest a drink.

Before we reach the pub he has asked about Rachel, and as soon as I bring his whisky and soda to the table he asks about her again. I drink my whisky neat.

Rachel is waiting in the small hotel. She doesn't like to be left there on her own. I've had the first signs of her asking where I go, what I do. "Seeing a man about something" is not much of an explanation. While I say this, Victor lights that cheroot of his and scowls at me through a blue fog. I ask if he is fumigating the room.

"This is a ridiculous time for you to become involved with a woman, darling. We are supposed to melt into the background. We've waited three years. We don't want to blow it now."

I consider how successfully I have melted into the background recently. There's a landlord with a broken nose in Brighton, and a DHSS hostel that kicked me out. I remember the official in the blazer, who wanted my name. I think about Rachel, who is beginning to ask questions. I remember meeting her, introducing myself by thumping some guy who was annoying her. In a trainful of people. I raise my glass to Victor, and give what's meant to be a shamefaced grin but probably looks like a careless shrug. "You're right," I tell him.

"And you must forget about your flat. You mustn't think of taking these people on."

"Of course not."

He gives me his tired look. We've known each other a long time. He has a few years on me — maybe ten — and sometimes he treats me like the son he never had.

Now he's leaning forward and patting my hand. You start doing that in an Earls Court pub, Victor, and *you'll* be getting yourself noticed too. But this pub is full of Australians, so perhaps it doesn't matter. Victor is playing the wise father again. "It always gets worse towards the end. It's like when you increase the tension on a spring: the pressure is straining to be released. You push the spring down and you can feel it quivering. But you have to hold it down like that, and not let it burst free and flop trembling onto the table."

He leans back in his pub chair and sucks on his cheroot. It's died. He takes it out and frowns at it, then he licks the end. It looks revolting, glistening like a puppy's fresh turd. "Licking ain't gonna light it," I tell him. He smiles, and fumbles in his jacket pockets for a box of matches. Shaking a match out involves a lot of rattling and scratching about, before he lights the turd using two matches held together for a brighter flare. It should help dry the thing out.

As his face disappears behind a pungent blue cloud he relaxes into a deep wreathed smile of satisfaction. Whether this is due to the cheroot or the fact he has done his fatherly duty I don't know, but we must look a lovely couple. When he gets up to leave me he pats my shoulder, and you'd think he was leaving early to boil up our late-night cocoa.

But when he has gone I buy another whisky, and sit there musing on being a crunched-up spring. Yeah, the tension is slipping a bit and I've done a few foolish things, but that's not because we're near the end of the wait. I was like this before I knew. It has just been too long. For a guy like me to hang around kicking his heels ain't natural. It's not as bad as being banged up in prison. I've had that, and I can tell you it is always a hundred times better outside. Even the boring days outside when it's raining and you've finished the paper and you don't know how you'll last till bedtime are days to savour, compared to drying up in a cell. Outside, you're in charge. You can walk out the door.

That's what I hate most about keeping my head down. I'm locking myself up voluntarily. And I resent what happened to my flat. A couple of guys think they can stake it out and wait for me, rub their filthy fingers on my clothes, piss in my bathroom, and I'm supposed to ignore it. I know what I said about possessions being like leeches, but that don't mean I'll surrender them to a pair of punks. If they want them, they can fight me for them.

I think I'll have one more small whisky to keep the blood from cooling, and then slip back to Deptford and crack a couple of heads. I'm getting enthusiastic till I remember Rachel brooding in the bedroom. My storming back to Deptford is gonna have to wait. I can see what they mean about women softening you up. You don't want to be thinking about someone else at a time like this.

I stand up with a sigh, like any husband coming home from the boozer, and I head back to Rachel with whisky on my breath.

10

Maybe it's the light in this train. But look at these people: they have dusty clothes, concrete-coloured flesh, dead eyes. They've stepped down here to get from one piece of pavement to another, yet they look like they spent their whole lives underground. It's as if the tube sucked the sunlight out of them.

There are men in business suits, men in working gear, and some who haven't been out of their filthy clothes for a week. You'd have to cut them off their backs, like off a corpse. There are office girls reading paperbacks. There's a mother and catatonic child. There's a woman about the same age, rigid in her seat beneath glued and dyed hair. She holds her novel like a hymnal. She's from an office somewhere too.

But half this carriage could be going anywhere, doing anything. They're not tied to a nine-to-five, that's for sure. The lives they lead don't fit into tidy patterns. They're not from regular families in regular employment. They're just people, leading their lives, their way.

The truth is: we ain't predictable. You think of schoolkids. You spend a few minutes in a classroom and you find there's budding farmers, policemen, bank clerks, bus drivers, mothers, harlots, fortunate and starved. They'll stay like that. No one's the same. Everyone is different — some are just more so. Politicians ignore that. Which is why they get us wrong.

You know how it is — you sit on the underground with nothing to read, and you either stare at your fellow passengers or you drift into thinking. I didn't bring anything to read, and papers bore me anyway, so I'm wondering if I'm the kind of guy who's cut out for relationships.

Rachel was OK last night. I mean, she didn't ask anything, she just gave me a look when I got back. She didn't object when we went to eat in a trattoria where the food and wine must have cost a week's dole. She doesn't question what I do or decide. I take her along and she comes. I call the tunes. It's like I was the DHSS. She does what she's told.

When I told her this afternoon that I was gonna be away till maybe tomorrow morning I don't know what I expected. We had Wednesday night in the Earls Court hotel, then I said I'd have to spend the next night away, and she said OK. She sort of curled up inside herself and said OK. If that's what you want.

What I want? What I want is she should shout at me. Shout where-the-hell-you-think-you're-going-you're-shagging-some-other-woman-you-lousy-bastard. What I want is she shouldn't shrink in her skin and say nothing. What I want is to see she's human. It's got me torn up inside. I mean, what I want is that she shouts and I shout and she shouts back, then I say I'm sorry and put my arms round her, then we kiss and make love maybe, and in the end we're both real people again. She knows about me and I know about her. That's what I want.

But this shrugging, accepting whatever life brings, it worries me. What happened to her? Where did she get this automatic shutdown defence mechanism? Give her a tiny problem, lay on a touch of stress, and zap! The tortoise head whips back under its shell, gets inside the armour plating, waits till the trouble goes away. What did life do to her, for Christ's sake? Just being out of work is not that bad. Jesus! She doesn't have to keep cutting bits off her hair.

I don't brood on this too long because this isn't a long tube journey. Change at Embankment. Down to the Elephant. As I get out of the second tube I see someone has been scratching letters off the sign above the door. "Obstructing the Doors Causes Delay And Can Be Dangerous" now reads, "Obstruct The Doors Cause Delay Be Dangerous". I like it. It cheers me up as I come up in the lift and stagger out blinking in the daylight. Not a bad day: watery sun, noisy traffic churning round the roundabout, pedestrians kicking through debris in understreet tunnels.

I wait outside the Coronet cinema, at the usual place. The usual south-east Londoners are hanging about the bus stop.

75

No one queues, because it's the start of the route. Traffic, traffic, traffic.

I catch a 199, pay on entry, and sit downstairs. I watch the passers-by in the streets outside, living their lives. For a few seconds you snatch a glimpse of them, doing nothing much: nagging the kids, chatting with friends, carrying shopping home. Sometimes you catch them laughing their heads off, running for a bus, meeting an unexpected friend. You see a little moment in their lives, something they'll remember with a chuckle over tea. And when it happened, you were passing by on the bus, tuning in to their moment from another reality, like switching through channels on late-night TV. Did you see that? That looked interesting. It's gone now.

I sit on the lower deck with my soft holdall heavy at my feet, behind two laughing women from Jamaica swapping advice about knitting. I prod my bag with my foot. Then I think about why I came.

As I approach the flats I don't try to hide myself. In fact I go out of my way (I mean I walk several streets out of my way) to make myself seen. I stop off twice to buy food. I use the left-hand staircase to climb up to the flat.

If you're out there watching, you guys, you must have seen me. I'm behaving naturally, not dancing a Gene Kelly in the streets, but keeping visible enough for tired eyes to see.

I'm surprised no one else has noticed me. I expected to bump into young Darius or someone. But nothing happens. I climb the stairs and hesitate at the front door. All I got to do is turn the key. There's no one in there, everyone has gone.

There's nothing to worry about, nothing to fear. They won't have booby-trapped the front door. They ain't that clever. But you don't live to draw your old-age pension by underestimating the enemy. I mean, what are the risks here? I've got better odds than I'd get at Russian roulette — twenty to one, at least. Twenty to one, easily. But what's the date today? There's a twenty-first day every month.

They won't have booby-trapped the front door. I could look a real idiot if I don't use it. But I won't get killed. Do I want to be a dead hero or a living idiot? I ain't that proud.

One thing about these flats: there's really only one way in. There's supposed to be a back fire-escape, but years ago, before I came here, someone unhooked it and took it for scrap. The council insisted on erecting another — this was about the time I arrived — and it got delivered in handy, fit-together sections. Before they could strap it up, it had vanished too. Another nice piece of scrap. Worth a few quid. Several fivers to each of the residents, and a good profit to the lads. I think they tried to persuade the landlords to bring another. It looked a good business.

So I shall have to slip into my flat by the front window. The people living here know it's my place. They'll think I lost my key.

The easiest way into a flat with aluminium frame windows is to use the little flap window at the top — the ventilator, only big enough for an organ grinder's monkey, but easily opened with a knife, slipped underneath to prise up the catch. Then you dangle something down inside to hook round the lift-up handle of the main window. You can use your tie, your belt or a piece of string. I use my belt. After a little manipulation, the buckle slips round the handle, I give a tug, and the job is done.

I drop my bag inside the window and hoist myself over the sill to follow it. When I'm standing on my own carpet I feel like you do when you come back from holiday. This is my place. Here are my things. Let me look at you and see if I remembered you right.

Some things have been moved. Just a little. Chairs pushed back along the carpet, small things like that. I never take much notice of how I leave things, so I could be wrong. The place hasn't been turned over, anyway. Not so you'd notice. I sniff at the air, and it's stale, lifeless, like the inside of an empty breadbin.

I leave the front door for last, and cross into the bedroom. No one is there. No sign of disturbance. I wander back through the lounge, into the kitchen at the back. It's clear. So is the bathroom. But I see they opened a new toilet roll.

I go back to the hall and examine the front door. It looks innocent. No wires, no apparatus. There's a free newspaper and two letters. No one writes to me much. Carefully I open the door and step outside. The precautions weren't necessary. But I'm still alive.

The trick now is to behave normally. I leave lights on, I wander about, I even step outside and clean the windows. If anyone is still watching this flat, they'll be doing it casually: drive by twice a day, walk along the balcony maybe, see if the milk has been taken. They'll need a signal that I'm back.

Around tea-time Darius comes by. "Thought you'd gone forever, man." We act cool, like we're not delighted to meet up again, then we sit round the kitchen table and talk.

The heavies stayed into Saturday night and left early in the morning. Maybe where they come from, creeping about at five-thirty a.m. doesn't get noticed, but it does here. Jancey was sleeping, but Darius is a bright-eyed little blighter, and by that time there's others in this block up and about too. This is the kind of place the milkman lives.

Darius checked with some friends and learned that the heavies were seen again Sunday evening. They sat outside shivering in a big green car for an hour and a half, and they ain't been back since. One or another young kid has been watching this place since I left.

I am slicing bread for tea when Jancey arrives. Darius lets her in, and she strolls into the kitchen and grins. We have a friendly hug and I tell her I was laying three places anyway. She says she has a nice cake next door, one she made last night. All three of us are grinning like it's an idiot's birthday party, but she keeps an eye on me like she thinks I may have a relapse any minute. I tell her to fetch the cake.

It seems a long time since we ate together in this kitchen. Jancey's cake is one of those ridiculous affairs you get by copying all the details of the *Good Housekeeping* recipe you usually leave out including the piped cream, split almonds, dates and cherries. In case we don't like the cake she brings half a tea-chest of biscuits and three different jams. I've sliced the bread too thick. Darius grabs a wedge, ices it with half an inch of butter, crams it in his mouth and washes it down with a can of Coke. Jancey and I share a beer. Darius now wants chips, but I tell him to make do with a biscuit sandwich. Jancey groans, because this is just what he does. He makes a sandwich so big even he can't force it in his mouth. So he puts it on the table and tries to squash it into shape, and by the time he's got his mouth full of that he can't make a sound. He's trying so hard to force his teeth through that wodge of food he's in danger of developing lockjaw.

I slide a bowl of fruit onto the table, and Jancey and I start on the bananas while Darius plays waste-disposal units with the bread. His eyes are streaming. While he's not looking, Jancey acts saucy with the banana. I laugh at first, and then look away, because though I know she's only kidding, it is sexy just the same. She strokes its white flesh against her black cheek, then slides it into her red mouth and rolls her eyes to make me laugh, and I think, Jesus, is that what it's like? *She* may be joking, but me, I just growl in a choked voice "Hey, why don't you cut us some of that cake?"

"You're impossible," she laughs. "Impossible." And she reaches for the knife.

It's one of those cakes that doesn't slice, it disintegrates. She divides it into great scoopfuls and fills a cornflake bowl for each of us. I tell you this is some cake. It may look like a crumbling chocolate sundae but it tastes like the finest birthday cake you ever had, covered with cream and laced with rum. "What'd you put in this?" I ask, and she says, "Darius, you don't get no more."

I ask if rum was in the original recipe and she says, no, and I say that's what stops the cake standing firm and has made it melt all over the place, and she says, "It's gonna do the same to you," and we laugh like we're kids.

She will have to keep half of this cake for tomorrow. Darius is struggling to finish his, and he's smearing it round the bowl so it looks like he's ate it, and I say I can't eat any more because I got to stay sober tonight. She hoots and is about to say something, but she holds off in front of Darius and squints at me to see what I mean. I pretend I don't notice — which is as much use with Jancey as a trellis against a gale. "You expecting trouble tonight? Think you gonna have visitors? What you gonna do if they come?"

I mutter something and start to clear the dishes, but she is not going to be brushed aside, so Darius crouches at the table with his chin on his hands, watching us like we're Punch and Judy, and I admit that someone might come.

"So what you do — tackle them yourself? Gonna be a hero?"

"I can handle it."

"And how many of them coming? If they come in the middle of the night, you ain't even gonna be awake."

"I'll wait up."

She shakes her head. "I despair of you, my man, I really do. I despair." She grins across the table, but her eyes are moist. "Hey, come on Darius, what you think this is — a café? You give me a hand to clear this up."

When they've gone I spend the rest of the evening on my own. I wonder if anyone will come tonight. I hope so. If I was in their shoes I'd hold off a couple of days. Let my quarry get nervous. Or careless.

But these guys ain't like me. They got a different background. They'll be round as soon as they see a light in the window. They'll think it's gonna be easy, and they'll want to get it done. They'll take the straightforward approach: two in the morning, when defences are low — in the front door — blam!

I hope I don't get any neighbourly visits this evening, from anyone else. I won't be answering the door. It could be the bully boys. They ring at the bell, hear me scuffling in the hall: one, two, and I die on the carpet. I don't even see the guy's face. It's been done too many times.

After ten o'clock I feel cold, and I turn up the fire. I don't play the TV because it drowns the noise, but padding around in silence makes the evening stretch out long. There are street sounds: cars, people calling, little flurries of activity, occasional voices next door. Jancey has some friends in. Darius will either stay up to gawp at them, or he'll curl up in bed and try to sleep. You can't escape the noise in these thin little flats, so maybe he's lying in bed, staring in the dark, listening to the personal stereo I told him fell off a lorry last Christmas, letting reggae drown the sound of grown-ups talking.

When I make the stake-out it takes too little time. I heave an armchair into the kitchen, lay out some light reading, and prepare a flask of coffee. I plug in the short-wave radio and tune it to the radio-microphone, then I leave the receiver on the table and walk out to stick the bug on the inside of the front door. It's the same kind of radio-mike they use in TV documentaries for outside location. You can buy them in your video store now. Folks use them for making nature films; bluetits in their nestboxes, badgers in their sets, intruders at the door.

Back in the kitchen the signal is loud and strong on the receiver. I turn the volume low, to stop picking up snatches of conversation from next door. I still get the louder gusts of laughter and the odd thump and clunk, but the mike will tell me when someone comes to the door. They'll use the door, because they'll have cut a key during their stay here. Windows are noisy in the middle of the night.

I pour a hot coffee, and sit sipping at it in my kitchen armchair. Keeping night-watch is the easiest job in the world. So easy you can do it in your sleep.

You have to give yourself things to do, to keep yourself awake. I've brought out a pack of cards, but when you know you've got them only to while away the hours, they are as exciting as a stack of washing up. Books and magazines won't grab me either. I might just as well clean the gun.

They are beautiful things, guns. Smith & Wesson is an old and fine make. Never a rough edge, no moving part that doesn't slide smoothly into place, nothing to baulk in that explosive split second you need the thing to work. The only differences between the expensive and other models is how truly they keep to target, how they behave in rapid fire.

The smell of machine oil reminds me of other guns I've handled in my time. Unbreakable Brens, trundled through the field by infantrymen all over the world. The old Lee Enfields — kept long after their time, because for all their heavy unsophistic-ation they could be relied upon to work. You could drop them, bang them, let the rain dampen them, but every night you'd pull them through and oil them, then every time you squeezed the trigger the boring old things would fire.

I preferred Belgian FNs. Lighter, smoother working, less kick when they fired, capable of a steady repeat-action to hold a one-inch group at fifty yards. I loved that gun.

For punks who like gangster movies there were hip-held automatics: skeleton-frame Sterlings, Uzis and Kalashnikovs. All useful destroyers, quick spray-killers in a crowd. But not for the *cognoscenti*. They have no delicacy, no class.

I pull my little piece of four-by-two-inch rag out of the barrel of the Smith & Wesson, hold the pistol up to the overhead fluorescent, and squint inside. It's as clean as a virgin's whistle. It shines quietly from the lubricating oil. It seems alive in my hands. I can almost hear it talking to me. I could swear I see it breathing.

The rounds are scattered on the kitchen table, and I'm moving the pistol from hand to hand like I was kneading a blob of putty. Every so often I raise it, aim, and squeeze the trigger. I'm moving easy with the gun, like a boxer, rocking and swaying gently in my chair, feeling the gun a piece of my hand, like the boxer's glove. We're growing familiar, like we've known each other a long time. This is a marriage we have here.

I find I'm breathing short and fast, like I'm getting sexually excited, and I recognize the way a firearm hypnotizes and becomes your friend. It's time to stop playing. You're masturbating with the thing. It's time to open the chamber and load up, then place the gun carefully down by your side. I slip the safety on. When you get light and trembling with that special kind of stage fright, you can't trust your fingers to do what they're told.

Loaded, the gun weighs heavy. When I rest it on the table it shudders and then sighs. The grey steel gleams against the laminated surface. I replace the spare rounds in the small cardboard box, look around for where to put them, then slip them into my jacket pocket, and ease back into the comfortable armchair.

It has grown quiet. Once I think I hear muttered words and a little chuckle, but it only trickled through from Jancey's, next door. Perhaps someone's still there, or she's tucking Darius up in bed.

I realize I'm sitting tense, as if something's going to happen in the next three minutes. So I breathe out long and slowly, and I shuffle my feet. I gaze at the unopened books with dead eyes, and the pack of cards is as uninviting as yesterday's milk. Only the gun glistens, waiting.

But it's still too early for these guys. People are awake. The heavies will want everybody asleep, including me. In Belfast, sure, you can go up to someone's door mid-evening, knock politely, and then blast the hell out of them as soon as their shadow darkens the frosted glass. You can lob a firebomb through the window. Either of these ways is easy; because your victim is carelessly drifting through another evening of everyday life. He isn't tensed and waiting, wondering if now's the time.

What'll they try? It won't be firebombs. They are bad news in a block of flats, and they can't be relied on. OK, so you set the flat on fire. So what? Do I come running out in the first ten seconds? No, I hold on in there till the last moment. Maybe I jump out the back way. Maybe I do a lot of things. You don't know. If I'm in bed, it might take me half a minute to wake up. And meanwhile, what do you do, out there on the balcony? Do you wait around with a gun in your hand to shoot me down when I finally stagger out? What do you think everyone else is doing while the place is burning — ignoring you? No, it won't be firebombs.

It might be a burst of bullets through the door as I answer their knock. It might be a silent death in bed after they've let themselves in. That's what I'd do. Slide through the front door, slink into the bedroom — they know the flat now, remember — and use a quiet knife, with one hand across the mouth to stop a dying scream.

I'm glad they know where the bedroom is. There won't be much doubt in their determined little minds. Open the door, three steps forward, turn right, there he is, catch him in his sleep. This is your early call, mister. Goodbye.

Yeah, they'll have it nicely planned. Except I won't be in the bedroom. I shall be in the kitchen, at the back of the flat, hard to get at. Wide awake, with a gun in my hand.

Half an hour later and it's damn cold in this kitchen. I've opened the cards and played Devil's Patience, but I didn't get excited when the game finally worked out. Now I get up and walk around the kitchen table a couple of times, do a dozen stretch-and-bend exercises, then pour myself some more coffee and flop back in my chair.

The coffee tastes like it was made yesterday. What is it about vacuum flasks that makes every drink taste like there's a chunk of dead mouse at the bottom? I throw what's left down the sink and swill out the flask.

Back at the table I practise making houses out of cards, to prove my hands aren't trembling, to show I'm really calm. OK, the houses stand up, but it's no way to spend the night. It lasts me about two minutes.

So I look at my watch and I see it's nearly midnight. The street sounds have died now. Just the occasional passing car. London is never completely silent, never quite asleep. Always someone is awake.

And midnight is *early*, even in Deptford. In this bleak kitchen it's the dead of night, but around me half the block will not yet be asleep. I can hear a muffled distant television, Jancey is still chatting next door, and someone outside is calling goodnight. I pick up the cards and deal a circle for Clock Patience.

It's a mindless game and the odds are twelve to one it won't come out, so I am left to think in the slow gloom. Why am I so sure they will come tonight? They have all the time in the world. What if they don't come? I can't stay awake in the kitchen every night. Why am I doing this? I'm supposed to keep my head down and stay out of sight. Especially now.

Victor won't be pleased if he hears about this. He'll point out all the things I know: it's self-indulgent, it's dangerous, and it tells the other mob I know they're there. But they know this already. When Victor and I gave them the slip at Victoria station they knew we were onto them. After that, what did they expect? They knew about us, we knew about them. Positions were declared. Lines were drawn.

This is my justification. Once both sides had revealed their hands there was no point carrying on playing the game. We could settle down to real life; they were out to get us, and we were out to stop them. And I know only one way you do that. You take them before they take you. Yeah, you could hide, but where's

84

the future in that? They're hunting, and you're hiding. The best you can hope for in that game is a draw — you ain't gonna win. If someone wants to get you, they'll keep trying — and you'll never be sure where they are. If you've got an enemy out there, you either buy him off or take him out; that's how I see it. Since these are not people I can buy off I only have one option.

The good thing about only having one option is it cuts out a lot of rubbish you don't have to think. It usually takes you longer to decide whether to do either A or B than just how to do A. All I have to think of is how to do A.

The problem is they have a lot of strong cards: I don't know who they are, how many they are, where they'll come from, or when. But then, they don't know I'm waiting. When you think a guy's afraid and hiding from you, you can get too confident. Careless. And then if you make a little mistake — like getting two of your men killed when they're busting a flat — you get a nasty shock. The kind of electric jab that stings you into pulling your tentacles back fast. I'd like to see the look on their top guy's face when that happens. I'd just like to see his face.

I'm smiling to myself at the kitchen table now. This is how I like things — me pulling the strings, getting them to dance to *my* tune. It's how I play chess with Victor. He sits there sucking on a dead cheroot, staring at the board like he's forgotten a phone number. Then he carefully moves a pawn one little square and leans back like he's changed the whole pattern of the game. Me, I can't be doing with all that. I move my knights and bishops out early and smash holes in his pawns as they crawl from their trenches. I seize control of the middle ground and let my powerful queen swoop across the board like a ballistic missile. I like that part of the game. There's some kind of fun at that stage — carnage and swopping pieces. Of course, it quietens down later. Victor likes planting his pieces so I can't move anywhere interesting. Even his pawns get in the way. And he always wins in the end. But that's because I get bored.

I'm feeling more perky now. I've come through that dip we all go through after midnight, when we're still up after we normally go to bed. The body is shutting down out of habit, but it's getting all these confusing messages about how it's got to stay awake.

For half an hour the fun goes out of things. But I'm through that now. I'm beginning to look forward to the rest of the party.

My mind is racing. So I take up a book and try to read.

How I could fall asleep at a time like that I don't know. But suddenly I'm looking round that kitchen like I never saw it before. I'm sweating and straining my ears, unsure what I'm listening for. Out of the short-wave receiver comes a scratchy hum, and for a few bleary seconds I think it's a radio station closed down for the night. Then I remember the mike on the door. Then I remember bodies fading like ghosts on the dark kitchen lino. Then I remember the dream.

It floods back to me in spasms, like blood spurting from a wound. The scenes surge back overlaid with a red mist not there when I dreamed. The end of the dream has seeped into earlier scenes and stained them with pain.

Nothing happened at first. My mother was preparing food for a party. I sat, bored, at a corner of the heavy wood table, picking at the pages of a book. She toiled at unending tasks. It was like watching someone else have that dream we all have: where we're already late and we've got to clear these last few things, but every time we try, something else gets in the way. Each frustrating chore piles on top of the one before, and you know you'll never finish them, but you must. Twice I rose and tried to help her, but I seemed to be in a different dream. She brushed me aside, hardly noticing I was there. When I opened my mouth to protest, I was like a goldfish blowing in its bowl.

She flittered in the kitchen, piling crockery onto the table. Plates overflowed with party food. Wine glasses sprang up like sudden marsh flowers. From teetering fruit-stands bunches of luscious grapes hung down — thick blobs of syrup glistening on their skins — so they looked like wet sea-anemones. Tiny rivulets of linen tablecloth trickled between the crowded china like lines of white sand between rocks, and dribbles of grapejuice splattered into shapes of crushed starfish.

Sandwiches curled open to show festering meats, junkets melted, cakes fell away from their icing, and a bright green lizard

86

slithered under a loaf of bread as the telephone started ringing, loud and insistent, out in the hall.

I strained to hear my mother's words as she answered the phone, but they were muffled, brief, as if responding to a death. We never had a phone in that cottage, so the words I couldn't hear were never spoken. And the woman who returned was not my mother. She was younger, thinner, more worried. This new, familiar girl fussed around the table, patting at the rotting food as if plumping a baby's eiderdown, waiting, waiting, waiting for the guests to arrive.

They too ignored me when they blustered in — hearty gusts of wind through the door; false laughter echoing in the rafters; shrieks bouncing off the walls. Their faces were like the grotesque masks of street carnivals, their clothes the cruel parodies of stamping clowns. Hoots of triumph crashed through the shrinking kitchen like the trumpeting of elephants, saturating the air.

A fierce drunken dance had started. Swollen guests thumped around the kitchen table, whirling their partners faster and more crazily. Sweaty men with hard eyes spun the girls round. Skirts swirled. Men's fists punched the air, brandishing flagons of beer. Foaming liquid sprayed above the dancers' heads and fell to the floor with the dry rattle of earth sprinkled on wood. Spilt drink stuck to my bare toes, and when I tried to wipe it off, it changed into blood.

In the dance, the guests had become soldiers. My mother's face as she spun from uniform to uniform shone with the frightened ecstasy of a martyred saint. In the frenzy of dancing they lifted and tossed her from one to another, effortlessly through the air like seaweed in the sea.

The room quickly darkened. Other guests scuffled in corners on the floor. Smoke caught my breath. I knelt choking, sharp thorns in my throat, acid tears burning my cheeks and dripping down to my young mother's face, staring up from the floor. The skin on her face had been scraped from one cheekbone. Her lips were gashed. Her mouth was black. Shreds of torn clothes disguised her battered body.

I saw the lizard again, darting from her matted hair to hide in a broken fruitbowl. Even as I stared, the violated carcase changed into the glossy pink china of my sister's doll, shattered on the floor into jigsaw pieces, stuffed with raw meat.

Among strewn cakes and oranges lay other corpses. Everything was sticky with mucus and blood. Then the smells returned: sour wine and vomit, the sweetness of puddings, the reek of charred cloth. When I looked at the broken bundles scattered across the floor, I recognized the faces. I remember them now: there was my mother, my sweet child sister, the old man I called grandfather, the funny couple from the farm, and the boy with one eye. As I woke from the dream I heard his glass eye roll like a marble across the cold kitchen floor.

I sit shivering in the armchair in this first-floor flat in Deptford, and I feel I'm still trapped in a cupboard, listening for strange noises, till I realize they are the last images of the dream, slipping away like ghost bodies melting on the floor. When I reach out to the big mug of coffee on the table, it is cold, and I wonder how long I've been asleep.

It is half-past one in the morning. There are no sounds for me to hear. Jancey has gone to bed. No one calls in the street. Distant cars pass by about once in three minutes.

I decide I am shivering because I am cold, so I stand up and exercise. Then I turn on the grill to warm the place up. I hold my hands over the cooker like I was a boy scout crouched over a camp-fire. Before making more coffee I stand silent for a full minute, to be sure there's nothing out there I should have heard.

A lorry staggers along the High Street, and even at this distance the vibration rattles the draining board. A cough and a murmur comes through from Jancey's, and a lone car crawls along the road. I wait to hear if it stops. But it doesn't.

So I make some fresh coffee. Each sound is exaggerated with a middle-of-the-night timbre, like it's in a film with the sound track too loud. The static from my receiver gives everything this electronic edge. I am sharply aware of every move I make, each crack of sound as I put down a cup, each dull ring as I move a spoon, each splash of water, squeak of the tap, thud of my shoe on the floor. The springs in the armchair ease rustily as I sit back down, and they creak whenever I change position. Every breath that I take is like a gust of autumn breeze.

The coffee grows cold before I finish it. I am curled up in the armchair, flicking through a book. From the hot grill a current of warm air wafts across my face. It's about two o'clock. I am relaxed and settled, capable of staying awake the whole night. These quiet hours are a time of peace, where every long soft minute is a luxury. My mind is barely ticking over. A gentle cleansing operation is quietly washing through the grey chambers, tidying away unwanted rubbish, turning off the background noise, smoothing out the crumpled fabric of my brain.

It's what happens when you dream, I guess. The night-shift cleaners march into your shut-down offices. They shake out your carpets and empty your trash. They tip out the ashtrays, swill unfinished drinks from plastic cups, rootle through the waste-paper baskets and empty them out. In your sleeping mind these images knock and scrape against each other, creating strange collages of familiar and distorted material. A lone clerk sifts through, consigning some to the incinerator and some to be filed. They will reappear in dreams and memory. They will lurk inside cupboards in murderous kitchens, spewing across the lino if you open the door.

I hear a car cruise by. It pulls up along the road.

A door slams shut. Then the other eases into place; trying to be quieter this time. When your neighbours come home late the man slams the door. His wife winces, and gently pushes hers into place. Then they both creep along the pavement, onto the concrete path, up the concrete stairs to the waiting concrete flat. It could be anyone.

From the comfort of my armchair I reach across the table and pick up the gun. I flick it open. I examine the chamber, as if I didn't know it was loaded. I leave the safety on: when they arrive I don't want to blast a nervous bullet through my table. My ear bends towards my receiver, and I keep my eye on the kitchen door as if they could come bursting through right now. I turn out the reading light, and the grill glows warmly. Transferring my gun to my left hand, I reach over and turn off the grill. Then I pass back the gun.

The radio hisses and the cooling grill pops loudly beside me as it contracts. It's enough to startle sparrows in the street.

While I wait in the darkness, the damn grill drags out its dying spasms like it was Jimmy Cagney on the steps of City Hall. Minutes drain away like blood in a hospital drip.

Through the radio's crackle I think I hear a noise. Picking out real sounds through the static is not easy, and I lean forward like an old crone to her knitting, staring at the box like it's a badly tuned TV.

Then there's a cautious cough.

Someone is nervous, clearing his throat as quietly as he can. I hear it clearly on the radio, and I stay leaning forward, close to the receiver, my weight moving to the balls of my feet.

Crack, goes the grill beside me.

I jump, but there's no reaction on the radio. In here, the noise was loud, but those people ain't listening through an amplifier. I catch a whisper through the static.

Oh yes, baby, this is the one.

I slip across the floor and stand in the corner of the room, so I'll be away from, but behind, the kitchen door when they open it. My gun is up. The catch is off.

A creak comes out of the receiver, and I know they're opening the door. It sounds like they're forcing it with a jemmy, but they're not. They're using a key. It's simply that the radio is turned up loud. I should have turned it off. Just as I'm wondering if I have time to nip across to silence it, there's a burst of shouting that nearly jolts it off the table. Suddenly I'm surrounded by a stereophonic cacophony — from the radio on one side and the hallway on the other. I decide they've crashed in like the SAS do after lobbing a stun grenade — barging in screaming to disorientate the enemy. I stand rock still in my corner. I have the Smith & Wesson trained on the doorway ready to blast the first guy to show.

What's happening? They're still in the hallway. It sounds more like they're fighting each other than coming after me. I stay in my corner like a boxer waiting for the bell. The clamour from hall and radio sounds like the fight's happening everywhere else except here.

Then the scuffles subside and I think I hear my bedroom door opening, so my finger tightens on the trigger and I hear my name and I shake my head and I recognize the voice and I know it is Jancey and she's shouting where am I and I think they've grabbed her and made her act the decoy and I'm trying to work out what to do when I hear what she's saying. She says they've got these guys and it's all right now, I can come out.

I don't move, and she starts up again: "It's OK," she tells me, "we know you're hiding, but for Lord's sake, man, don't go for us. We on your side, man, and we got them. It's safe now."

A man's voice chips in: "It's OK, man. No crap."

Jancey sounds anxious: "You in the kitchen, ain't you? I'm coming in there, so for Lord's sake don't you hurt me." I say nothing.

The other voice — Caribbean — says: "I reckon he gone out for a packet of chips," and several guys laugh.

Someone says: "Hey, no one sleeps that hard."

The kitchen door moves slowly open. Jancey is talking all the time, like she's coaxing a wounded dog. She switches on the light. Then she appears round the door.

We stare at each other. She has her hand on the door, and I have my gun pointing at her chest. "I was beginning to think this room empty too," she says. "When you weren't in your bed, I wondered where you gone."

Quick as lightning, someone outside makes a quip about my bed and Jancey, and she grins and tells them to be serious and asks, don't they think of anything but sex? One says he don't think so, and someone else makes a crack about reggae, and I realize this gun I had pointing at her seems to have drooped like soft rubber, so I relax my arm and let it point to the floor.

Then she breathes out and gives a real smile — one of those big things that brightens her face like a starburst — and I see she's been frightened, and I sigh, and suddenly I've got a lump in my throat and I'm trembling and I don't think I can move away from this wall. I fiddle with my safety catch like I've just finished on the firing range, and I lean back looking nonchalant because I'm too weak to make a move.

But when she takes a step towards me I find I've crossed the kitchen to meet her. I grab her in my arms and hug her like I thought she'd run away, and when I come out of that obliterating kiss I find the kitchen is full of blacks, and though they're grinning like the sun's out, I demand what the hell's been going on?

11

It's all right for you, reading this in comfort. You think I'm some kind of dumbo. You knew immediately that Jancey had stuffed these guys into her flat because she knew I'd come for a showdown, and it had to be tonight. So she crammed six big fellers into her front room, sat them down with rum and blankets, and the whole bunch snuggled up like they were queueing all night to buy tickets for the Test Match.

They even set up a neat military system of two-man sentry duties, to make sure they stayed alert. They could teach me a thing or two.

It's still organized, even now. Four of them are bubbling around the kitchen and the other two are in the front room keeping an eye on the visitors, roped up on the floor watching two blacks the size of quarter-backs shaking through their jackets. But the pockets are empty. even the makers' labels are cut out.

So one of my giants saunters over and kicks the two miserable chickens into positions suitable for having their shoes and trousers pulled off. Without them they look like a pair of fat, homosexual schoolteachers tricked into an awful mistake by a bunch of wily schoolboys. If it wasn't for their guns you'd laugh.

The pistols have impressed the rescue gang. When Jancey persuaded them to sit in next door, none of them were too sure how heavy these guys would turn out to be. A spot of rough stuff in the night; that's all they expected.

So Jancey's half-dozen were ready for a punch-up: element of surprise, weight of numbers, move in fast. And these are big boys. Three of them I recognize, but the whole gang has been grinning at me and clapping me on the back like I was their kid brother pulled out of a scrape. The two human parcels screwed up on the floor could have fared a whole lot worse. Many a bunch of vigilante bully-boys would have worked them over into lumps of fillet steak, twitching and staining the carpet. But these six descended on them like the Dynamos on a loose ball, flattened them into the floorboards, and trussed them in sash-cord in twenty seconds. It must have seemed like they dropped out the ceiling. Very professional. Must come from working casual at the post office. You learn to wrap parcels.

Anyway. I have this kitchen full of people, all looking to me for instructions like it was me who organized this. They say they'd appreciate knowing what I originally had in mind, so they can see if it still sounds suitable. I say it depends what they mean by "suitable".

A guy called Rufus — who I know because he lives round here — he talks to me like an uncle: "Let me tell you why we here. Not just because Jancey say you need helping, but because she say these are people who ain't from round here. They come and act like they still at home. They think they have a right to come and cause trouble. Like they live here. Well, this is our place, right? All of us, we live here, and we decide what happen. Not some strangers who come from God knows where. They should stay out where they belong — keep their hands off our people. You are one of us, so we look after you."

I nod. What do you say to that? If someone pulls you out the river when you're half drowning, you just lie on the bank coughing and spluttering, and no one expects you to say anything. But when they're standing round you in the kitchen, saying you're one of their warm family, you feel kinda helpless. I ain't used to this sort of thing.

Jancey strolls up smiling and squeezes my arm. "You should tell me when you're in trouble. Don't keep it bottled up." I look into her eyes. A thousand words burst in my brain, but I can't say anything. I feel like I was behind glass, and for a moment I am reminded of my dream, but Jancey pulls me by the arm back into reality and asks, "You want to come say hello to your friends?"

As I follow her into the front room someone whispers to Rufus: "She got him under her thumb, I think."

I stand in the doorway of the front room, looking at the two bundles against the far wall. They stare back, giving as good as they get, and I think yeah, these two and me: we're the professionals here.

It's like a coded signal — the Mason's handshake — that tells you they're in the brotherhood too. They are lumps on the floor, ridiculous in their underpants, but when our dead eyes meet, a message is passed.

The trouble is, I don't know what to do with them. Rufus asks me what I'd had in mind, and I shrug. Only Jancey saw the Smith & Wesson in the kitchen, because I stuffed it inside my jacket before the big boys came in. I feel safe enough to bounce the truth off him like it was a joke. "I thought I'd shoot a hole in their heads and mail 'em back to their bossman."

Rufus nods amiably, because he doesn't take me seriously. "Return To Sender. Sound good to me."

"If we don't return them," I say, "Mama's gonna notice her boys ain't back, and she's gonna send someone looking for them."

"You think Big Daddy might come down here himself?"

"Maybe he'll send his cousins."

"So who this family is?"

"We could try asking them." I don't hold out much hope on this one, but the boys might as well find out if the visitors speak English. We saunter over, and Rufus squats by one of the two parcels and grins coldly, about six inches from his face. "Now tell us where you from."

Rufus holds himself within head-butting distance, and I guess he's daring the man to spit in his face or something. Idiots and National Front supporters might try that, but our man's face has frozen. He's like a policeman taking evidence, and it occurs to me that it's just what he might be. But he had no labels in his clothes. And he carried a gun. So he ain't a cop. Not standard issue. No.

"You come to see my friend?" asks Rufus pleasantly. It's an easy question. It helps the guy to answer, starts the vocal juices flowing, passes air through the throat. I'm impressed. Rufus might make a good interrogator. "Your ropes not too tight?" he asks. He lets the silence linger for ten endless seconds, during

95

which his bulk seems to swell in the room. Then he flicks back his head like he's gonna deliver a head-butt, and as the prisoner flinches to avoid the Jamaican Farewell, Rufus says simply: "Take him in the kitchen."

The idiot in underpants is trundled to his feet and prodded out the room like a beef to the abbatoir. I know what is needed at this point, and I start to follow. But I've just reached the door when his escorts do it for me in the corridor. Out of sight, they crash his bulk to the floor and put the boot in, twice and loudly. It's followed by more noise, sharp and ugly, as they drag him into the kitchen. The man is not enjoying this, but he's not meant to. It's a piece of sound theatre designed to scare the shit out of his companion, waiting his turn on the front-room floor. I add to the atmosphere by coming back into the room, closing the door and leaning against it, staring. Rufus shakes his head. "Sorry about that," he says to the parcel on the floor.

We both gaze at the lump for a moment. Another thud is heard from the kitchen. "You not from round here, are you?" Rufus asks casually. "Tell me, are you paid to do this, or you got a problem with this man?" The lump says nothing, like he was told. He licks his lips, and Rufus chuckles. "Round here they call me Mr Niceguy," he says. "These others, they want to cut you with their knives and throw you in the river. But me, I think you just earning a living. You not married, are you?" Still no answer. "But you have someone who care for you? Someone gonna miss you? Or is you a lonely man?"

He looks lonely to me. He's staring at the carpet, and you can see his muscles melting. Rufus whispers, "Look at me when I talk to you." Their eyes meet. "Now, we gonna waste no more time. What your name anyhow?" The man is shrinking from him, but he doesn't look away. "You come by car?" The silence after this question is filled with fear. We hear a muffled cry from the kitchen, and some scuffling noises. "You come by car?" Rufus asks again.

The lump is not ready to answer, so I turn up the pressure: "He ain't gonna say nothing. Work him over while I fetch my car. We'll dump him in the river by Rotherhithe."

"Give me more time," replies Rufus. But he knows this is part of the game. He probably remembers I don't have a car.

I swing out of the room and into the kitchen. The other punk doesn't seem badly hurt. I think they've had it easy so far. You have to remember they came round here to kill me. We're letting the kettle go off the boil.

Three huge blacks sit round the kitchen table, skimming the pages of my magazines, and the pasty-coloured Lump Number Two lies on his belly on the floor. They've made him lie with his hands behind his head, which is a trick they probably picked from a *Miami Vice* afternoon repeat, except it looks stupid when the guy's hairy legs are sticking out from the tail of his shirt. I stand on his heel and ask the others if he has gone to sleep or what, and one of them responds on cue and asks what happened to the bozo in the front room. "He's started talking," I say.

But it won't cut any ice with the crumpled shirt-tail. He knows that neither of them will utter a word till they're hanging by their balls from Tower Bridge. And the only word they'll say then won't help.

The truth is that Rufus and his friends are keen, but amateur. The two captives have simply unplugged their voiceboxes from the mains and shut down all systems. If I had some time on my own with them I might squeeze something out, but I'm inhibited in front of the neighbours. And torture ain't one of *my* strong suits either. I'm likely to be sick on the floor before the victim is. I've seen enough violence in my life to know the only way I can deal it out is in sudden fast dollops — a well-aimed kick or punch, a gun if I have to. It just ain't something I can savour or enjoy. If I really had to spend a long time hurting someone slowly, I'd have to use a blindfold: them or me, one of us would have to have their eyes hidden. I know the look in a victim's eyes and I don't want to see it again.

So I mooch out of the kitchen telling myself that these two won't have much to tell anyway. They're just guns for hire: tough guys sent on a job. As I pass the door to the front room Rufus is still talking sweetly. He is getting no response, and his patience will soon go.

I stroll out onto the balcony and breathe in the night air. The rest of Deptford is asleep, unaware of the drama in this one wideawake flat. But even if they were awake they wouldn't ask questions. When you cram people into flat-warrens, they can't start running around poking their nose in every time they hear a noise next door. They'd never stop running. Maybe it's different where you come from. But this is Deptford. This is where the poor people live. We drive buses and man the trains, we sweep the streets and empty bins, we dig the drains and mend the roads. But we have seen your firm brick houses. We have seen your foreign cars. We come on bikes to clean your windows, and we tell our families what we've seen. Lurking in unfamiliar corners of your class-divided towns, men like me are gonna smash your fortunate houses down.

The light waits inside Jancey's curtains. Her door is unlocked.

She is clearing away the last glasses from the vigil, and when I come into her living room she has a cloth in her hand. I am looking thoughtful, but she is in no mood for meaningful gazes across the room. She shakes her head, smiles, and clucks her tongue. "Well, boy, this is a mix-up. You want some coffee?" I shake my head.

"There's no liquor. I bought some rum in special, but those boys finished that. You have to have coffee." I follow her into the kitchen. "I didn't come for coffee. I came to say thank you."

"Well, thank *you*. I don't want no pretty speeches. You can buy me flowers sometime."

We are standing in that kitchen where I've shared her meals and laughter, and she finishes drying the glass and places it carefully on the table. "So what you going to do now?" she asks.

"You mean what am I going to do with these guys, or what am I going to do right now?"

"Whatever."

"Well, right now I was going to say thank you, but you didn't want that. Then I was going to kiss you, but I don't think you want that either."

"You always had too much lip."

I start edging round the table when I see little Darius gleaming in the doorway. We grin at each other. "Don't let me stop you," he says.

"Darius," she scolds, "what you doing out of bed? I told you to stay there. I tan your hide."

"The trouble's over now." He shrugs like he was putting on a jacket. "A man can't sleep anyhow." He slouches up to the table.

"You excited?" I ask.

"Yeah, but I knew we'd win. No-o contest."

We are all standing there with our hands on that table like it was a boat we were trying to launch in the river, so little Darius at the head looks up at us both and asks, "Are you two gonna have this kiss or not?"

When I reappear in my flat I am not surprised to learn that the two doughballs have said absolutely nothing. Rufus is annoyed. He wanted to show me how much he'd got out of them. "I'd toss them in the river in sacks," he says, and I pretend to believe him. "Except I want to know where they from. Who sent them? Someone has a lesson to learn."

"True."

"Anyway, if these men won't talk, I got to ask you. You must know who they from. They did not pick on you for the hell of it. And you knew they was coming."

"Seems to me that half Deptford knew they were coming."

"Only we. So where they from, man? Where's the rest of them?"

"I don't know. You guys left any of my whisky?"

"I and I didn't touch it, man, I and I wasn't invited. But if you offering . . ." So I pour seven whiskies, hand them out, then wander off to stab each of the captives with my foot and check they're still awake. They are lying in separate rooms with no trousers on. They don't look in bad shape, and the guy in the kitchen no longer has his hands behind his head.

I lead Rufus out onto the balcony, and we stand with our whiskies looking into the darkness. "What did you do with their guns?" I ask.

His face shows no expression. "We found the car they used," he says, as if this was what I asked. "Probably stolen. No way to find out. It didn't have documents inside, but that don't mean nothing. My car don't carry documents either."

"How did you know it was their car?"

"We can spot a strange car. Anyway, the keys fitted."

"I never said thank you, Rufus."

"I told you — you one of us. One thing we learn years ago: you let them touch one of your people, and the floodgates open. So for every one of us they hurt, we will get ten. Like the Israelis."

"You modelling yourself on the Israelis?"

"Do me a favour: they learnt it from us. Come on, man, all this flip talk — who these people from? Is this a gang you gave some shit? Tell me."

"I got no neat story for you, Rufus, but this is what we have so far." I drain the last of my whisky and look into the empty glass. Rufus won't drink any more of his till I spill some details. So here goes: "You know, I don't have what you'd call a regular job." He raises one tired eyebrow. Here in Deptford half the male population don't have what you'd call a regular job. I continue: "I do a bit of this —"

"And a bit of that —"

"And one of those times I must have crossed into someone else's territory."

I look into his patient eyes. We stand wrapped in the night while I continue talking. "The sort of things I do, well, they're nothing special: some driving, a spot of shopping — you know, specialist stuff — odd jobs really. It don't sound much, but I like to do it properly, not to get caught."

"Like we see tonight, when we have to bust you out of your flat?"

"OK. OK. I'm just telling you what I do, and why people use me."

"Like who? Shoot me some names."

I give him three names — guys he will have heard of, who live around here. Guys I really have worked for, briefly, doing odd jobs. Guys he can check with, after I've gone. I don't give *you* these names, because if I spell them out I should never need to waste money on a return ticket again.

"You in trouble with these men?" he asks me.

"No, I always do a good job for them."

"So what was tonight about?"

I sigh, to let him see he is dragging this out of me. "I was asked to deliver a threat. A guy I ain't worked for before said he wanted

100

to use someone from up here to call on a man in Brighton and advise him to lay off some property. And to show we were serious I had to leave a little reminder."

"Such as?"

"Two or three bruises."

"Kneecap?"

"Nothing like that. No bones broken. He wasn't a young man."

"I didn't know you do this kind of thing." Rufus's face shows nothing, but it tells me plenty. Because he doesn't like my story he's beginning to believe it. So I invent some more: "I ain't proud of it. It's not what I usually do. But he gave a ton payment, and the old guy only got a shock, so where's the harm? I have to eat."

Rufus sucks on his lip. "So you paid a call in someone else's patch, and now two of them have called you back?"

"It ain't that simple. I didn't really hurt the old guy much. I hardly roughed him up at all. Anyway, there I was in Brighton. So I hung around in the sun a couple of hours and when I got to the station there's a car in the car-park with the old guy in the back, and he has friends."

"So?"

"So I ran. There's a maze of alleys round that station, and I lost them."

"Then what?"

"I couldn't use the station and it's a hell of a journey by coach, so I took a cab up to Preston Park, waited around, and caught a London train from there. I thought that was the end of it. But next day I'm coming along the High Street when I meet little Darius — you know him? — and he says there's two guys broke into my flat and they're waiting for me."

Rufus stands licking his teeth and thinking. We've been out on this balcony a long time, and no one has come to interrupt us. They are waiting inside while Rufus finds out what is going on. "Seems a lot of trouble they've gone to," he says, and I nod. When he stares at me again I see flecks of amber in the brown of his eyes. "All you do is hit this man a couple of times, and he sends two shooters to stake out your flat. How they know where you live?"

"I don't know. Maybe they were on my train and followed me. I wouldn't recognize his friends."

"They should have been waiting on Victoria station, checking each train that came in." I make an encouraging grunt, to help him get involved in the story. "There again," I say, "maybe they are not from Brighton at all. Maybe I put the wrong two and two together. Maybe they're from the London end."

"Why would that be?"

"Well, when I pick up my money for the job, they didn't seem too happy. They said I didn't lean hard enough."

"No one's gonna shoot you for that."

"No . . ."

"But what?"

"Drugs are a vicious business."

"Drugs? These were drugs people?"

"I found out later, in the pub when they paid me off. This was drugs all right."

"Which pub?"

"The Crown, Southwark Park Road."

He looks sombre. Now that I've mentioned drugs the story suddenly sounds believable. Just. You have to be black and live in a place like Deptford: then it sounds believable.

"The Crown — that's Bermondsey, right?"

"Right."

"So who are these people in Bermondsey? And what's the address in Brighton?"

"That's a different gang."

"You ain't been thinking. These guys in London, they tell you to go all the way to Brighton just to hit a guy. What you think they mean by 'hit'? These are men who shoot people, right? If they pack you off to Brighton, they want you to put a bullet in him. Or if you right and they just want you to smack his face, then he is not in another gang — he is one of they. You was delivering a message."

"So where does that take us?"

"You know too much about they gang."

I stand on the balcony, apparently musing on this very credible story, but really wondering how soon we can step back inside.

I'm shivering to death out here. It's only my fevered imagination that keeps me warm.

Rufus keeps both hoodlums separate and talks to each one quietly so the other cannot hear. He tells them that we are getting somewhere now and it's time we heard *your* version but there's no need to hurry because we have all the time in the world. We are going to have ourselves some nice hot coffee and you can lie there and watch. He was a great loss to the police.

When the coffee is poured and steam is rising from the mugs I invite Rufus to bring the rest of his guys into the bedroom so they can hear what's been going on. With two rooms used up holding the heavies, the bedroom's all that is left. Rufus leaves one guard on each prisoner and his other three come with us. I don't like leaving those two killers lying there with only one guard each. Even though each has a confiscated gun dangling from hands as big as Caribbean haggis I am still uneasy. If I was lying on that floor I'd be as hungry as a cat outside a birdcage. But Rufus tells them they shouldn't get within six feet of their prisoners, and they both hang their heads sideways like he was telling them how to open a can of beer.

In the bedroom Rufus retells my story, condensing it like it was *Reader's Digest*. Everyone accepts it. They're hardly listening. As far as they're concerned, it's three in the morning and the dancing has stopped. A guy with a face like a tired wrestler says, "Let's do them over and dump them somewhere. They won't want to come back."

Rufus isn't satisfied. "These is messengers. They boss is just gonna keep sending messages until one finally gets through. We got to get our message back to him, and we got to make it clear. We got to say: You making a mistake coming in Deptford. Stay away and don't come back."

"These two won't come back," says the wrestler.

"But they not the boss. They nobody. We want to know who the boss is."

"They not going to tell us. Maybe they don't know."

"Then we keep hold of them. Make him send to find them."

This is an idea that raises some chuckles: "We *kidnap* these doughboys? Where we gonna hide them — under the bed?" Rufus gestures for silence like a compère killing applause. "You stop fooling and turn on your brain. Put yourself in his correspondent shoes. What you done? You sent these heroes in the middle of the night to sort out a man who is asleep. You wait to see them next morning, but they don't come back. You say to yourself, 'What's with these dumbos — they can't find the street? They lost their *A to Z*?' Then you begin to worry. What happen out there? So you got two choices: either you send someone to look for these clowns, or you say, 'Oh well, I don't know, something must have happened, and I'll forget all about it. I didn't really want that man anyhow.' Now you tell me — which option he going to take?"

There's a display of shrugging, nodding and stroking chins, so Rufus keeps at them: "Well, what's he going to do — put it down to experience?" Grunts of acknowledgement, wary looks. Rufus takes them on to step two: "So he going to send a search party, isn't he? We going to wait for them."

"How long that'll be?"

Rufus smiles lazily, "Well, this boss-man may like to stay up till past three in the morning, but more likely he under the blanket. I think we won't see no one till lunch-time at the earliest."

"Good," says the wrestler. "Because you ain't going to see me till lunch-time. I'm tired." He is not alone. I ask, "Where you thinking of keeping these guys?"

"I have somewhere. We take them away from here. It's a waiting game now." He turns to the others and gives the good news: "We going to need two guards at a time, starting now. Who's first?" He gets no response, so he continues: "And in the morning I need some street lookouts for their search party. Right?"

A mournful beanpole with Rasta dreadlocks asks me: "Where's your phone, man? Time I and I woke up some friends."

I tried, but it was too late for sleep. I didn't offer them more coffee, and when they'd gone I mooched around the flat hoping to wind down. It's a trick I never learnt. Victor: he's one of those guys you used to see in spunky films about British Tommies — sit him on an ammo box in the back of a rolling three-tonner and he's asleep in a twinkling. Me, I'm too edgy. Here in the flat I take off my shoes and pad about in slippers because maybe I'll find it calming. I look at a book, and I drink warm milk.

And I listen at the wall for sounds from Jancey, but it's as quiet as a pillow, and she's obviously gone to bed. What she did has drawn us closer. I have to ask myself it it's right we should keep a wall between us and pay two rents. We could slide together as easily as a train halts by the platform. It wouldn't be dramatic, just a slipping into place. And if that sounds unexciting, I have had a life full of turbulence, and I don't need any more. I could melt into her flat, and keep my slippers by the fire. I would cherish her like an old man who's caught a barmaid. I'd wrap her in security and never cause her pain. In the middle of each night I would smooth away her loneliness, and sometime in the day I'd bring her flowers.

Darius would have a father. He would love his mum and me to get together, and I can't pretend I wouldn't want to have him as my son. To hug him in my arms is something I can feel so strong it's just like it was happening right this minute. I'd like the boy to have a father. I'd like him to grow up happy. Not be like his dad.

I mean — you know what I mean: I know I ain't his dad really. I mean if I *were* his dad . . .

But I ain't, and I won't be. All this crap about love and security. How much of that can I give him? Security is a word I found in a dictionary. I've never had security since I was an eight-year-old kid. He has more security now, huddled into that cosy, poky little flat with Jancey, than I'll get in my whole lifetime. I can't give them nothing. I don't have things to give. I just take things away.

If you're lying in bed trying to go to sleep and you're screwing yourself into a ball of self-disgust, you're gonna find the sheets get colder and your limbs get stiffer, and if you don't break the mood you'd be better out of bed.

Yet when I tumble out and start pulling my clothes on again, my spirits rise like it's a sunny morning and I've had ten hours sleep. It's five in the morning and I can hear the first cars swooshing through empty streets. Lights are on in some of the windows as milkmen and postmen swallow mugs of hot tea. They say goodbye to wives who wear curlers, and they ride off on bikes with their scarves trailing behind like pennants. Those scattered bright windows mean home and family in our concrete flats. There's peace and purpose in Deptford at this hour.

I stand on the balcony, sniffing the dawn air. A breeze cuts across from the river, bringing that faint Thames aroma that floats up only when cars are off the road. Nobody is around. I wonder where Rufus has placed his men.

I find one down at ground level in what the council calls our courtyard. He's lounging in a doorway, invisible in the dark. "You give up a nice bed to come out here?" he asks.

"The sheets are still warm," I tell him. "You can swop if you like."

He laughs. "I think I smell them from here."

"Go on up," I say. "I can't sleep. And I'm embarrassed having a bodyguard."

"We ain't bodyguard. We is the trap." He is happy to chat in the lonely darkness. The chance of anyone coming this early is remote, but when one car does rumble by at the end of the road, we both slip into his doorway and stand silent and still. The car fades away. I bring the conversation round to our prisoners, but he doesn't know where they were taken, or what we might do when someone finally comes. Rufus is playing it close.

A muffled crackle splutters out from a walkie-talkie inside his jacket, and he pulls it out to log in. There's a routine check every ten minutes. "Just to see I'm awake," he says.

I stay through two more routine calls, and we've run out of subjects by five-thirty. Then a call comes in off-schedule. Someone has spotted a prowling car. It's a Ford Sierra, dark green, two men inside. It has a CB aerial. Rufus's boys are tracking it, street to street. Now the car is making its third circuit. Either it can't find the address or they're checking the place out. When it finally pulls in to a kerb up a side street a hundred yards away, a voice supplies commentary from his second-floor window. The voice says two big white men have got out wearing suede coats. One definitely has a grey suit underneath, and the other is probably the same. More voices join in on the radio circuit. It sounds like a mini-cab station at Christmas. Nobody travels in suits at dawn. Not in Deptford.

The guy beside me in the doorway calls in and mentions I'm there, and I get an immediate order to fade. They don't want these guys to see me. I warn over the radio they'll be carrying shooters under their suedes. Whoever is running this stake-out says they realized that: they picked up two guns in my flat. I hope they're in safe hands.

Nobody is surprised when the two coats turn down my street. Voices are signing off all over Deptford as guys quit their lookout duties and come rushing over. They ain't gonna be in time — I live in a short street. We've only just flipped off the radio when two tons of suede appear round the side of the building. As the coats separate to take a flight of stairs each, there's a screech of tyres round the corner and a big old-style Granada lurches to a halt behind them. The two heavies spin round to see four lethal-looking blacks gliding swiftly from the limousine, and they both freeze for a second like cowboys ready to draw. I hear the next car arriving a second before they do. As I start forward out of the shadows I feel an arm of steel across my chest. "Keep out of it," he says.

The two coats make a dash. They are built like South African rugby forwards, and they'd cut through most opposition like a spoon through custard. Except that this time the custard has set. Like cement. Four great panthers crash into them at the pavement with a thud like a sledgehammer hitting a mudflat. There's another screech of brakes, and a van that should never have escaped out the scrapyard collapses shuddering in the road. Guns come out from under the suede coats as fast as at the OK Corral. One has a pistol and the other a short shotgun. They raise them to shoulder level, and back off from the small crowd. After ten paces, they seem to lose their nerve and start running down the street.

I can see what's gonna happen. My belly cramps. The blacks start chasing, and they're catching the gunmen up. At the corner of the cut-through the one with the shotgun turns. In the mouth of the alley he holds them back.

The coats did their homework in circling the block, and now it pays off. They have the place sussed out. We hear the Sierra switch on — down the alley out of sight — and we all see the shotgun move a split second before he fires it. Those blacks were hitting the deck as soon as it moved, and in the reverberating seconds when we all look to see who's been hit, the suede nips down the alley and into the car.

Someone gets to the entry damn fast, but he don't stick his head round the corner, since with daylight behind him he's gonna feel like a bullseye on a firing range. He even holds back when we hear the car pull away, and I wouldn't blame him for a moment. There's a time to die and that ain't it.

Now everybody starts chattering and telling each other what they already know. Then two more cars arrive. Out of one spills Rufus. Either he's wearing pyjamas under his jacket or he's changed his taste in shirts. He scolds them for not disabling the car. "You should have shut the stable door so the damn horse don't bolt."

A lookout comes through on the radio. He's in an outpost up on Evelyn Street, and he's seen the Sierra burning by. Evelyn Street is the escape route from Deptford. Rufus tries to arrange a car to pick them up in Bermondsey but he's having no luck. There's a limit to how organized these guys can be. I look at this bunch of bruisers bouncing around my street and I tell you I'm impressed. Getting them round here is good. Getting them out of bed must have been a miracle.

This guy Rufus appears in a new light. He is a big likeable feller who looks as if he belongs in a jazzband playing the stringbass. We've had a few lazy laughs in the past, and I knew he carried clout, but I didn't give him the respect he deserved. I'm glad we're on the same side.

I start musing on how it is we *do* find ourselves on the same side. After all, these guys are no part of my battle, most of them don't know me, and they've turned out in numbers only because Rufus said they had to defend their territory — but I decide this ain't the time for that, and it would make more sense to invite these gift-horses in for coffee and what's left of the whisky. But Rufus is Area Commander now. He wants them back at their posts. We must expect another visit fast. "And they gonna come in numbers this time."

While they all climb back into their ancient cars I take Rufus aside for a talk. "You ready for this next visit?" I ask.

"We will be."

"This is a vendetta aimed at me, not at you. You'd better let me fight my own battle."

"You going to take on all these people?"

"That's my problem."

"Listen. We know you a long time, right? Everybody get trouble sometime, and this may be the first for you — the first we hear about. Now, I am concerned about only one thing: we don't want other people's fights in our streets, and we ain't having their drugs here."

"That's two things."

"Being clever? Right. A lot of men smoke hash — that's OK. Some are on mainline, which is not. But it's controlled, right? Now, out there, in other areas, north of the river mainly, there is gangs would like to come down here and set up organization. We don't let them. You and they have to understand this: it is not going to happen here. Right?"

"Right."

He walks back to his car, and they drive off. I feel suddenly alone in the courtyard. Then I see that my radio ham is back in his doorway. We grin at each other. I ask, "You want some coffee?"

He shakes his head. "Not while I on duty," he says.

12

The day wakes up looking grey and undecided. Now that all the usual street noises are back in place it's hard to think this is not a normal day. Scattered around the streets is a tiny army of scouts waiting for a battle, but you'd never know. I think I'll pop out after breakfast and feel the vibrations in Deptford High Street.

That's if I *can* go out. What have I let myself in for here? Am I to stick in my flat like bait — the tethered goat waiting for the tiger to pounce? If I was on the tiger's side — running the other mob — I'd be in no hurry to pounce. Now I know there's sentries out, I'd hold back. Wait a few days till dumbo gets bored and strolls in the streets.

So where does this leave dumbo? I can't stay cooped up in here. I ain't even supposed to *be* here, for Christ's sake. Victor will go bananas, and Rachel will think I got laid.

Rachel.

I cast my mind back. What did I tell her? Yeah, one night's OK — that's how long I said I'd be away. One night. That must give me till about lunch-time. She'll hang around the Earls Court guest house till then, waiting for me to turn up and whisk her out for a spaghetti. She'll give me till lunch-time.

And Victor? There's no real reason he should contact me at all. We're simply lying doggo. But Victor, being Victor, knowing me, being me, will be round the hotel checking, sometime in the day. He may give me till tea-time.

How about Rufus? He just wants to keep the goat tethered — here, where he can see it. And the other mob? Unpredictable. Maybe they'll wait now till nightfall. So maybe I should try an experiment. Maybe I should stroll out the front door and take a walk. Three to one my friend in the courtyard is there just as much to stop me leaving as to stop others coming in. He's awful close for a lookout.

This was not what I had planned. I was gonna march into the flat, turn on the lights, make a noise, act dumb, spring the trap. If Jancey hadn't tried to help, it would have been fine. The two biffos would have come sneaking through the door, rubbing their hands and telling themselves they'd got me by the balls, and I'd have pointed the extinguisher and put out their fire. One, two, goodnight to you. It seemed simple enough. I didn't anticipate how it would turn. It's like when Victor clunks me at chess. I storm across the board and topple his bishop or something, then turn round and find he's closed the back door. Changed the picture. I sit scratching my head wondering what's happened, and he puffs on one of those stinking cigars, telling me it was obvious this would happen right back when I moved that pawn. Me: I usually don't remember touching the thing.

I got a stupid feeling I just moved that pawn again.

Jancey.

I shake my head. Somewhere buried in my brain is a puzzled little voice that keeps trying to ask a question but keeps getting shushed by everyone else. But I can hear it. I don't want to, because this is a question I can't answer. Time may sort it out for me, but meanwhile I have to live with its niggle. It's asking what I'm gonna do about Jancey and Rachel. It's asking do I want to keep a hold on one of these two, and if so, which? And it's asking how am I going to do that anyway. There's no place for women in my life. Girls, yes: skirts, crumpets, pieces, frails and one-night stands. But women you want to keep a hold of, to share and build a home with, these are not allowed. Absolutely no-no.

Which does save me from having to decide which one I would choose.

When the telephone rings, I move to answer it without thinking. I've lifted it to my ear before my brain switches to caution, so I hold onto the handset without speaking. I shouldn't have picked it up.

It's probably Rufus. It can't be Rachel, it won't be Jancey, and if it's Victor I'm not at home. I say nothing. Neither does the phone. I stand without breathing, listening to line noise.

They're bound to say something, even if it's just Hello. But they don't. So I wait for them to put the phone down. But they don't.

We are waiting at both ends like a pair of bookends and I get impatient and ask, "Who is this?" There's another silence for five long seconds. Then I hear the line go dead.

This is not going to be my day.

All I feel is regret. I open the fridge to defrost it, I pack a bag with my favourite clothes, I switch off the power at the mains. When I close the front door behind me I have a lump in my throat. I turn right, and walk along the balcony that way, so I don't pass in front of Jancey's window.

When I cross the courtyard my friend from the shadows intercepts, like I knew he would. "Rufus say he prefer if you stay indoors."

My smile is genuinely sorrowful. "Tell him thanks — thanks a lot, but no thanks. It's better if I leave. Tell him for me." He isn't sure. "Get him on the radio," I say.

It takes half a minute. I get the feeling Rufus has been dragged back out of bed. He sounds weary. I tell him: "This is my fight. I can't drag you guys into it any deeper, so I'm heading out. If you leave my place empty, they'll back off. I'm sorry, Rufus."

"It ain't that easy, man. We need you to bring them in."

"I know. But it's only me they're after. It's my fight. I'll take it to them."

"Maybe they come anyway. We still have to wait."

"Don't let people get hurt for me, Rufus. I'm not worth it."

"What you gonna do?"

"Flush them out. But not here."

"You need help?"

"Thanks. But I'm on my own now."

I head off along the road and make for Deptford High Street, swinging my bag of clothes like I was going on holiday. Turning left into the shops I wonder if I am under surveillance from Rufus's boys. They'll feel like I've taken my ball back and spoilt their game.

I feel kind of cheated myself, and I stare at all the shops and people knowing this time I really won't be back. This is a place has sunk its claws into me. Usually where I live leaves no mark, but this is different. For the first time since I had to leave home, this is a place that will leave a scar.

I trudge up the High Street and pay no attention at first to the sirens. They're a familiar sound — police, ambulance, fire engine; electronic donkeys braying. When I look along the road I see them coming. Four police cars. Two pairs, two abreast. Jesus! What do they think they're doing? This is a high street, for Christ's sake. People are doing their shopping.

The cars slew to a halt, blocking the traffic. Cops jump out and start grabbing Rastas in the crowd. Aggravation flares like a lit blowtorch, and a Black Maria cruises out from round a corner to pull up behind the cars.

I can't believe what I am seeing. In just ten seconds a peaceful shopping street is transformed. There's no rough stuff from the police — nothing you could file a complaint about — just an unexpected public display. They ain't behaving out of hand; they're just questioning suspects in the street. But this is an exhibition. It has to be deliberate. Reaction is swelling all around me, and I'm tempted to join in. I move onto the kerb to cross the road. Then I feel a tap on the arm. I turn to face the cop, but find I'm looking at a black guy I ain't seen before. I can tell he belongs to Rufus. "Don't do it, my friend," he says. "Come listen to this instead."

We move under a greengrocer's awning, and he raises his walkie-talkie. There's a mess of yelling and confusion coming over, and I ask him what is going on. "Chaos," he says, "chaos everywhere. And by coincidence, while this little episode is happening in downtown Deptford, in uptown we have very much the same thing."

"Whereabouts?"

"Well, would you believe? How about that? They's doing the same thing outside your flat. Ain't that amaze? You better accompany me off the main street. You like yams?" he asks as he hurries me through the West Indian greengrocer's and out the back. No one in the shop seems surprised at two men slipping away from a police raid. The guy says his name is Des.

We stand in the greengrocer's backyard among piles of broken concrete and cardboard, and we try to tune to Rufus on the radio. Messages are flying through the ether, coming from every side, like we were listening to twenty stations at once. Des transmits that he found me, and I say that I'm going over to the flats to see what's happening, but both Des and the radio warn me off. "You stay out of this," says the radio. "It maybe you they looking for. You disappear now, before the filth tune in to our Station Of the Stars. Seein' Rasta?"

Des inspects me like I'm a record he's thinking of buying. "So, is you who these filth are looking for? What you think?"

"I doubt it."

"Is you is or is you ain't the reason? That is the question, my friend. We best get you out of here."

"I was on my way to the train."

"They like that. You a sitting duck there."

"I could try a bus."

"What you gonna do — wait at a bus-stop? See which come along first, a red one or a blue? Don't be foolish, friend."

"I'm not spending the day cooped up in this back yard."

"Did I say that? Come on, friend, we go by car."

We slip out the back gate into a high-walled alley, me denying again that the police could be looking for me, and him smiling. At the end of the alley he looks both ways and signals me out. We hop across some more intersections till we find his rusting yellow Ford Capri. "That's unobtrusive," I say.

Des lounges against it and switches on his walkie-talkie. They're all still shouting. He keeps calling in till he's acknowledged, then he asks for a road report. It's not good. The police are scattered around the area with several pairs of squad cars and at least three Black Marias. In Childers Street, outside the Rastafarian Community Centre, a van-load of rozzers has appeared in face masks and riot gear. Blacks are pouring out of flats all over Deptford. Sirens are wailing, and the shouting is like at Millwall when the team's gone to sleep.

Des stays tuned to the brotherhood. A new voice has interrupted and is howling slogans like a revivalist preacher. His message is not for peace and goodwill. But information scrambles through as well. Someone says that up by Molins, Evelyn Street is

114

closed. That's my exit route gone. When I suggest we head the other way, for Greenwich, Des shakes his head. "Half the police come from there."

"Not too sure about your car," I say. Nor is he. I think he's growing into his protector role. He'll be holding my hand soon. He has it firmly in his head that this whole fracas is on my account, and nothing I can say will sway him. I hope he ain't right.

Now we're off along some alleys, cutting west till we reach the railway viaduct. We are making fast progress till suddenly a black van pulls out of a lane twenty yards ahead, brakes, and spills a sackful of coppers out the back. We freeze and I think they've got me, but we see they're ignoring us and clipping on their riot-visors. Then they're off at a rush, underneath the viaduct, and Des says, "Childers Street on the other side."

That's where the radio said the rest of the riot squad landed. It's getting more serious. We stand there with two choices: either we turn back the way we came — which may be safer but ain't gonna get us far — or we go straight ahead past the police van, pretending we are lawfully about our business.

We take the bold route, and walk forward. I feel like I'm creeping past a sleeping bull — nice and steady, don't run, be prepared. When we stroll past the front of the van I peep up to check the reaction, and I guess that the two cops hunched inside see these two anxious faces glancing nervously, and they decide it isn't worth climbing out the van for, and I reckon that if I was them I too would lock the doors and stay inside.

Ten yards ahead we are passing the cut-through beneath the viaduct. Des relaxes his shoulders, and suddenly there's a roar like a dragon dying, and about twenty visored policemen come backing into the far end of the tunnel under a hail of bricks and missiles from their front. They pay no attention to us, so for a moment we can gawp in safety behind the scenes with the boys in blue. Then an orange light flares in front of them, and I know some joker has thrown the first Molotov. Another explodes before we run.

"Ugly," grunts Des.

"Speak for yourself," say I.

We are running up Trundleys Road across the Surrey Canal

when I suggest that this running could get us nicked by the police. Trundleys Road is not a tucked-away back lane. But Des points out that everybody else on this road is running anyway, and if we want to stay unnoticed we'd better do the same. We arrive at the Surrey Docks tube. "Down you go, friend," pants Des, but I get obstinate. "I ain't walking out on this," I say.

"That's right, friend. You go by tube."

"I'm part of this battle. I'm not running away."

"Yes you are, my friend. And my job is make sure you do."

We stand glaring at each other, and I notice the traffic has snarled to a standstill on Lower Road. But where we are on Rotherhithe Road, it's empty. So Evelyn Street is blocked. Nothing is leaving Deptford. I need an escape route. Well, here I am standing by a purpose-built hole in the ground, a drop into another dimension. Forty feet below lies the underground, busy and blind as a mole. "You got change for the machine?" asks Des, and I step inside.

You'd think they had another road block down here. I sit on this platform fifteen minutes waiting for a train. Everything's quiet, apart from the draught blowing. You could sit here doing your *Daily Telegraph* crossword puzzle, and never know there was mayhem upstairs. This is where to be when the Bomb drops: snug as you like. Settle down with a good book, and let them blow themselves to bits.

What would you need? Food and drink, sleeping bag, pile of books, transistor radio — well, you never know: *someone* may be broadcasting up there. "This is the BBC. Here is the news. At approximately one o'clock this afternoon, World War Three was declared. According to Washington, the President regrets the decision, and says it was forced on him by the intransigence of the Russians. Radio Moscow has not mentioned the war yet.

"Here at home, the Queen has appealed for calm. Today's racing has been abandoned, and the rest of the day's sporting programme has been badly affected.

"Now, before our next programme — which was recorded several years ago by the Central Office of Information — we go over to Bill Giles in the London Weather Centre for the twenty-four hour forecast." And on would come dear old Bill, or whoever was stuck in the Met. Office basement when the bomb dropped, and he'd invite us all to chant with him: "A deep depression, centred over Europe, shows little sign of lifting . . ."

And I'd sit here, deep underground at Surrey Docks station, buried alive beneath fifty million dead, doing my crosswords, listening to public service announcements on the radio, wondering if a train will ever come. Very much like now, come to think of it: bored and fidgeting, breathing stale air while time stands still.

But even London Transport can't keep every train north of the river for ever — eventually they have to let one across. So I wake my feet up, stop fantasizing about the bomb, and invite the East London Line to ferry me up to Whitechapel.

Then there's another ten cold minutes waiting since the East End service is only twice as good as ours, and twice as good as nothing is not much. But finally a muddy old train trundles in from deepest Essex, chattering to itself like the Little Red Engine: "I'm a *good* little engine, I climbed *over* the hill." It creaks to a halt by the platform like a middle-aged jogger at the end of his first half-marathon.

I'm on my way to Earls Court.

13

I wouldn't say she gives me an ecstatic welcome. I bounce out of Earls Court station, hop round to the boarding house, and find Rachel sitting in the lounge with the TV off. She's looking cold, and she's been cutting her hair again. Poor kid. She could have picked herself a better boyfriend. While I've been out in the fresh air enjoying myself she's been stuck in this featureless boarding house, wondering if I'll ever come back. The lounge is grey, cosy as a doctor's waiting room. "This furniture looks like they dragged it up from a shipwreck," I say. "And it hasn't dried out yet."

She sits stunned, as if she was dragged out the same water, half-drowned, an hour ago and hasn't got over the cold. "Like some lunch?" I ask. "Spaghetti?"

By the time we tuck into our main courses, the place has worked its charm, like an Italian restaurant should. We grin at each other through forkfuls of spaghetti. I lean back in my chair and dab at dribbles of juice with a linen napkin. She asks where I've been. I bring out my wide-eyed honest look: "I had to check on the flat. And I was on night-shift."

"Are you ever going to tell me what you do?"

"It's nothing special: odd jobs, helping out."

"Anything legal?"

"If I can. Why do you keep hacking at your hair?"

"You tell me your secrets, I'll tell you mine."

We look into each other's eyes like card players wondering what's hidden. But she can't bring down a screen like mine. Behind that smile she's vulnerable. She's grown up and left home and wonders who the hell she is. She's no work, no money, she don't exist.

I don't exist either, not in your statistics. I'm anonymous. I live in your shadows, spending my pennies, talking to neighbours—as warm in the fabric of your society as a moth larva in your coat.

118

But watch me loiter over coffee with my Rachel. Thawed by the meal, we've eased back together. Our smiles grow wistful. It is time to leave this place. While I pay the bill she waits by the door.

When we dash from the street into the hallway of the boarding house, someone calls my name. I turn at the foot of the stairs. Rachel is half-way up. She drums her fingers on the banister as I edge back to the lounge.

A fifty-year-old lady is twisting her thin body round the lounge door. Her crinkled hair looks like she knitted it when she made her cardigan. She keeps one watery eye on the television, and half of one on me. "Telephone message," she croaks. "You're to phone a Mr Fictor. Came half an hour ago."

"He came, or the call did?"

The woman is oozing out of sight behind the door, back to applause on her TV. "He telephoned. Said it was urgent." And she is gone.

"It's not that urgent," Rachel pouts. And I say "No" like an obedient husband, and chase her up the stairs.

Half an hour later my thoughts switch suddenly to Jancey. Some kind of flicker crosses my face. "What is it?" Rachel asks, touching my cheek as if to capture the thought. I mutter "Nothing", like every lover does when he thinks what he shouldn't, and I bury kisses in her throat to hide my face.

We lie together beneath the crumpled warm sheet, and a tear trickles from the corner of my eye as if Jancey was dead. I turn back to Rachel to nestle in her warmth.

When we make love for the second time this throbbing afternoon it is like lingering over liqueurs by a log fire. We lie close, listening to each other's heartbeats. The stickiness round my loins is like syrup. Out of strength comes sweetness.

I sit up in bed and swing my legs to the floor. Rachel stirs beside me. She stretches out a hand and strokes my backside, but I stand and move away from the bed, dropping a wad of screwed-up tissue on the worn carpet. She murmurs, but her words are indistinct. I tell her I have to make a phone-call.

*

"I thought you'd never call."

"You know me, Victor. It's been a busy day."

"I've been watching television. It's been on the radio for hours."

"What has?"

"Your Deptford riots, darling. I guessed it was you immediately."

"Me?"

"Yes, you. You have seen the news?"

"No. They haven't mentioned me, have they?"

"Not by name, darling. But both channels have a camera outside your block of flats."

"Why?"

"That's where it all started, isn't it? Who fired the shotgun?"

"I didn't fire no shotgun —"

"*Any* shotgun. Don't talk to me as if I was one of your Deptford pals. I'm mad enough already."

"This wasn't my fault —"

"But you were involved?"

"Not in that last fracas. Not in the riot."

"Only in the earlier fracas? Well, well. And there I was, hoping you'd have an alibi. I thought it was just possible you weren't involved — given the area in which you live."

"Look —"

"I'll see you in the same pub we used last time. Same time."

"All right. All right. What time was that? I've forgotten."

"I told you twenty times."

"Oh, yes."

"Goodbye."

Twenty times. I turn a rusty handle in the part of my brain that handles mental arithmetic. Twenty hundred. Less one. Seven o'clock. So I've got till twenty to seven. I hope I can remember which pub.

I shall have to lie to Rachel. First, because I have to slip over to the pub without her. Second, because I have to go down and sort out Deptford. It could take all night. When I get back to the room she is still in bed, lying naked on her belly beneath the sheet. I shut the door, and she turns round to talk. She doesn't hold on to the sheet. Her breasts swing in a way I defy any artist to capture in paint. It takes my breath away, so although she is half asleep she gets in first: "Did you get through?"

"Yeah." My throat's all dry.

"Were you making your report?"

"In a manner of speaking."

"Mission accomplished?"

I try to make a joke out of what she's driving at, and lean forward to poke her in the belly. "You're just dying of curiosity, ain't you, pussycat?"

She takes hold of my forearm. "Of course I am. I care about you, stupid — whatever you're doing." Her eyes hold me like magnets. "Talk to me."

Even my hesitation is part of that open and honest act I usually put on when I'm telling a lie. I hate myself for doing it, but it comes so naturally I have no choice. "When I was out last night I got mixed up in something. It's blown up into some kind of news story, so I better check the bulletins. I may get a mention."

"Oh, God," she says softly. "What did you do — rob a bank?"

"I told you before — I ain't that glamorous."

"In ten minutes there's the five o'clock news. Come back to bed and we'll listen together."

"I ain't taking my clothes off again."

I keep them on for the programme. We switch between the BBC and LBC, and catch some actuality reports from Riot-Torn Deptford. It's a blazing news story. All over London, folks will be snuggled up in their cosy little nests, far enough away from Deptford to feel safe, but close enough to feel a *frisson* of excitement.

Minor disturbances linger on. On-the-spot reporters time their pieces to coincide with police sirens and people yelling. They shout urgently into their microphones to increase impact. Less than half a day old, and they are already "The Deptford Riots".

This is the official version: Disturbances started in the early hours of the morning when police were called to investigage complaints of youths fighting, and a gun being fired. When they

121

tried to make an arrest, the police were subject to vicious abuse and assault. Reinforcements were called. These too were angrily resisted in the streets. Then, police claim, someone took a shot at them, and they had to withdraw for their own safety. The gunshot is disputed by locals. Police are adamant they heard it. No one else did. No one got shot. During the rest of the morning a state of lawlessness existed throughout Deptford. Gangs of black youths roamed the streets unopposed.

"Hear that, Rachel? Suddenly 'local residents' become 'black youths'. Just because they walk in their own streets."

Through the middle of the day the pubs remained open and hostilities grew worse. Shortly after two o'clock the police returned in strength. They encountered little opposition, and restored order within the hour.

"Because nothing was happening."

There were several arrests.

"A few lads staggering out of one of those pubs we heard about." Investigations are under way.

After the reports some political worthies spew out the same old phrases they parroted last time the natives grew restless somewhere. I sit on the side of the bed and decide maybe Rachel is right: I'd be better off between the sheets than listening to this dross.

She throws in a clincher to help make up my mind: "There's half an hour before the television news starts," she says. And she grins.

We miss the headlines, staggering into the back of the television lounge about five minutes after the news starts. The presenter is now droning on about another minor leak of nuclear waste at Sellafield. She is reading a PR statement from her autocue. It's as bland and unruffled as the one she read last month: There's no danger to the public, radioactivity levels are inside the permitted safety level, the three workers are perfectly well and undergoing routine tests. The world is returning to normal, and I wonder how far down the news Deptford will have slipped.

But it's still the main story. We see another bunch of outdoor reporters huddled into their coat collars, clutching mikes like they

122

were chocolate lollies. They rattle off their prepared pieces to camera, and look like football commentators who've edged onto the turf after the big match.

The story hasn't changed since we heard it on the radio. I'm listening for clues as to why the fuzz came so fast; you wouldn't think they knew where Deptford was. I'm developing a suspicion that the heavies who raided me might have been their cronies. Maybe when they didn't phone home, the alarm bells rang. After all, there are a lot of divisions in the police — they don't all wear uniforms and some don't even shave. These guys could have been from any one of them.

Anyway, it seems the police have a story that roughly hangs together. They piled into Deptford because someone heard a shot and phoned them. Personally, I'd have thought that anyone who heard a gunshot round our manor would have just moved away from the window and kept his head down, but I've got to accept that someone may have phoned. We are *connected* to the phone down there. And certainly there was a gunshot. You may remember the last thing the suede coat did before crashing down the alley was to blast off his sawn-off shotgun and watch us diving to the ground.

Maybe someone did think this was a bit strong, and phoned the filth. Sounds unlikely, but it's possible. Usually the Law ignores what we get up to down in Deptford, but firing off shotguns is something they have a duty to respond to. It gives them an excuse to use the riot vans — and it beats booking drivers for speeding. They can soak women with firehoses and bash curlytops with truncheons. But they came in force. It was a hell of a response to one gunshot.

On the TV screen there's a guy padding around in front of my block of flats, pointing out the scenery. I almost blush with embarrassment, like it was me in the picture. He says this is the place the gunmen ran from. It's not strictly true, but close enough for the news. He's showing us where the first confrontation occurred. Yet the TV camera seems more interested in my building. It stays trained on the front like it was expecting something to happen, while we hear a recorded interview with some policeman who probably never left his desk, saying it is possible one of the residents knows rather more about this, and investigations are in hand.

So that's that. He knows and I know that well before the six o'clock bulletin started they found that one of the flats was empty, and they asked where was the guy inside. He'll be back soon, Jancey will have said. I stare into the TV picture to see if I can see anyone moving in my flat.

No. But the light's on.

They'll get no help from Jancey, nor from anyone else. She'll say I'm a travelling salesman and I often spend a night away. The neighbours will say he's a nice young man, well, not so young really. He keeps himself to himself, he likes kids and is kind to animals.

Jancey. How is she coping with all this? She ain't used to this kind of pressure. All she did was get some friends to help a friend, and now look what's hapened. They turned the big light on.

She'll be OK, unless someone else says something. Nobody from her handpicked half-dozen is going to utter a mumbling word. So there's no reason the police should be interested in her. But if some nosey neighbour says she often spends a lot of time with me, those policemen are going to pile into her like teeth tearing into a peach.

14

At twenty to seven I breeze into the pub feeling spruced up and sharp as a Porsche purring from a 12000-mile service. I wear a tang of aftershave and a clean shirt. Rachel has told me that if I'm not back inside the hour she'll have my suitcase on the pavement.

Victor is at a dark little table in a gloomy corner. He's puffing out enough cigar smoke for a railway marshalling yard, and he lurks behind his Guinness like a gardener burning leaves. I wave some smoke away and ask if he's selling roast chestnuts. He doesn't reply. He just stares at me, sucking on his cheroot like it was marijuana. His head has sunk into the upturned collar of his black wool coat.

"Guinness," I say pleasantly, "I didn't know you drank that. What're you doing — practising for another trip to Ireland?"

"I knew you'd be late, darling. I can nurse this cockroach juice for hours."

"Late — me?"

"I thought you might be otherwise involved — signing up for a television series, perhaps."

"Television?"

"You've seen the news? Oh of course, I forgot. You *are* the news."

"I've seen the news. I saw the six o'clock. There was nothing about me."

"Just a matter of time, darling. I've been listening and watching all day. As soon as I heard the word Deptford my ears pricked up. It's not a place is often mentioned in the news."

"Every dog has its day."

"The story is that there's an irresponsible, bored lunatic in Deptford, and I ought to keep him in a cage until I need him."

"Victor —"

"So I watched the screen with what programme-makers call mounting horror, knowing that somewhere behind all this smokescreen about gunfire and rioting was a little chirpy face I'd recognize —"

"Talking of smokescreens, Victor —" But he just blows a mouthful at me and jabs the end of his cigar into the fug. "By mid-afternoon they had a television camera cemented in front of your flats. What the hell have you been doing down there?"

"It's a long story —"

"Summarize. Give me the fly leaf, not the whole book."

"Well. You remember those guys who were following you — the ones we shook off? And you remember they were following *you*, not me, so don't blame all this on me, well, they showed up at my flat."

"I know this. You've told me already. And I told you to keep away from them."

"That's right. And I did keep away. I went back to Brighton."

"For how long?"

"Two days."

"You didn't come out of Brighton for those two days?"

"No."

"Why was that? Did you feel like some bracing sea air?"

"Something like that."

"You're holding back on me."

"Yeah."

"Oh, of course. Your seaside romance."

"It kept me quiet."

"But after two days of passionate panting you dragged yourself away, back up to town?"

"We stayed tucked up in bed in that nice little hotel across the road."

"So why is there a riot in Deptford?"

"Because though I stayed in Earls Court the first night, I popped down to Deptford last night."

Victor sighs, and blows a swathe of air through his cigar smoke. "And were these people still in your flat?"

"No. But I put out the flags — let them see I'd come back. Then I waited up till they called."

"Which presumably they did?"

"I knew they would."

"I suppose you didn't wait to hear what they had to say?"

I snort. "They didn't call round for a chat, for Christ's sake. They came to kill me."

He sips suspiciously at his Guinness, and doesn't seem to like it. "You're sure they were going to kill you?"

I am surprised at him. "Of course I'm sure. They had guns."

"So had you."

"And I was gonna use it."

"Did you?"

"No. We'd both made plans, and they both went wrong. I got some unexpected help from the neighbours." I tell the rest of the story. He sits wreathed in smoke, taking my confession like a Catholic priest. When I've mumbled my way to the end of it he stares into his Guinness with the glum patience of a headmaster approaching retirement. Slowly he shakes his head, as if he'd just read my school report. "You really cannot be trusted, can you?"

"Hell, Victor, what was I supposed to do? They had me cornered. Was I supposed to wait till they picked me off? It's not my way."

"That's true. So you tackled them head on."

"It's the best way."

"And now your . . . neighbours have taken them prisoner."

"That wasn't in my plan."

"Let's suppose your visitors *were* Special Branch. No wonder Deptford was crawling with patrol cars."

"You think these are the Law? I bet they're the other mob. You know we got competition."

"You think they're clever enough to trace your flat, to post watchers on two-man shifts, to bring out half the police in London to rescue them? This time, darling, I'll have to insist: You must vanish."

"I can't. I feel like a prisoner who's just got parole. You can't stick me inside again."

"Think of it as a rest cure. For God's sake, darling, we move tomorrow night. It's virtually over. But for the next twenty-four hours you've got to come out of sight."

"Where?" As if I didn't know.

"My place will do."

"What about Rachel? She's not gonna like me disappearing again."

"Spin her a romantic tale. You've always been good at that."

"She won't believe no tale, no matter how romantic. Don't forget I was out all last night. Once she will accept, twice is too much."

"Tell her you work shifts."

"You think she's some kind of idiot?"

"Maybe — she puts up with *you*. I don't care about your Rachel, darling. Get rid of her. We're working now."

I know he's right. What am I doing, tangling myself up with a girl at a time like this? It ain't sensible. It ain't allowed. But I always did hate rules. "I'm not gonna ditch her, Victor."

"What do you mean — have you fallen in love?"

"I don't know nothing about love, but I'm fond of her. I'm not gonna dump her like yesterday's paper. I care what she thinks."

"This is foolish. It's dangerous."

"I know. It's the story of my life."

"It is not. It's because you are not foolish you have lived this long. We've known fools, and they're all dead."

"So are some smart guys. You don't have to be foolish to die."

"It helps."

"I am not giving her up. Let's change the subject: when do we start?"

"We start now. And you give her up."

"You're bringing out the mule in me, Victor. Give me orders I can obey."

"Listen: tomorrow evening we move out of town. I shall have a car and the equipment. Once we've left London you'll *have* to leave Rachel. You do realize that, don't you?"

"Yeah, but that's tomorrow. By then she'll understand, and she'll wait for me."

"How do you mean 'she'll understand'?"

"I got time to tell her something."

"The truth?"

"No, but —"

"And she'll wait for you?"

"Yeah."

"What makes you think we'll be coming back? We could get caught, we could get killed, we could have to disappear."

"I'll tell her to keep a light burning."

He thinks for a while. He blows ripples in the top of his stagnant Guinness. He hasn't really got a choice. He says, "Make me a promise. Go back to the hotel, climb into bed with your Rachel, don't leave your room till nine o'clock tomorrow evening. I'll bring the car to the front of the hotel. At nine o'clock you leave the room, you come outside, and you get straight into the car without stopping. Is that clear?"

"Yeah. What's the car?"

"Some kind of van."

"Can't you be more specific?"

"Not yet. Now, I'm serious: do you promise?"

"I promise."

Well, you have to say something. My whole life is a series of broken promises. But I mean it when I tell him. Isn't that always the way with promises?

The problem is, of course, that Rachel is starving. I can hardly send her out for sandwiches, and from the way Victor was talking this could be our last proper meal together. Certainly it's the last one we can linger over.

I don't make this too clear to her. In fact I just stand in the middle of the bedroom looking like a favourite rich uncle on a flying visit from South America, urging her to choose where she'd like to eat, and not worry about the cost.

"It sounds as if whatever you did last night made a profit," she says archly. Which shows how little she knows about what I get up to in the small hours.

"Choose somewhere romantic," I purr.

Two hours later we clatter down the stairs of a West End restaurant feeling like two plum puddings on legs. Somehow we float into Charing Cross Road and stand on the pavement swaying like penguins, waving our flippers to attract a taxi. When we collapse into the squashy back seat we both belch, and we giggle the length of Piccadilly. By the time he drops us in Earls Court, the back of his cab smells like we dropped a bottle of brandy.

We wave him off like we knew him, then we lurch arm in arm to the hotel. I give as good an impression of a drunk as I ever will, but when someone calls my name from the shadows I spin to face the darkness where he stands. I'm sober again. If I'd been carrying my gun I'd have pulled it.

All I can see is empty pavement. The nearest cover is the hotel door, ten yards away. He speaks again, and something stirs in the gloom. "Where you been, man? I been here ages."

Little Darius comes forward. He looks tired and cold, younger than his twelve years. From his expression I see he has no idea the jolt he gave me. His main concern is his message. His next concern is Rachel. He hasn't seen her before, and perhaps the only woman he's seen me with is his mother. He gives Rachel the blank stare he'd give a truant officer. "I got to talk to you, man, alone." I smile to show Rachel's OK, but she moves away. She says she understands and will wait for me inside.

Darius watches her go until her back disappears inside the door: "Well, it's your affair," he shrugs. "Listen, what we gonna do with these two prisoners?"

"You still got them?"

"What you think — we give them their bus-fare and let them go?"

"Where are you keeping them?"

"Rufus found someplace. He ask do you want to talk with them?"

I'd forgotten them. They were out of my hands. Rufus and his boys had taken them over. I don't want to talk to the bozos. What's the point? They'll be as forthcoming as a Swiss bank manager. But Rufus has held them close, and I can't tell him he's wasting his time. That's not how you repay a favour. So I forget the promise I gave Victor and tell Darius I'll come down with him. "You got to say goodbye to her?" he asks.

This will not be easy. Rachel is inside the hotel lobby, waiting for me to walk her upstairs and round off our meal. She was

130

cheated out of last night, and though she does not know it she is going to lose tomorrow night too. I may not be good at long-lasting relationships, but even I can see this is not the way to become those Folks on the Hill, Darby and Joan, who used to be Jack and Jill . . .

I leave Darius shuffling in the litter while I ease up to the bedroom and try on a smile like when the Pink Panther gets caught in a scrape. It's about as helpful. "If you're going to tell me you've got to go out on business," she snaps, "I'm going to give your secretary the once over."

I slip some things into my holdall and work through five different ways to say I'm sorry, but "How come you only work night time?" she wants to know.

"I work shifts."

This may be the line recommended by Victor, but on Rachel it works like one of his cigar-ends hitting paraffin. I back toward the door trying to shush her, till she stops shouting long enough to ask, "What sort of business are you in that uses kids as errand boys?"

My mouth jams open, and she says that if I really am going, then either she comes with me or she is staying here to pack.

This is the time when a professional knows he has to cut sentimental connections and kick close friends and women back into the world of clerks and shopkeepers. They always tie you down. You have to smack them in the face and leave without saying goodbye.

And when I slam out of the hotel to face Darius in the street, I have Rachel right beside me. Which may make *her* happy but means that I am losing my marbles, and Darius thinks I've betrayed him, and Victor would swallow his cigar.

15

To get from Earls Court to Southwark Park Road you take the District line tube to Embankment. You change onto the Bakerloo and catch that down to the Elephant. There you hang around opposite the Coronet till a bus comes. You stay on that, staring out into the dark, till you're half-way back to Deptford. Which at ten o'clock at night is as much fun as starting a fire with wet tinder. Which is why Londoners north of the Thames think going south of the river is like stumbling into the left-over servants' quarters, down in the basement where decent folks don't go. Which is why we take a cab.

Darius says I have to show up outside Deptford in an Irish pub called The Colleen Bawn. It was thoughtful of Rufus because it's on the bus route. But here we are instead, snuggled up in the back seat of a taxi: me on the left, Rachel on the right, and Darius bright-eyed and eager in between. He tells us what's been happening in Deptford since this morning, and it sounds like I've been away seven months.

The police piled into the borough all through the day. Every time the next van spewed out its string of pink and cocky sausages the temperature flared like when water hits hot fat. So then they'd have to call another van. But by mid-afternoon the hostilities had settled into the familiar pattern of "racial disturbances", where constables clout coons, and blacks stone vans. Our streets were invaded by two or three hundred coppers who normally wouldn't be able to find Deptford on a map. They surged up and down in packs, clattering and scared in their riot-gear, lamming into anyone wearing skin darker than a ginger biscuit. It was worse than soccer hooligans. Behind them came reporters in taxis, TV crews and black vigilantes. Also there were the inevitable sewerfuls of National Front and similar white trash, wrapped up nice and warm in their West Ham and Millwall scarves.

Edited highlights of this Match Of The Day dominated the news.

"Our place is under siege, man. We have more coppers than we has windows. Your flat's like the police canteen."

"Hope they brought their own sugar." Rachel sits quiet in her corner, putting pieces of the jigsaw together. She has a lot of blue sky yet to find.

"It gone quiet now," Darius continues. "But so what? People is still down the pub or in they flats putting we kids to bed. It all liven up soon. About half-past eleven maybe." I suppose he's right. Though it's not the kind of thing should be second nature to a kid.

I pay the cab, and the three of us squeeze into The Colleen Bawn. The noise is louder than at a dog track. This is the last half hour of legal drinking time, and staff are pulling Guinness from every tap. Customers clamour at the counter as thick as if they were handing out free tickets to Dublin. From the Micks returning from the bar with rows of slurping porter glasses clasped against their chests we get some hard glances. We don't look as if we belong. Since Darius's tousled head reaches up only to my chest, I can see why. We look like we came to the wrong party — like we brought our adopted son to his friend's birthday, and called at the wrong address.

Before my brain untangles enough to see how to retrieve this situation, Des has appeared and is blowing in my ear. "Much better outside," he shouts. "Is a special Irish celebration night — one of their saints got married or something. When the landlord call 'Time' he going to start another big racial disturbance."

We squeeze back out the pub door onto the cold pavement, and stand reeling, like we were belched up by a drunken giant. Des hurries us off the main road down the alleys, past some interesting graffiti to where his yellow Capri has collapsed beneath a lamp-post. "Should have picked a quieter place to meet," he chuckles. "What a crowd, heh? But you not famous when Darius sent to fetch you."

"Famous?"

"Why, yes, man. You not seen the TV?"

*

133

He breaks the news as we cruise through the dark streets in his Capri. I'm in the front, and Rachel's in the back with Darius. I hope they're making friends. When I peep in the mirror, I see him squint across at her. She smiles back.

The TV put out my name in the nine o'clock bulletin, and by ten they'd added a picture. I'd like to know which picture this is, and where they got it.

The story is that I'm ringleader of the Deptford rioting. Well, it was my flat got busted, I was the guy they came to kill. But the story goes way off-beam when it says I was the guy started the shooting. Someone has said I'm a well-known gangland figure, and I probably ran into an ambush when I tried to return home. Who, me — living in a dump like this? And how it led to a race riot and running battles in the street is something no one tries to explain. "But you big news, man. Dangerous and armed."

"Chauffeured in a yellow Capri."

"It beats walking. And is private."

He doesn't ask about the gangland story. But Rufus will. When Jancey asked him to help me out, he thought it was just a neighbour under threat. He said he was happy to help a friend, but not to take sides in gang warfare. So does he believe this TV story?

When we draw up in a pitch-black stonewalled alley I wonder about his reaction. He's a tough guy. I'll fight tough guys if I have to, but not my friends. I did that once before, and it left a taste I won't forget. Victor and I spent a month in the sun trying to drink it out of our systems, but the hangovers only made it worse.

We climb out the car. Rachel looks quietly excited, peering round this dark alley like it's the entrance to a new nightclub. Darius starts to yawn.

We're at the base of a greystone railway viaduct. Each of the round-topped arches is closed with a crude wooden door. Small businesses and lock-up garages cling to these spaces like limpets in a cave. Down at the far end someone has fitted a neon sign, but the rest of the sites are anonymous in the night. While Des raps at a flaky green door, a train rumbles overhead, going south, and I wonder if they heard him knocking inside. Then, like in a cell door, a six-inch square panel slides back, and part of a face looks out. I'm surprised: you could ram a shotgun through that hole in half a second. They should have fitted one of those glass bead peep-holes. But I remember these are borrowed premises. You have to take what you can find.

The wooden door creaks open, scraping on the cement floor. We step inside. I don't recognize the guy who let us in. We are in some kind of indoor builder's yard: bags of cement stacked against one wall, assorted timber against the other, and a concrete mixer, lathe, two power saws, and a battered van that looks welded to the floor. Over near the far wall stands an ancient McAlpine portacabin, stolen from some building site twenty years ago. The only light comes from there. Out here in the main space, bare bulbs hang from long flexes. None have been switched on.

Two white men and a black sit in the portacabin, watching us. We cross the floor, climb three steps and enter the terrapin. Our two white heavies are too big for the straight-back chairs they've been tied to. They look like overgrown kids strapped to their chairs for a penance. The guy who let us in flops down on an old divan. The other nods at me from the comfort of his cracked-leather chair. "Who she?"

I turn to Rachel. "I think you should take Darius home. It's way past his bedtime."

He chips in fast. "I not tired."

"We're gonna need some privacy." I say.

Des touches my elbow gently. "She can't go. Only folks who live there can go near your flats now. They is alive with vermin."

"So what should she do?"

"I take them my place. We wait till you're finished. Darius can walk home from there."

I consider this. There aren't many options. "OK?" I ask Rachel, and she nods. I turn back to the guy in the armchair. "Meet Rachel," I say. "She's a friend."

"Hello, Rachel. Welcome." He is Trinidadian. She smiles. The other feller looks up from the divan. Behind the copy of the *Gleaner* that he's reading is a pistol in his lap. He throws Rachel a wicked smile. "You come here often? The joint's really jumping tonight." He is Jamaican.

"I'm not wild about the music," she replies. But before this repartee develops into a full cross-talk patter she turns back to me and shrugs. "So this is where you work. I'm reassured about the secretary. Come on, Darius." She starts for the door. Darius opens his mouth to object, but Des takes his arm and leads him away. "See you later," I say.

"Don't be too long," she calls over her shoulder. Darius stomps down the three steps without saying a word. The Jamaican with the gun follows them while they cross the gloomy concrete floor. He forces open the door and lets them out into the night. Then he scrapes it closed, and comes back. We all let the silence hang.

It's down to me to break it, so I ask, "They said anything yet?"

"No."

"Too bad."

We sit looking at each other. "Well," I say, "we can't stay here forever. When Des gets back we'll take these two for a ride."

The Jamaican laughs like Dracula from the divan: "They last ride."

One of the captives speaks. He delivers his lines slow and easy, like the hero in a cowboy film. "It's gonna *have* to be our last ride, isn't it, Sambo? Because we already know *your* names, and we've met this geezer before. Now we know his friend Des, and his girlfriend Rachel, and a cute little piccaninny who I'll pick out easy in the schoolyard. Looks like you're gonna *have* to kill us, and hope you don't get caught. If you got the balls."

Now that is calling a bluff. He must be impatient to get back home. Maybe his shift is over.

When someone calls your bluff, you best ignore him. Don't look at him. Act like he already does not exist.

Use silence. At first he'll be confident: you are saying nothing because you have nothing to say — he's got you beat. Then he begins to wonder. He needs you to say something. He wants dialogue.

Most likely he'll taunt you. To get a response. It becomes important to him: you started this game, you laid down the rules, so he has to beat you at it.

I try the silent treatment now. But one of them keeps trying to needle us into a response. When a train rumbles overhead he leans towards the Trinidadian and sneers, "Hey, Sambo, hear that? It's heading for the coast, taking scum like you back where you came from." For the moment, the two blacks follow my lead. They don't say nothing. They just stare at him. But it won't be long before one of them cracks. "Bloody blacks don't deserve to be here anyway. Only half human. Can't even crap like white people. They don't have proper bogs in wogga-wogga-land."

I'll have to stop this. It's all pointless anyway. They are not going to squeal, and we are not going to kill them. We are acting a charade. But I am going to find out who sent them.

I stand up suddenly. "OK. We'll take them out in the car, go for a ride, and leave them somewhere with their throats cut. Who wants to thump them first?"

The two blacks don't like these men. But they are not eager to pitch into two helpless dummies strapped to chairs. I'll have to handle this myself: "You tell us who sent you and we'll skip all this."

"Get stuffed. You ain't gonna kill us."

"No? Well, first we're gonna beat the hell out of you. Or don't you believe that either?" He holds my gaze. I say, "You're gonna get a load of pain, just to protect someone else. Is it worth it?" He looks bored.

"Take one of them outside," I say. "It don't matter which. But leave him strapped in his chair."

The Jamaican unfolds from the divan. He stuffs his pistol into the top of his trousers, tilts one of the two heavies back onto the rear chairlegs and drags him out the door, clumping down the steps to the gloom outside. I follow him out. The Trinidadian stays.

We drag the guy, still strapped in his chair, round to the back of the portacabin into a three-foot gap between it and the wall. There's a smell of urine. I borrow the gun and hold it to the big guy's head. We can't see much in this dark gulley, but he can feel that barrel. "Tell me who sent you," I snarl in his ear, "or count up to three."

The only sound is our breathing. "All right," I say. I swing the gun back from his head and crash it down just above his ear. I kick the chair from under him, and as he falls I fire the gun into the floor. Inside the portacabin that should have sounded pretty good.

I walk back up the steps and stand in the open doorway with the gun smoking by my side. Behind me the Jamaican is breathing heavily, adding to the effect. "Your turn, mister."

He sits in his chair looking at me as if he ain't scared. But I can see a tightness round his eyes. The blood has drained from his cheeks. "On your feet."

The Trinidadian carries a haunted look. He watches the guy shuffle to his feet. He has to splay his legs either side of the seat and heave himself upright with a jerk. There he stands crooked, pushed forwards with the chair legs sticking out behind, like an old peasant woman carrying firewood. He ought to be wearing black.

"Get him out of that chair," I say. "We don't want to bust another one." They are both giving me dry, end-of-the-day stares. Bozo thinks he is gonna die, and the Trinidadian doesn't want to get mixed up in murder. He hesitates as he unties the ropes. "Hey man, you sure this is cool?"

The Jamaican behind me moves forward snarling to untie the chair. He knows I'm bluffing. The big white creaks upright and stands flexing his hands. With the borrowed gun I keep him covered while I back to the cabin door and open it. "Come on. Let's get it over."

I wait two yards from the foot of the steps as they bring him out. From the corner of my eye I can see his partner, tangled with his chair in the dirt behind the portacabin. He is still unconscious. I turn the second beef round to take a quick squint, then I pull him back before he sees the guy breathe or something. "I'll give you five seconds," I say. "Who sent you?"

It seems a long five seconds. He stands silent, waiting for the gun to go. The Trinidadian looks more scared than he does. The Jamaican stays blank, and I'm hoping the corpse don't stir. I only count to four, then I move in close and stick the barrel of the gun in his throat. "Against the cabin wall," I say. "You can watch it coming or turn your back on it. I don't care." For one hostile second our eyes lock. Then I glance away with a smile. I ease back with the gun so he has room to move.

Which he does. His left hand flashes upward, and he knocks my gun aside with his forearm. He follows through with his right, wasting no time on punches, just grabbing for the gun. His right shoulder crashes forward as he spins, to jolt me off balance and let him come in close. It's a well-executed disarm, straight out of the book, as I expected.

Because I've read the book too. When he knocks my gun aside, I don't stand there surprised. His blow sends me to my right, and I slide with it, fast, and dive away to the floor. For half a second you might have thought his fist had smashed me across the room, except that I follow through my dive into a roll and end up squatting on the floor, eight feet away, with the pistol pointing straight at his guts. I straighten, rise, and look like I'm angry. "You want it the hard way? So be it. We're gonna knock some shit out of you before you go. Take him apart, you guys, while I keep him covered."

Now I ask you: would you move in there? If there was six foot four of muscle, tensed and angry in the last minutes of its life, and your only protection was some lunatic hoodlum standing to one side with a loaded pistol pointed in the general direction of the fray, would you leap in there?

Neither do they.

So I toss the gun to the Jamaican, and I approach the muscle with my hands in my pockets. He has half an eye on where the gun went. A loaded revolver flying through the air brings extra instability into an already volatile situation.

I take my hands out of my pockets, and step forward the last pace. I say, "Want to try again?" and I rabbit-punch him in the throat. It's a hard blow to stop. It's fast, and it comes from low without warning. He buckles and chokes, as you'd expect. I grab him by the lapels, and as my fingers scrabble for a hold I drop my little micro-transmitter into his breast pocket.

Now you know why I had my hands in my pockets. While I have him by the lapels I head-butt him across the face, to give him something else to think about. It should loosen a couple of teeth — and it feels like I have one stuck in the middle of my forehead. Because my head landed on his teeth it hurt me more than if I'd smacked down on the bridge of his nose. But it's good to see his mouth dribbling blood. And he sure is breathing bad.

I relieve the Trinidadian. "As soon as Des gets here we're taking this doughboy for a ride. The guy behind the cabin ain't dead. He'll come round soon. You two drag him back in the cabin and keep your eyes on him. Keep him well tied up, because he is not leaving. OK?"

He stands nodding. He doesn't know what the hell is happening. "Right," he says. "Right."

Des sits in the front of the yellow Capri like he's a chauffeur again. In the back there's bozo and me. He has blood caked round his mouth, a blindfold over his eyes, and his shoulders are hunched. I think he has switched off. He knows we ain't gonna kill him, since we haven't already. For the same reason, he can hope we don't even kick him around. It's drive about, play a few games, get dumped, long walk home. There's nothing he can do about it. So sit back, turn off, save your energy. It's part of a professional's training. Swim with the tide. In any battle situation most of the time you have no choice, you hardly count, so relax. Just occasionally you can seize the initiative, do something unexpected to transform the whole picture. Bozo feels he had his moment back there under the arches when I let the gun waver. He tried, but his luck didn't run. He thinks I reacted too fast. He doesn't know I was drawing him out, like taking the sting from a bee, sapping his tension and leaving him flat. All he is left with is a sore face. There were other ways I could have planted the radio-mike. But I want the man like he is: tired, fed up, off his guard. He doesn't even tilt his head and try to see round the blindfold.

We are driving through parts of Brixton that look like they've never seen daylight. Then we wind through interminable streets of Edwardian terraced houses converted to flats and rooms. The drabness continues. You'd think we were driving in circles, but we're not.

In the dark I don't recognize Clapham Common at first. I'm only sure because of the name on the tube station. I let two more minutes pass then tap Des on the shoulder. He slows down. I tell him to turn left. We go a hundred yards and I tell him to stop.

He gets out and holds our door open. I bundle the blind dummy out. He finds it awkward, relying on touch. On the pavement he stands, wary. He's waiting to see if this could be his moment again.

I jab the pistol hard in his ribs and say, "Don't try nothing. You could live to remember this, if you're lucky."

I get Des to untie his hands and then slip back inside the car. I motion him away and he glides the car twenty yards forward and round the corner. It is now as quiet as it ever gets in Balham. "Just you and me," I say quietly. "Want to talk about anything?" He doesn't react.

"You're going to walk along this pavement, keeping on the way you're facing. I'll cover you with the gun. For twenty paces you can feel your way along by the low walls to your right. After twenty you can take off your blindfold. Not before. Understand?"

He still says nothing, so I add, "The only reason you're still alive is I didn't want to involve these guys in murder. They ain't part of our battle. They are clean, and well out of their depth. When you get back you can tell your boss two things from me: one, I am keeping your friend as hostage, and two, I want Timmy back. Give me Timmy and I'll release your friend. Understood this time?"

Again we get nothing. So I lose patience and decide to skip all that stuff about twenty paces. I thump a rabbit chop on the back of his neck, and he crumples like a stabbed bull in the ring. Then I turn and run after the car.

We don't go far. We take two sharp lefts and stop again, on the main road fifty yards up from the road we left him. In the front seat by Des I fiddle with my receiver till I pick up the signal from the mike in his pocket. We can hear him panting as he walks. "That no good," says Des. "Sound like a heavy breather."

"Must be a wrong number," I say.

My guess is that the bozo could make a half-hearted attempt to chase after the car, but more likely he will not. Either way he will then head for this main road. He'll count himself lucky that the rabbit-punch only stunned him and didn't lay him out. It ain't easy delivering an effective chop to the back of the neck on a guy who's taller than you. You can't get your weight behind it. But I had to delay him while we disappeared.

Now to see if he is true to form. Over the radio we hear him snorting around, and we get too much scratching from when his jacket material rubs against the mike, but in less than half a minute he emerges onto the main road. He looks like a night-shift worker who's just woken up. Our car is parked with the lights off and is one of many. Bozo stares up and down the road and wonders what to do before he finally fixes his bleary gaze where I hoped he would, and trudges away towards the phonebox.

I say, "I hope those guys left his small change."

"What you think — they criminals?"

Bozo enters the phonebox. Bozo rattles phone. Bozo swears and hits it. Bozo leaves.

I say, "I hope the other bastard's working."

"In Balham? They just works of art here, man, street furniture, not functioning machines."

We listen to the radio. This time he's out of sight. From the rattles and clunks it's difficult to tell what's happening, but I switch on the cassette recorder in case. We hear him dialling: seven digits — a London number.

He sighs, then we hear his money go down. "Hi. This is Casey." We can't hear the voice the other end. He continues: "Yeah, Casey. I got out." Pause. "It's a long story but —" Pause. "What d'ya mean? I just got free. I been there all day." Pause. "I *know* I shouldn't phone, but it's important, isn't it?" Pause. "Well, thanks a lot." Snort. "Look, are you sending someone after them, or what?" Short Pause. "I don't know where it was. But I'm in Balham High Street now." Pause. "I'll *have* to manage, won't I? Listen: he knows about Tiemens. He said he wants him back. And that's not all: he's keeping Patterson till we release Tiemens." Pause. "I'm just telling you what he said." Pause. "I thought it was important." Sniff. "Yeah, but this is kinda exceptional, isn't it?" Pause. "Yeah." Slower pause. "Yeah." No pause. The receiver

142

clatters into place. "And thanks a bloody bunch. Welcome back."

The guy we now know is called Casey stomps out of the phonebox and glares up the road in our direction so hard you could swear he sees us. He curses again over the microphone and clumps along the pavement towards us. I slide down out of sight. "You staying up, Des?"

"Yeah, he probably not recognize me. All blacks black at night." I crouch on the floor while Des whispers a commentary. I needn't have bothered; Casey crosses the road before he reaches us. He passes by on the other side of the road and once he's well past I pop up to watch him through the rear window. The mike transmits his breathing nice and clear. "This sure a dull programme," says Des. "What on the other side?"

"We should be able to track him for about half a mile, but with all these buildings we'll be lucky to get two hundred yards. Give him a few more seconds, then turn the car round. I want to know where he goes."

It's Des who realizes first: "That man gonna catch the tube. We'll lose him."

He's right. Casey is twenty yards from Balham tube station. Once he's down there I'll lose radio contact. I'll have to get after him. "Hold it," Des warns. Casey has slowed at the station entrance and is looking around. When he's satisfied, he slips inside. I start opening the door but Des says, "Quicker by car" and switches on.

He wheels the kind of u-turn he's been longing to do since he saw it on *Hill Street Blues* and he roars up to the entrance. I'm out of that car before it stops moving, and Des is behind me without even turning it off.

A ticket inspector wakes from his slumber and Des shoots past me waving his tube pass. I follow him through, calling something about a last train. The man shouts, "There ain't no hurry, you got another ten minutes", but by then we're both hammering down the escalator. It's a long straight run. We turn left at the foot and come panting onto a platform where there's only one old man sitting in his grandfather's overcoat and he looks like he's settled for the night.

Des is through to the other platform while I'm spitting out phlegm. So I'm still there when Casey appears suddenly from a cut-through up the other end. Seeing me sends him back again.

I steam up the platform after him, knowing Des can block him the other side. By the time I've got up there and slithered through the cut-through, Casey has found himself in a fight. He's a big man. It must have taken a full five seconds for him to crumple Des, but he needs another three to get moving, and by then I'm at his side.

I whip out the gun and point it, but he grins. "Come and get me."

"You're coming back, Casey. You've told us what we need to know."

"How d'ya know my name?"

"I know everything about you. Stand by the wall."

"Get stuffed."

"Where do you want it, Casey, head or heart?"

He shrugs. "You can't use that here."

Des has moved into a groaning squat. He sounds in real pain. I guess he's exaggerating. But Casey feels confident: "See your friend here?" Casey tilts his head towards him, rocks back easily on his heel, then swings a sudden powerful kick at his face.

It wasn't wise. Des is not that badly hurt. He sees the kick coming, sways sideways and grabs at Casey's foot. He makes contact but can't hold it. There's an untidy second in which I dive forward to knock Casey off balance, and he lurches against the wall but keeps upright while Des scrambles to his feet. I'm hampered by the gun. It's like having one arm out of action. Casey brings a double-handed chop down on the back of my neck, just off target but enough to send me reeling in a flood of numb red nausea. He yanks me up by the hair. As his fist crashes over, Des thumps him. I still get half the blow — and half a blow from Casey is ten from anyone else. For another second I flail like I'm drowning, and Casey grabs at the gun and wrenches it upwards from my hand. I lose the damn thing and crash blindly against him, but he skips backwards, and as the mist clears I see his eyes blazing and his teeth bared and the gun is comfortable in his hand and pointing at my chest. "That's better," he spits, cocky as he deserves to be. "Now it's me taking *you* in, sunshine, just as I was told."

I freeze and think I've blown it. Then there's a bat fluttering in a cave, and Des's shoe comes hurtling through the air aimed straight at Casey's head. As he ducks he has Des diving for his legs and me closing in, and this is the moment we all discover the benefits of my upbringing because like a promising cadet I'd left the pistol's safety on.

Well, I wasn't going to use it, was I? It had slipped my mind in the last awful seconds, but it all goes to show the value of a good education. I must write Victor a thank you.

Casey lashes out as he kicks his legs free. I duck and come inside. He tries a head-butt which I dodge, and I clip a neat jab across his chin which rocks but doesn't fell him. From somewhere down round his ankles he heaves a massive haymaker punch, using the dead pistol as a knuckleduster. If it had landed, my head would have flown like a shied coconut. But I sway back and chop another satisfying crosspunch on his ear to send him stumbling after his haymaker, and when he shambles round to face me he's as wide open as a mother's welcome. The punch I place on his chin arrives with the full weight of my body and jolts his head back as if it was on elastic. He topples back after it with his feet and arms splayed, and sails off the platform onto the electric rail.

It's a sight I never saw before. He sprawls across it and shudders like his back's broken, and there's a crackling noise like sizzling fat. He is staring at me as he dies, and my face will be the last image seared across his brain. The body twitches after he's dead.

Des stares at me blankly as he puts his shoe on. I pick up the gun and pocket it. "Nice of him to die tidily," I say.

At the bottom of the escalator we meet the ticket inspector riding down and frowning as he approaches us. "What happened?" he asks.

"Man on the line," I say. "Suicide I think."

"Why this time of night, for God's sake? Come and help, will you?" he says as he passes. But we're off up the stairs.

In Des's flat the three of us are behaving like those sexual stereotypes the Brent librarians used to complain about. Rachel is making coffee, I'm fiddling with my cassette recorder, and Des is lounging in his armchair like he owns the place. Well, he does pay the rent.

Before we left Balham I made Des wait the car at the phonebox while I recorded dialling sounds from zero to nine. He kept staring out the car window like he was a cat had broken a saucer. By the time I jumped back inside he looked like he was down with flu.

It doesn't improve his nerves now to see me sitting on his carpet timing Casey's phone rings with my stopwatch to work out the number he dialled. Though I can run this machine half speed I have to be meticulous with the timing. I play each whirr the dial made as it wound back, I clunk the recorder switches, I fidget with the stopwatch, and it gives him a pain between the eyes. Even my pencil scratching on the paper makes his teeth grate.

Rachel hasn't been told. She asks if we'd like whisky or rum in our coffees, and the tension eases. I say whisky and Des says rum. She joins me on the carpet, and we all sit blowing on our coffees and warming our hands on the mugs. "Glad you finish unscrambling that number," Des says. His eyes stay shut.

We're about half-way down the mugs when we hear the front door go and someone on the stairs. "What the hell the time is?" asks Des. The footsteps stop outside his door.

The knock is soft, little more than a rapid series of taps, like if you beat your fingernails on the table to get attention. Whoever is out there will have seen our light, and knows we're awake. I glide to the side of the door, Des stands up, and Rachel sits among the coffee cups wondering what to do. I pull the pistol and hold it within my jacket. This time the safety is off.

When he reaches to open the door Des licks his lips. "Who there?"

"This is Jancey. Open up, man."

I interrupt them. "Who's that with you?"

"Only Darius. Come on, let me in."

She comes into the room like a shy actress making a bad entrance, to find us poised round the door like actors on the set. Even the coffee mugs look arranged. She stares at Rachel like it's Rachel's cue. Darius looks as if he's stuck his eyes open with superglue, and because he's too tired to stand waiting in the doorway he slouches in and says, "Hi." Des shuts the door.

Jancey and Rachel quit staring at each other. Rachel looks up at me, and Jancey looks at everyone except. We're all waiting for someone else to speak. I sheathe the gun and walk over to Darius, and place my fist gently on his chest. "You working night-shift, or what?"

"The filth had me, didn't they?"

We all react to that, and Jancey explains. "They see him walking in the street late at night. He on his own. After this bad day, anyone not tucked up in bed is making them suspicious. Especially his age."

"I not a kid any more."

Placing a hand on each of his shoulders, I look him in the eye and ask if he is all right. "Sure."

"What did they do?"

"Just waste a lot of time. Keep asking questions. Where I live. Where I been."

"What did you say?"

He shrugs. "Nothing they want to hear. I tell them where I live. I say I live *here*. I can't help that. I say I been out for a walk because I can't sleep. No law against that."

"Then they ask him again," continues Jancey. "And again. Keep asking the same questions. They tell him he is lying, keeping something back."

"Ver-bal har*ass*ment," drawls Des, back in his chair.

"So I clam up," says Darius. "I tell them I tired now. Ready for bed."

"Sure," says Des. "Is reasonable. Is why you went out, because you could not sleep."

"But they not see him go out," interrupts Jancey. "They got

147

people posted on our block of flats. They watch who go out and who comes in. But they not see Darius because he not been in since five o'clock. Had me worried."

"I say they just didn't notice me," Darius says. "I ask if I supposed to check out and hand in my keys, like a hotel." Des laughs.

"They only stop pestering because he a child," Jancey declares. "They know he lying, but so what? He been up to something but it not what they after."

"I am not just a child."

"Well, you not what they looking for either." For the first time she looks at me. Just a glance, flashing by, but I have time to see the accusation and hurt. I can't let her carry on pretending I ain't in the room. I stride over and take her by the shoulders in the same way I held Darius. "I'm sorry, Jancey. I know it's my fault, but me feeling guilty don't help any. The police think I started this trouble."

"I don't know who else did. Was they police come to your flat last night, or villains?"

"I'm not sure."

"Not sure! You don't know who your enemies are? What kind of thing you done?"

I try to pull her in to my chest, but she turns away. "And you haven't introduce me to your new friend."

She spits this out like it's a boxer's left jab. I flinch, and Rachel starts up from the floor as I begin stumbling through some kind of introduction. What should I say? All I can manage is "Yeah, this is Rachel. Rachel, Jancey. Yeah."

Not that what I say makes any difference, because these two are still eyeing each other like welterweights at the weigh-in, and Darius stands between them like a referee. Jancey sniffs over the coffee mugs on the carpet. "You all been having party? Looks cosy, I must say."

Des starts to offer coffee, but it gives her another opening: "No, I'll go make my own, thank you. This your kitchen through here?" And she flounces out. Or if you like, she stalks to her corner smiling at the end of round one.

In the middle of the room Darius grins. "She cross because she have to come fetch me from the police station. You should have seen her sail in there."

"*Darius!*" Jancey's call cuts through the room and must have woken the folks upstairs. "You gonna let your Mama do this all herself?"

16

I'm getting used to two o'clock in the morning. What you need is a reason for being awake. Take sentries — they sit squinting into the dark, waiting to see something move, and naturally their eyes droop. But if you've got excitement — and that's anything from romancing to stalking in the dark — then you'll be alert in the wee small hours. No one's around. The street glistens in night rain. Shadows are soft in the streetlamps. Movements happen singly, so you can look at them: flurries of waste paper on empty pavements, a sudden darting cat, a lone car humming its mantra.

Des's Capri doesn't hum, it gargles. He coasts it through Southwark to the Old Vic, crosses Waterloo Bridge, heads west along the Strand into Trafalgar Square — empty of pigeons in the dove-grey light — mooches out through the West End, glides round Hyde Park Corner as if it was always free of traffic, and drops us in Earls Court like it was just the street next door.

He is gone before Rachel fits her key in the hotel door. We are softly up the stairs and into our room with less noise than a pair of cat burglars. I open the curtains to let the night in. But there's no sky, no stars, just the opaque blank wall next door.

I sit on the bed and take off some clothes. Rachel kneels behind me whispering in my ear, "You never told me about Jancey" and I tell her she's just the woman next door and Rachel says, "Oh yeah?" and I push her onto her back and sit astride her in the dark. She runs her fingers through the hair on my chest, and her eyes glitter in the dimness. Absently I stroke her body, and the colours of her skin drain into the monochrome of the blankets. Only the whiteness of her bra stands out.

I am fondling her like a memory, in the way you stroke a cat: knowing it's there, glad it's purring, but letting thoughts wander like your fingers tickling the fur.

Even when she strokes my inner thigh, back and forth like

rocking a cradle, I hardly notice what she is doing. The lazy warmth of a tropical evening flushes through my limbs. Only when she fumbles with the tiny metal flap of my zip does my mind shake back to the present. I think I should do something, take some kind of male initiative in what's happening. But she is comfortable on her back. It would break her mood to lift her. So I sit docile above her, upright and male, unresisting as she delves with her hand.

Then we move at the same time. I slide sideways from her as she sits up, grabbing at me to stop me moving away. We hug each other and kiss. I feel the precise shape of every vertebra, the mole between her shoulders, the rough seam at the fastening of her bra. I loosen the clips and pull her towards me and her breasts melt on my chest. Then she stoops forward. Her spiky hair scratches down my front.

When I lift her gently away she asks didn't I like it, and why must she stop? When I push her off me and over she whispers that she thought I'd be tired at this hour of night.

But I am bursting like an overstuffed sausage, and every thrust I make inside her is like I'm seventeen slow inches long and growing with every stroke. Suddenly we are no longer human, we're some desperate machine crashing and pumping before exploding through the room.

The reverberations fade until the only sound in the room is our breathing, slowing down.

I was standing in the back of a small boat, drifting down some English river I've never seen — the kind with dappled, overhanging leaves reflected in the water — grasping a punt-pole in my hands and propelling the flat boat like it was something I'd done for years. Colour seeped into the scene like turning up the control on TV.

The water was gun-metal blue, with greens and browns rippling on its surface. My pole was varnished, and I was wearing white. Bird noises faded up as if I had found another TV control. Laps of water slapped against the boat, like wine trickling from a bottle.

I looked down into the punt and saw Rachel gazing up at me from beneath a wide straw hat. Billows of muslin and soft material filled the seat all round her. Then a long glass appeared in her hand, and a straw, and she sipped at an amber drink, and ice cubes clinked.

I glanced away, back up the river from where we'd come. It was wide, tree-lined and empty, curving out of sight beneath a brilliant sky. A huge sun throbbed overhead. An African sun. The warmth was not English. It sapped my strength and made sweat trickle into my eyes.

When the corpse floated past, it was as unremarkable as a branch drifting in the water, and once we had passed it, it stayed bobbing in the water as if tied to our stern. I prodded with my pole, but somehow the current made it cling, and I found I couldn't shake Casey away.

He lay grinning up at me on the water, spreadeagled on his back with his arms splayed. I waited for him to speak. But he just stared. There was no malice, no reproach. His eyes gleamed, as if he was happy to be dead. Then I realized he was looking forward to something. He rested on the water waiting for what he knew was going to happen.

I turned back to Rachel still sitting peacefully in her seat, sipping her drink. She smiled, and her eyes shone, and her lips parted in mockery of Casey's smile.

Behind me his body began to beat against the stern of the boat, and as I turned toward him I saw Rachel from the corner of my eye begin to clamber up from her seat and I called out to her to stay sitting and not to stand but she laughed lightly and tossed back her head and I felt Casey behind me clambering into the boat. In the last frenzied seconds as the boat tossed I thought Rachel held a pistol pointing at me, but then I saw it was only her glass. The liquid had turned bright red.

We rocked wildly on the water, then pitched soundlessly into the stream. It wasn't cold. It was tropical water — warm, seductive, fatally dangerous. I swam round the boat, looking for Rachel, but both she and Casey were gone.

When I crawled onto the shore I came out of the English stream onto sand. For perhaps one second it remained a river bank, but then it became the shingle and sand beach fifty yards from my childhood home.

Maybe I wasn't fully asleep — you know that half-waking state where you try to control the direction of your dream? I knew I didn't want to walk up that beach. I tried to make myself turn away. But I had no choice. I had to go on to the usual horror. The dream lingered through the endless moments while I trudged up the clinging sand, seeing our little cottage grow larger and more ominous, till suddenly it was if the film director grew tired and cut to me opening the cupboard door and peeping out.

It was the same terrible ruin. Familiar chaotic ground. The kitchen table turned on its side, party food tumbled across the floor, broken glasses, smashed plates, crooked bodies, blood. Drip, drip, dripping wine. Rustling in the far corner. Two people, two bodies churning among splintered crockery, two animals copulating in the dirt.

Rachel's face glistened in the gloom as she urged herself to her climax — sweat and staring eyes, tongue darting between dry lips, breath panting. And he, even as he turned his damp face towards me, pink and stupid in his unbuttoned uniform, could only be Casey, rooted in my dreams now, the same leering grin that will haunt me for years.

I was a child again, and Casey turned away. He was secure enough to turn his back, to show me the two foul moons of his backside, heaving up and down as he ground her into the floor.

As I picked up the knife from the rubble by the table I was waking. I remember thinking that the soldier had a face now, and though his head remained slobbering in her breast when I plunged the blade through the thick khaki, I saw the sudden sharp pain jolt through his eyes.

I kicked him aside as the dream faded. His body rolled away and uncovered the blood-spattered broken body of my poor dead sister, and even as I raised my hand to my mouth to stifle the scream, I saw the vicious green lizard dart into her hair.

Warmth.

Closeness.

Rachel hugging. Real, living, Rachel holding me tight. Naked bodies, like mother and child. She strokes my hair and soothes me like a baby. I may have whimpered.

I'm sure I didn't scream. I don't scream when I waken. Maybe I groaned.

Rachel holds me as the minutes tick away in the darkness. My breathing slows to normal. "You're all right now. You're with me. It's all right. Only a dream."

I ask what time it is, for something to say. She leans to the bedside cupboard. "Four o'clock. Four in the morning. Good job it's Saturday."

Saturday. The word rattles in my brain. Saturday. This is the day. Victor said it would be Saturday. "What time is it?"

"I told you. Four o'clock."

I lie down, and she draws first the sheet over me then the blankets. She snuggles closer, but stays on her side to watch me and ask: "Better now? Do you want to talk about it?" I shake my head. "Those dreams are the worst. What were you doing? You were speaking gibberish."

My mouth has dried. I take two cracks at saying, "People can speak gibberish in their dreams."

"It sounded like a foreign language."

I'm shivering now, and she slides closer to warm me. I can't shake a lingering vision of her straining eagerly against Casey, and I half blame her for it as if it were true.

"I'm not surprised you had a nightmare. You've had a terrible day."

I snort.

"I know that's a lame thing to say."

I pat her arm. She takes a deep breath, but doesn't use it. She wants to talk, but doesn't know how to begin. I won't help her. I'll make like I'm going back to sleep, or maybe I'll get up and do something. The last thing I want to do is talk.

So she does instead. Her tone is soothing, her whispers slide like sighs, but gently she is uncovering the reproach she's been hiding for days. When a guy like me, she says, wakes with bad dreams in the night, he has something worrying at his mind. Everyday horrors seep into his unconscious like stains on a sheet. He can't settle. He whittles away at what troubles him, trying to absorb unwelcome thoughts. She avoids the word conscience. "Can't you give up this living?" she asks, and I stare at the invisible ceiling.

154

"What life?" I mutter, and my mouth is still glued up. If I act catatonic maybe she'll go back to sleep.

"That gang you're with. Those men in the flat."

"It's not a gang."

"When you went out, did you take those prisoners with you?"

"Prisoners?"

"From that garage, or whatever it was. That place under the arches."

"Oh, them. They're OK now."

"What happened to them? Who were they?" The inquisition is starting. The long slow hours of four in the morning, when a man and a woman lie awake in the dark, and one of them keeps on talking, while the other turns away and groans out for sleep.

"Are they from some other gang?"

"We're not a gang. They're just friends."

"You had a gun. Why are you hiding from me?"

"I'm not."

"You are. What happened in Deptford today — yesterday? There was a riot." I grunt. "Were you involved in that? You were, weren't you? Did you even start it?"

I have to say something. "It blew up, got out of hand. I was just there when it started."

She starts to speak, then stops. We lie on our backs staring upwards, our eyes and throats dry. This is why I hate getting involved with women. If you let it last, if you let sleeping together become regular — the way you live, instead of unexpected and just for sex — sometime you will end up having one of these four-in-the-morning, lay yourself bare, skin-peeling torture sessions. Women won't be content with companionship and sex, they have to flay you with emotion and tears. For them, crying is enjoyable, therapeutic, something to look forward to when the relationship matures.

It's the catch in her breath tells me she is weeping in the dark. The wet snuffle that says: I'm trying to suppress my tears . . . I don't want to disturb you . . . Just go back to sleep . . . Ignore me, and I'll cry in the night alone.

So I have to turn over and take her in my arms. I stroke her hair and burble fine words, while she sobs out her questions and

155

accusations. Before I know what I'm saying I've promised I'm not a criminal, that it's a different kind of mission. She fastens on the word: "Mission? What — are you some kind of terrorist then?"

I snort, and twist my face into a don't-be-ridiculous expression. But it's too dark to see, and she has her head buried in my chest. "What *are* you doing then? Why are you here?"

"No reason."

She pulls at the hairs on my chest. "You've got to tell me."

My mind races back to when I met her. I even wonder if she could have been planted on me. But I remember the train and the guy with the personal stereo, and I know it was just chance that we met.

She scratches at my skin, and asks again. She's like a favourite daughter, wheedling her dad. I say, "You sound like my sister."

"I didn't know you have a sister."

"She's dead now."

"Oh. Oh, I'm sorry. When did — don't you want to talk about it?"

"I just want to go to sleep. It's helluva late."

But I can sense her blossoming into that relaxed wakefulness you can get in the quiet hours. She's found something to probe at. It has silenced her tears, and I bet her eyes are shining in the dark.

"Was it recently?"

"No. It was a long time ago. I was just a kid."

"But you never forgot her?"

"No."

"Of course not. How did she die? Was it an accident?"

I should tell her I don't want to talk about it: it's too painful. She'd understand. But what the hell, there's nobody else awake in this sleeping world. "She was raped to death by a bunch of soldiers."

You would expect this to shock her, and it does. She stammers a kind of apology and wriggles up the bed so her face touches mine. We can see each other now. She places her hands on my cheeks and stares into my eyes. I look away. "Yeah. Well, I'm alive. They didn't get me."

"Were you there?"

Jesus, I'm tired. Every word stops me turning away and closing my eyes, to block it out, to let me retreat into sleep. I squirm like I'm trying to shake off a mosquito.

"You weren't there, were you? You didn't see it?"

"I saw it. The end of it, anyway."

She kisses me softly on the forehead and wraps me in her arms so securely I'm reminded of my mother. My Adam's apple swells in my throat, and for a second I think I'm going to join her in tears. But I won't. You don't lead my kind of life if you can't damp down emotions. I stir, and think about getting out of bed.

"It was before you came to England, I suppose?"

The question jolts me, and I stiffen. "What d'you mean?"

"Well, you're not English, are you?"

"Of course I'm English."

"Not really. I mean, you weren't born here."

"Why d'you say that?"

"I do know you by now. You're not . . . native English, are you?"

"We moved around a lot when I was young. My accent got mixed up."

It must be fully twenty seconds before she speaks again, and she ain't sleeping, that's for sure. I'm getting nervous. It's a powerful weapon, silence. "If you're really pretending to be English, then you *must* be a terrorist, I suppose. Have you come here to bomb people?"

"Do me a favour!"

"What then?"

"It's nothing to do with bombing people. I'm a pacifist, if anything."

And she laughs at me. I tell you, she actually laughs at me — breaking off from this inquisition to laugh at the thought of me being a pacifist. I'm gonna argue with her, but then I realize it does sound pretty ridiculous, so I smile too. I don't laugh, but I do smile. "OK. So I'm not a pacifist."

"Then what are you?"

How do you tell the girl? I lie there light-headed on the pillow at half-past four in the morning, knowing that anyway it's nearly

157

over, that by this time tomorrow we'll have done it, that by this time the next day I'll be out of the country. Rachel's face will fade into the kind of indeterminate image it is now, in the dark. I shall have flown into who knows whose airport, or I'll be sleeping on a ship steaming slowly out the English Channel, or I'll be dead and rigid on a lonely piece of ground.

Rachel, this is our last night together. These dark creeping minutes are the climax of our game. We'll drift entangled into sleep, wake and make love one last time, then part so softly you'd never know it was goodbye.

Because it is over, darling Rachel. In these last few days we have anticipated different futures. You knew I'd move in with you — perhaps you already felt our child kick inside your belly — you saw us wave it off to school. But I betrayed you. All the while you were building this future I knew there'd come a morning like this, when I'd smile sadly as I left you, when I'd give a last half wave at the corner, when I'd set my face to the reality of the serious work ahead.

17

I stab a fork into my fried egg and it bleeds yellow over the bacon. The egg has been gleaming up at me, cold and slippery as an oyster, daring me to eat it. Alongside, a slimy sausage glistens like a dog's turd on the side of the plate. The coffee is tepid.

"Do you want more coffee?" I smile at Rachel in a slow, sad way she is bound to misinterpret. We gaze across the breakfast things like an old married couple, and I remove a smear of marmalade from the tablecloth. I wait till she has finished and gone upstairs. Then I phone Victor. It's as well there's two miles of telephone cable between us, because if he could reach me he'd wrap it round my neck.

"You've put everything in jeopardy, you realize that?"

"I know."

"As if it wasn't enough to start a major race riot, you kill a blasted policeman."

"Policeman?"

"What were you thinking of, for God's sake?"

"What policeman?"

"The man in the underground. You did *know* he was a policeman?"

"Casey?"

"Detective Sergeant Casey, idiot. Who did you think he was?"

"I didn't know. He was one of those guys came to my flat. He had a gun."

"What was he doing in Balham tube station?"

"It's a long story."

Victor doesn't want to hear it. He tells me to stay where I am because he's coming to fetch me.

"What do I do with Casey's friend?"

This doesn't please him either. "What friend?"

"Didn't they mention Patterson on the programme?"

"Patterson?"

"Casey's friend. There were two of them, remember?"

"And where is he?"

"I've got him prisoner. What should I do with him?"

"Christ."

"I'm sorry, Victor."

"Sorry!" He sounds like his cigar's disintegrated.

"I'd better release him."

"You'd better get over here."

"I can't just leave him. The guys will want to know what to do with him."

"Which guys?"

"I have two guys guarding him."

I stand clutching the receiver while he lets out a sigh so long I have to feed another ten pence into the meter. When the pips stop he still doesn't say anything. So I break the silence: "I'll go sort it out. Don't worry about it."

He is starting his reply as I put down the receiver. I can imagine his tired voice continuing unheard. I stare glumly at the coinbox. A wasted ten pence, really.

Call number two: the number I rarely use. A noncommittal voice — male — says, "Hello."

"It's me. I'm phoning from a coinbox. Sorry."

"It's probably safer than most places. How are you?"

"You been watching the news?"

Of course he has. Sometimes I think the Big Man has the TV permanently on. Maybe he has four of them, silently playing different channels. Four quiet windows onto an alien world. He says, "No one seems to know much about you."

"I should hope not. Anyway, about all this: there was nothing I could do. Two guys tried to break in at three in the morning, and they woke the neighbours."

"Light sleepers, your neighbours?"

"They were awake already. They were waiting for them. Trouble is, they didn't tell me."

"And you didn't know?"

"I ain't proud about it."

"No. What was this shooting in the street?"

"The first two guys had friends. They came after them when they didn't show up."

"And who were these people?"

"Christ knows. I thought it might be the other mob, or . . . But then they said this Casey was a cop."

"An ex-cop. A very different animal."

I consider this. "So what does that mean?"

"He's not a cop any more, but he's working in a similar line of business."

"A bent cop?"

"I doubt it. He's an ex-cop. My guess is he's moved across to some private security firm — the sort they use for unattributable jobs like this. But someone is onto you. It's bad news."

"They were onto Timmy first. But I'm out of sight now. I'm gonna hole up with Victor. But look, I still have one of their men: Casey's friend. You want him?"

"Where is he?" I tell him about the old garage under the arches. He says, "Just get rid of him. Let him go, shoot him, anything."

"Well, which?"

He sniffs. "Does he know where he is?"

"No."

"Does he know *anything*?"

"No."

"Then let him live. Make some woman happy."

"Why not? Listen, That guy Casey: before he died he rang a number. I know what it was. Can you get it traced?"

"A number? You got it right?"

"Sure. He was ringing home. I heard what he said."

"Anything interesting?"

"Not really. He confirmed they've got Timmy. Nothing else. You want the number?"

I saved this gem for last. After a whole night of me being a first-class liability I have pulled one big juicy plum and handed it to him. It's more like an apple than a plum — an apple for the teacher, to keep him sweet if he was gonna get mad at me. He is delighted. He says he'll have the address inside half an hour. So I

161

say I'll ring him back. I want to know where these guys are coming at me from.

When I stick my head round the door and tell Rachel I have to go out again, she sits down on the bed without a word. I bounce a few more cheery sentences off her, but she has withdrawn into her shell. I say I'll be back by lunch-time, but I can't tell if she believes me, because she don't seem to have heard a word I said.

So I leave her. I just hope she won't start cutting her hair.

I keep squinting out the window of the 188 bus to recognize where it was we hid Patterson. Even when I jump out in Southwark Park Road I ain't certain. But I slip down a couple of back roads and I find it soon enough.

I knock at the wood-plank door and it sounds as empty as a politician's promise. You'd think the last occupant went bankrupt and left years ago. Then someone peers out the little square panel, and finally some bolts are drawn back and a Rasta I never saw before beckons me inside. "Thought you gone off on holiday," he says.

We pick our way across the cement floor and into the battered portacabin. Patterson is still there, still tied to his chair, staring at the floor. He looks a lot worse. He looks like I feel on a very bad morning. "Make yourself some coffee," the Rasta says, and he picks up the phone.

Rufus and Des arrive within ten minutes. I stay in the cabin sipping hot coffee while the Rasta slouches over to open the door. For a moment they are snapped like a photograph in a flash of daylight. Then they are inside, waiting while he scrapes home the bolts.

Rufus says something, and the Rasta comes into the cabin alone. "He want to see you outside."

I leave him with Patterson. They're as talkative as two sacks of cement. I step out onto the main floor where Rufus stands waiting. Des shuffles his feet, like he's just the driver and didn't oughta be around. I try a smile, but it splutters out like a candle in a draught.

"You have some explaining to do," Rufus says. He looks tired.

"Yeah." I shrug helplessly. "I'm sorry, Rufus, I really am. I didn't want any of this. It just got out of hand."

"That's true. That is true."

"What can I say? Look — hand this guy over to me, and I'll deal with him. I'll release him. Then I'll clear out of the area. Things'll quieten down in a week or so."

"You think? The police are not going to forget this. They will have it in for us in a big way. Make us pay."

I sigh, because he's right. "OK. I can't put the clock back. But let me take over from here. It's my job now."

"Too late for that. We involved, like it or not. But what we involved *in*? You did not talk straight with me, out on the balcony."

"Straighter than you think. I didn't know who these guys were then."

"Now we hear they police. You didn't know that? You not dumb."

"Well, maybe I am. Don't believe this crap about them being police. They didn't act like police, did they?"

"There's police and police. These has no uniforms, but they carry guns. What you been doing?"

"Not a lot. Look, that other guy, the one got killed, he wasn't police, he was an *ex*-cop. He left. And look, I got to say this: I didn't ask for you all to get involved. I was dealing with this myself. I coulda handled it, without all this. It was my fight."

"And this is our manor. I tell you before: we keeping our streets clean. So I ask you again, what this about? Is it drugs, gangs or what?"

"A kind of gang fight. There are some guys want me out the way."

"So why the police come?"

I could tell Rufus to stuff his questions, but I like the guy. A lot of people round here have put themselves out for me. They have a right to feel I owe them something. The trouble is, I can't pay. "I don't know the answers," I tell him. "Let me take this guy away — I'll let him go — then I'll disappear. And when I get this all sorted . . ." I peter out.

"You'll what? You gonna pay back all they people got arrested

163

for you? You gonna get prisoners out of jail? You gonna repay the fines, mend the broken glass? There's nothing you can do, man. You tell me this all your affair, you deal with it yourself. Well, this all *our* affair — right? We deal with it ourself — right? We don't need your help, because there ain't nothing you can do, and we don't want you round here anyway. You don't live here any more. So you piss off, and you don't show here again. You lied to us, man, and you brought trouble. You ain't fit to live with decent people. Go find a sewer of your own."

The silence falls like a guillotine. We stand like three old trees in winter, quivering in the gloom. Then I inhale long and slowly, because it's for me to make the move. "I'll take him and go, then," I say. Rufus shakes his head. He stares into my eyes. I try to think of something I can say that's better than just I'm sorry, but my brain has dried up. I have a ringing in my ears like I've been smacked around the head.

When I trudge to the door, only Des comes to let me out. I want to reach out and touch him, to put a hand on his shoulder or something, but he avoids my eyes. When he scrapes back the bolts I wince.

Then I'm out in the street where the daylight hurts and the wind kicks dirt and paper round the kerb. I think I got something in my eye.

I sit watching Victor's television through stale air thick with tobacco smoke. He drags morosely on the cheroot while we wait for the pretty young newsreader to get through the latest government verbals on the self-pitying unemployed. There's jobs there if they'd take them, the Minister says. Despite the other millions out of work. All they got to do is have faith.

"Can you open a window in here?" I ask.

"Here it comes," he nods at the screen.

"The Deptford Riots" the newsreader says, making it a sentence on its own. She's shown us the label so we can recognize the packaged news story like it was a familiar soap powder. The Deptford Riots means the tut-tut tale about dirty black people beating up innocent policemen. Bloody immigrants. Ungrateful bastards going too far. Anarchy and danger in the streets. Somewhere round a corner near you.

I stare at the screen while they show a grainy old black-and-white photo of me, younger, with longer hair. I look grimy, bad-tempered, just the sort of guy you'd expect to find hiding in a woodpile in Deptford when there's trouble about.

"Was that photo in your flat?" Victor asks.

"Do me a favour. Must have found it in someone's file."

"It doesn't look like you."

"Thank you."

She is telling the viewers that the fuzz would like to talk to me "in connection with the death of ex-Detective Sergeant Casey at Balham underground station last night. It is believed that this incident may be connected with the riots yesterday in Deptford."

They cut to a drone in uniform with a face like leftover porridge. He wheezes ponderously into his chest-mike about a breakdown in law and order. A male interviewer with sleek hair sits awkwardly on a high-tech chair, agreeing with him. The young prune wears his tie crooked, and I keep expecting the policeman to lean forward and straighten it. Someone ought to. Then we cut back to the newsreader. She treats us to her speciality sad gaze to camera, so we can see that either society's collapsing or her piles are hurting, and then we're off to the next item.

Victor kills the sound, and I challenge him: "So it's all my fault?"

"You're a useful scapegoat, certainly. It gives them an excuse for piling into Deptford, and it lets them target you for a national man-hunt."

"You think people will recognize me from that old photo?"

"I hardly recognized you myself."

I pick up my coffee and stare at the cold dregs. I've let Victor down. Even if what happened was not all my fault, I contributed. I didn't slip away. I roared in head first, like a schoolboy boxer who won't make the grade. I wasn't professional. "I'm sorry," I tell him.

"Don't keep apologizing, darling. It's out of character.

Anyway, now that you've psyched yourself up you might as well stay there. It's only a few hours now."

"What are we going to do till then?"

"Stay in. I shall pop out for an hour this afternoon, to fetch the van and pick up some things. You'll have to stay in. It'll be dark when we leave."

I rattle my empty mug on the table. "Another night job. I ain't had a good night's sleep since God knows. Reckon I'll start sleeping in the day."

"That sounds very wise." He says this in the kind of dry voice that ought to mean he is smiling. But when I glance up, he is pacing round his old armchair with his lips pursed. He drums his fingers on the chairback as he passes. He flicks me a look, and keeps walking. I wait. He keeps walking. I say, "Tell me," and he stops.

"There was a phone call before you arrived. It was the Big Man."

"I spoke to him. He saw me on the telly."

"That's not why he rang. It wasn't the main reason." He seems to catch his breath, and he stops. He won't look me in the eye. Just as the pause edges towards the ridiculous he reaches into his jacket for this packet of cheroots. I watch him concentrate on licking the end of a little cigar. He holds it in his mouth, he picks out a match and he strikes it on the box. As he disappears behind a safety curtain of blue smoke he starts to say something, but he coughs on the smoke. His face reappears through the swirls and his eyes are sad. He takes another smouldering drag then jerks the cigar away and lets his arm droop to his side. "He phoned to tell me they found Timmy."

An outstretched tentacle of smoke tickles at my nose. "Who did?"

"Oh . . . the police, or somebody. He's dead, of course."

"Yeah." I stare at Victor's carpet, and see the pattern for the first time. It has something to do with grapes. "Where'd they find him?"

"On the underground line. He fell under a train early this morning. On the Northern line. It seems he'd been drinking."

I don't say anything. Victor paces about for a bit. "They killed him, of course."

I'm thinking about this. "How did the Big Man hear so fast?"

"Apparently Timmy carried identification in his wallet."

"He wouldn't do that. They planted it on him."

"Of course. They were sending us a message."

"It wasn't Balham again?"

"No. Somewhere north of the river. Same line though, Northern."

"They colour it black on the tube map."

"I've been here long enough to know the colours of the underground, darling."

"Black is the colour of death."

"Don't talk like an old woman in a village. The colour is unimportant. But perhaps they chose the Northern to make sure we understood."

"Yeah. Well, I understand. You think Timmy talked?"

Victor sucks in a Hooverful of cigar smoke, then strains it out through tight lips. "Who can tell? Perhaps they'd finished with him. Perhaps they decided he had nothing useful to say — which isn't far from the truth. All he could say was that we were waiting for something to happen."

"Just like us — waiting in the dark."

"Until now."

"Good timing on their part."

He glowers at the butt of his cigar like it's a broken fingernail. "Coincidence, darling. They got onto Timmy just as things were beginning to move. But they didn't know that."

"Think they do now?"

"I can't see how. They didn't know what they were looking for, any more than we did. They just kept waiting, listening, watching. Timmy must have made a wrong move, drew attention to himself." Victor pauses, and raises his eyes to meet mine. Then he smiles a slow sad smile. "He beat you to it, didn't he?"

I smile back. There's no humour in these smiles. They're just to show we still like each other. We're all we've got now. "Yeah, it could have been me," I say.

"Burnt to death on the underground line. Like your friend Casey."

I chew on my lip. "My mother was burnt to death, in the cottage."

Victor sighs and looks away. He wants to change the subject. "Timmy will have been dead before he got there. Anyway, it's happened." He grinds the end of his cigar into a glass ashtray littered with previous crushed remains. A lingering sweetness of tobacco in the air is destroyed by an acrid smell of stale tar. "Did you check out that telephone number?" he asks me.

"Yeah."

"Did you get an address?"

"Yeah."

"Do we recognize it?"

"No."

"What was it?"

I tell him. It's a place in North Finchley, Woodside Park. It's an address engraved in my brain. These are the people who got Timmy.

"Woodside Park is on the Northern line," observes Victor.

"I know. Who do you think they are — plain-clothes cops?"

"Hardly."

"Why not?"

"The police don't go dumping bodies on the underground line."

"Oh, really?"

"Darling, where do you get these ideas? If the police had Timmy, he'd be in a cell. Even if he died there, they wouldn't be able to just throw his body away. He'd have been signed in. He'd be on the record. This is England, darling. It's not like home."

"These ain't bobbies on bicycles, Victor, I've met 'em."

"Which ones?"

"Casey, Patterson, goddam riot squads in Deptford."

"Different animals. You really think it's the police who've been hounding us? Haven't you thought about this at all?" I catch a piercing look I've seen him give other guys; Gregory, when he wouldn't jump a six-foot gap on the fourteenth storey; Nick, when we learned about his drinking. It's a look I never thought he'd give me. It makes me cringe into the smelly upholstery of his battered armchair. It's like he's squinting down the sights of a rifle at me. I feel like I stepped into a fridge.

Then he relaxes into a sorrowful smile, like when you remember someone you loved who died a long time ago. And maybe that's what he is doing. Or maybe he's remembered some other time in the heat and dirt and anger when there was only the two of us, and the world had burst into flames.

When he reaches back into his jacket pocket for that inevitable pack of cheap cigars I'm watching him as carefully as a dog with a drunken master, unsure whether he'll get a kick or a bowl of food. Victor's face as the match flares in front of it has the rapt attention of a man lighting a fuse. But the smoke seems to soothe him, and when he glances up I think it must be how a father looks at his son just a couple of times each year.

18

We listen to the ten o'clock news on the car radio, slumped in this Japanese van he's hired, staring glumly out the windscreen at a million cars defecating exhaust fumes into a wet evening in Hammersmith Broadway.

According to Victor, there are two possibilities. They could be another cell after the same thing we're after, or they could be the British end, out to stop us getting our hands on it. "It has to be the second," he muses. We agree that the chance of any other group coming over for these things is remote. Most people don't realize Britain has any, and nobody knows where they are. Few people realize they exist, for Christ's sake. But they will.

So this has to be some bunch of legalized mercenaries lurking round the underground of criminal society, sniffing for scents that are foreign and bizarre. They are looking for guys you'd think would stick out a mile: terrorists, assassins, cut-outs and plants. But these are the guys who never stick out. That's the whole point. The only ones who ever stand out are the one-touch men, over for a sudden, hurried job. Get in, get it, get out. They don't wait to blend in. They're on a short-dated return ticket, they don't hang around. If you don't pick them up when they land on your soil, it'll be too late when they go.

You can console yourself that the battle they're fighting is usually their own. It doesn't concern you at all. The only reason they're here is that they've blown in from someplace that's tearing itself apart, to hunt down a compatriot. Maybe he's fled, or maybe he wants to return in blood and glory, but they intend to end his life in a foreign land.

Just occasionally the one-touch man has come for *you*. He has come because this is where you live. He isn't looking for you personally — unless you happen to be shopping in the wrong store or strolling past the wrong parked car. He is looking for someone symbolic, some*where* symbolic, where the folk who die matter less than the sign above the door.

He is difficult to stop, this one-touch man. He's like an express train that crashes through the barrier, sudden and dramatic, tragic and rare. You don't see him coming because he arrives looking like everyone else. He comes out the immigration terminal in crumpled clothes, carrying an ordinary suitcase full of ordinary things. He travels by public transport, rents a bed for the night, strolls in the streets to check if he's followed, then finally makes contact with his cut-out.

Victor and I arrived like that. We stepped off different boats — ferries from the continent — looking tired and a little vulnerable, and we dissolved into the crowd. There was no reason to look at us, nothing to suspect. We carried nothing unusual. You could have shredded our suitcases and not found a thing. Even our passports were perfect. Almost.

But we weren't here for a short trip. We'd come to stay. It ain't easy to soak into the ground of a foreign country, to become just another scrap of litter in the streets, printed in the same language, bearing the same marks, holding the same smell as the others scuffling in the dirt around you. We took our time.

We chose to live south of the Thames because we had to be in London and this was where immigrants hid. The capital is divided by imaginary lines. Boundaries are unclear. The only clear boundary in the whole dirty capital is the grey Thames. When you stand beside it you see an industrial river a hundred yards wide. You lean on black iron railings and you smell the diluted sweat of eight million people, mixed with the steel of commerce, the smoke of the barges, the warm fumes of city life, all dissolved in the grey-brown water.

It may not be as wide as many rivers in the world — there are bigger ones even in this little green island — and it may look on the map like a crazy bent rivulet in the sand; but when you stand beside it you know you're against a barrier. When you cross one of its broad and busy bridges you move into another world. One short bridge uproots you from the strained opulence of riverside Chelsea, where every brick has been scrubbed clean with a ten-pound note and repointed in charcoal cement, where the heavy wooden doors gleam like bank vaults, where the windows are double-glazed, burglar-proofed and framed with pâté — that one bridge transports you out from where the paraded money drips like fuchsias off Georgian balconies, across to where successful tradespeople live. They call them Yuppies now. They call them*selves* Yuppies even. Yuppies are the butlers of yesterday, running the masters' houses, and dressed nicely for doing so.

Across Victor's bridge is a starker journey. It jolts you from the Strand and Savoy hotel to the grimy dark railway arches where the homeless sleep with dossers in the slums of Waterloo.

Out in Deptford, of course, we don't get a bridge. The last one going east is the picture postcard split-in-the-middle Tower Bridge, way back past Jamaica Road. It separates the black suits and black money of the self-satisfied City from the honest black skins of Bermondsey. Your pinstriped carnation-sporting florid financiers never dream of popping over the muddy waters for a dekko at the real world and working people that prop up their plate-glass casino-land. They wouldn't want to get their turnups dirty. And since no one on the south side can afford the price of a pint across the water — assuming you can buy a pint there among the bloodstained clarets, double brandies and fizzing fart-inducing fancy Perrier water — I can't see what Tower Bridge is *for*, except to please the tourists, or to say "You made it" to motorboats trundling up from the sea. They should have sold it to that American who thought he'd bought it back in the Seventies. They let him cough up the money, sign all the papers, turn up with his demolition men — then they told him he'd bought London Bridge, not Tower Bridge, and that though London Bridge was the most boring one across the whole river he was stuck with it and could take it, brick by crumbling brick, to America and stick it where he pleased. The City was happy to be rid of it — dull, grey, utilitarian; designed by accountants and built on the cheap. It was natural they should sell it and pocket the loot.

And not a bent ha'penny found its way to the south side. All the unremembered ordinary people, cramped in the crowded tenements and back streets of Deptford, New Cross, Peckham, Catford, Charlton; we don't warrant a measly little bridge; we have to squirm underneath the stinking river in dark depressing tunnels like rats in the sewers — the underclasses, underground. Where we belong.

You notice I've gone back to saying "we"? You see how I identify with these people? Perhaps it's because so many of us there are foreigners. We know we don't belong, because you keep telling us so. But we're digging ourselves in, just the same.

Millions of you in this huge grinding metropolis hate the bloody thought of us. You resent the air we breathe. We can't even cross the mucky river in the fresh air; we might dirty up the skyline. So you stuff us down the rat-holes, ram us down the drain, cram us all together in the damp dark underground.

Well, every time you hear a traffic-flash on your radio, every time you hear there's a tailback and at least an hour's delay for anyone using the Blackwall or Rotherhithe Tunnel, then you just remember this: there's a mile-long queue of angry put-upon hard men with nothing much to lose, and they're all sitting fuming, and they're all glaring viciously, and it's all in the same direction, and that direction is up at YOU.

All of which lasts me nicely till we're out of the London traffic and coasting west on the M4. It's dark now. For a while the capital keeps a hold on us, lighting up the motorway with a million wasteful streetlamps. Then finally they stop, and we plunge on through the dark, relying on headlamps. Suddenly it's more peaceful, as if someone turned down the sound. I decide the time has come to tell Victor exactly where it is we're going.

We have to follow this M4 motorway due west for about an hour, out through Buckinghamshire, across Berkshire, and well into Wiltshire. Then we head off onto a trunk road for a few miles. Then we start on the back lanes.

Now I give him detailed directions. We cruise away from occasional traffic into the quiet of the countryside. In less than ten minutes it's time to pull into a verge. I open my door and step out. As my eyes get used to the dark, memory completes the picture. It's a month since I was here.

The cool breeze refreshes me. I stretch myself to relieve the cramp of two hours' driving, and I cross over to the gate in the hedge and open it. As I push the gate through its heavy arc, my feet sink into churned wet mud. Victor drives the van through. He eases it slowly across the muddy entrance, onto the firmer ground in the field. I close the gate and wave him on. He can't see me in the dark, and waits with the engine running. I appear at his window and tell him to drive on while I follow. My feet are filthy with mud. The van bumps gently across the meadow, while I tramp through the ankle-high wet grass behind him. In the breeze there's a taste of rain. One or two stars glint through breaks in the clouds. A cow groans in a nearby field.

When he reaches the dark copse of trees, Victor kills the lights and switches off the engine. The trees grow up the side of a small hillock no higher than a house. When I opened the gate it was a black smudge in the dark. You might just make out something solid, like a water-tower, on top. But now, sheltered in the field at the bottom, we can't see through the trees. Victor sits in the driving seat with the window wound down, and before he gets out he lights up a cheroot. Then he joins me on the damp grass. "There's no real path through the trees," I say, "But it's easy enough, apart from nettles and brambles. It's easier in daylight."

"You came here with Timmy?"

"We went up the hill."

"Nobody saw you?"

"No one would care. There are no guards — nothing like that. Not even a fence."

"This is definitely the place?"

"This is the one."

All that protects it is that no one would be interested. It's just a clump of trees on a small hillock in the middle of a farmer's field in the middle of nowhere. An old tower stands on top, but by the time you've driven out here, crossed the field, fought your way up through a tangle of brambles and branches, you have to ask yourself what was the point? It ain't exactly a site of architectural interest, and if you're really looking for archaeological mounds in Wiltshire I have to tell you that the county is smothered in the things like a kid with the measles, and this one's gonna come four hundred and ninety-nine down your list.

"Quiet night," I say, like I just made some poetry.

174

"Good," mutters Victor, and he draws on his cheroot. I smell the tobacco and wet grass. "We're early," he says. "There's nearly an hour to kill."

"I should have brought a book."

"That would make a change."

I scowl at him in the dark. "Maybe I'd better run you through the plan again. We might as well have it perfect." Victor nods and takes a last drag on his cigar. It lights up his face like a pantomime devil. Then he grinds out the butt beneath his shoe, frowns, and bends down to pick up the crushed end.

"You think someone could find it?" I ask.

"You never know."

"And what about all those tyre tracks?"

He hesitates, then grins. "Yes. Silly of me, darling." He turns back to the van, but I see he slips the butt into his jacket pocket all the same. Old habits die hard.

After quarter of an hour sitting in the van, listening to the light wind in the trees, we decide to get ready and start early. It's grown cold in the van, and we're bored. We don't play the radio because someone might hear. More important: we wouldn't hear them. Not that anyone's around.

So we climb out the van and stand beside it, straining our eyes in the dark as we peer across the fields. We have sat here long enough to draw out anyone watching. But nothing stirs. No one even drives down the lane.

Outside in the cool breeze we can hear leaves shushing each other in the night. Occasionally the horizon lights up from the headlamps of a distant passing car. It looks like when someone crosses an unlit street with a torch — the long thin beams feeling through the air, emphasizing the dark.

We open the back of the van and pull out the equipment. There's a bag with a couple of pulleys and some clamps, there's the bag with climbing gear, there are two planks of wood, and there's a hell of a lot of nylon rope. Victor slams the door, and a disturbed bird rustles the branches somewhere in the wood. We shoulder our bags and trudge into the trees.

This tangle of undergrowth was bad enough by daylight, but

now, underneath the branches, it's as dark as in an unlit tent at night. Brambles catch at our trousers and wrap around our feet. Twigs scratch our faces. We take several dead-end paths, and have to turn round and stumble back the way we came. Both of us carry small hand-torches. We flick them on and off briefly to help show the way. My bag catches in some saplings. When I pull it savagely free I snap off a young tree. Ten years' growth wasted.

But I find the clearing. "It's easier from here," I whisper. "There's a kind of path from the right-hand corner." I shift my load to the other shoulder and plunge into the undergrowth. At every step another bramble snags my trousers, and I think I shall arrive either with my pants ripped to tatters, or with twigs and creepers hanging off me like I'm a scarecrow with its stuffing falling out.

Suddenly there's a screech like a klaxon. My hand dives inside my jerkin for my gun. But it was only a stupid pheasant, startled from sleep to rise squawking and flapping its wings among the trees. I glare after it in the darkness.

When we reach the other clearing up at the top I am cursing like a wasp in a jam-jar. For all I care, you can stuff the countryside into the cellars of the Natural History Museum. I thump my heavy bag down on the ground, and stand panting like I just ran up the stairs.

We're on that flat grassy bit, the old stone tower looming black before us, ringed by scruffy trees rattling in the breeze. It isn't raining yet, and a few stars flicker damply among the clouds like coins at the bottom of a well. The place looks like no-one's visited for several years. "I'm gonna look round," I say.

I pick my way round the base of the tower. It's as interesting as the outside of a warehouse: black stone walls, no windows, just the one door where Victor waits till I'm back. "How high is it?" he asks.

"Ten metres maybe. In the daylight you can see it from the road, peeping over the trees like a castle on a chessboard. The black rook."

"How old is it?"

"I don't know. Could be twenty years. Could be two hundred."

This place doesn't serve any purpose, it just sits here. It could have been built by an eccentric baron, or it could have been fabricated just a decade ago. The wooden door doesn't open. In the finger of torchlight it is heavy and drab. It has no handle, no keyhole. It is not the way in.

Victor squats by his bag to unzip it. He hands me up the pitons one by one, and I clip them to my belt. I carry the karabiners separately in a canvas bag, and when he passes me the hammer I slip it into its pouch on my belt. While Victor squats in the darkness, I take one end of the eight millimetre rope and tie myself in with a bowline knot. Then I turn to face the cold brick wall, and at shoulder height I knock the first piton into a crevice between two bricks. I attach a karabiner, and thread my rope through. Victor gives me a leg-up to start me off, and I'm on my way.

It's a technique of ascent your true rock-climber disdains. I'm relying completely on rope, pitons and karabiners, making no attempt to conquer the natural surfaces. Pitons crunch into mortar between bricks, the swivel-hooks snap onto the pitons, the rope threads through, and I pull myself up a metre at a time. I'm not even wearing my old Carter nailed boots, because I get a better grip in my rubber-soled scarpetti.

It's a lonely job, despite Victor being just a few yards below. Darkness wraps around me, the breeze chills my fingers, I concentrate on tapping in the pitons and working my way up. The tapping of my hammer will be dispersed in the breeze. It's too high above the deserted countryside to disturb light sleepers, and although the thumps will resound hollowly inside the tower, no one is in there to hear. I could play a radio if I liked, and only Victor would complain.

But I just whistle tuneless snatches, and tap rhythms on the wall. I don't count the pitons. I don't peer up or down. I work on each one steadily: knocking it in, testing for strength, snapping the karabiner in place, threading my rope, pulling it taut, easing myself gradually higher in the dark.

The tower is only about thirty feet high. It doesn't take long to haul myself to the top. I slither over the edge, onto the flat concrete roof inside the mock battlements, and I sit for a minute to relax.

It's strange how the temperature thirty foot above the skyline becomes colder. The breeze is sharper. The air seems fresher. This thirty foot is on top of a tower on top of a hillock, so maybe I am seventy foot up altogether. It's a hell of a view. Beads of light glisten from villages and farmhouses all over the area. Parts of the horizon are blanketed in orange where the massed lights of small towns warm the sky. Faraway lines of streetlamps look like runways of distant airports, thousands of feet below. I can see cars moving, their headlamps trickling through the night. If I listen carefully, I can hear the drone of their engines.

And there's that persistent hum seeping up from inside the tower — a faint deep resonance, like when you wake in the middle of the night and hear the fridge switch itself on in the kitchen. I step in from the edge at the top of the tower, towards the huge flanges covering the central shaft. My eyes have long since adapted to the dark, and I can see as comfortably as a cat.

The tops of the flanges have been camouflaged. You can't see them from below, and if you flew over you'd think there was just a solid flat roof. You'd have to fly really low and slow to realize your mistake. But here on the shaft's perimeter you see a gap three foot high where the raised flanges overhang the concrete ledge. I can feel warm air seeping out.

I return to the outer edge and give the last piton a couple of thumps for reassurance. Then I slip the spare coil of rope off from round my neck, secure the end to the piton, and drop the coil down to Victor below. I hope he's standing well back.

Within half a minute the rope twitches and I start to heave it up. Victor's bag scrapes between the battlements and flops onto the inner concrete. I wonder if it's worth using his pulleys, but I just drop the rope back instead. Again it twitches, and again I heave it up. The noise of two planks clattering against the stone wall is like we've been joined by an insomniac carpenter.

With the planks stowed, I drop the rope one last time for Victor to climb up himself. He comes wheezing over the top as I'm fixing the pulleys to the planks of wood. He pulls up the nylon rope and threads it round a pulley. Then we heave the bits over to the edge of the great protective flange, and fix a crude block and tackle on the rim of the shaft. We both tug at it, tighten it up, tug again, tighten, and then to make sure it's secure we jerk it all about. Oh, oh, the hokey-cokey.

Victor sits on the concrete, leaning back against one of the flange supports. He looks at his watch. "We're still too early," I tell him. "We can't go down for nearly half an hour."

If you ever want to find out which numbs you first — boredom or cold — try sitting on top of a thirty-foot tower, perched on a hillock, between midnight and half-past when it's trying to rain. No wonder the sentries at Elsinore thought they saw a ghost.

They didn't even have Victor's disgusting cheroots to keep them warm. He sits huddled inside a kapok-filled anorak, filling his cheeks with blue smoke, while I cringe against the outlet from the ventilator shaft, trying to feel the benefit of a little warm air. Every five minutes I do exercises. By the time we drop down there, either I'll be as fit as a footballer or I'll have fallen asleep.

Victor grinds out another cheroot and again he puts the butt in his pocket. He stands up. I'm bent double, touching my toes. I stay in this chimpanzee position, looking up at him. "It's half-past twelve," he says, and I unbend. He stretches lazily, like he's just out of bed on a Sunday morning — which it is, by thirty minutes. He beams across at me.

"Me first?" I ask.

"If you don't mind, darling." I stoop under the flange. It's darker. Round my head it's as stuffy as in the tube. Round my feet there's a draught. I fumble towards the lip of the ventilator shaft where a low retaining wall stands about nine inches tall round the top. I straddle it, and sit with one foot lying along the concrete, and the other on the grille inside.

The inspection cover in the grille is padlocked and chained. Do they think that'll stop us, now we've come so far? I slip my little jemmy into the hasp of the lock, twist it to tighten, then smack with my hammer on the edge of the lock where the hasp hooks inside. It falls open like a broken toy. I lift the grille cover, slide it aside, and sit on the edge with my feet dangling into the void.

From the block and tackle we have tied off the rope to the flange upright, I let twenty feet dangle inside the shaft. When I get to the bottom of that, Victor will loosen the rope and start to

179

play me down. Maybe by then I'll have struck lucky and found a workman's ladder fixed to the wall. But knowing my luck, I will not. I take hold of the rope where it spills from the pulley, and I yank it tight. Then I wrap the nylon cord round me to act as a rappel rope. It passes through my left hand, round behind my left thigh, up from my right to cross my chest, then round the back of my turned-up collar to return to my left hand. Like this, I can sit on the loop of rope, using my left hand to control it. My right hand stays free. We have a separate thin signal cord, and I wrap its end round my belt. Instinct tells me to take a deep breath before I drop, but the air is so fetid I put my instinct on hold and just slip through the hatch.

The rope tightens snugly round my thigh, and I sit on it for five seconds to test the strain. Letting myself down the first twenty feet in the dark, all the old skills come back. Now it really is black. The air has changed to a warm stale draught. It's like swimming round a sewage outlet in the sea. I am rubbing against the inner wall of the shaft, hanging on my short rope. I flick on the torch, and its thin beam of light illuminates the wall. Every few feet there's a built-out ring of concrete, a kind of framework for the cylinder. Each one makes enough of a ledge for me to rest my feet and relieve the tension in my arms. This won't be such a hard descent after all.

The rappel method lets you down slowly at first. But as you slip further down, your weight pulls you ever faster, until in a sudden panic you realize you can't brake. The most I can drop will be about a hundred feet. I did it once in snow on Campanile di Val Montanaio in the Dolomites, but I don't fancy it now.

I keep wiping my torchlight round the walls of the shaft. About seventy feet down I see the top of the iron hand-ladder. Didn't I tell you there had to be something? They had to provide some way engineers could climb up. I work my way round the walls, thick with sooty dust, till I get my hand on the first step. It'll be easy from here.

Now that I'm this deep down I can see light coming up from the tunnel at the bottom. Between that light and me the air seems to shiver. It's the blades of the giant fan, extracting stale air.

I climb down the ladder, hand over hand, gradually working

lower, closer to those whirling blades, feeling the breeze stronger in my hair. The thought of the spinning blades helps me keep a tight hold on the ladder. I pause for breath near the foot. There's a hell of a lot taken on trust from here on in.

We have to rely on what we've been told by our mole. Appropriate, to have a mole working for you underground. Somewhere down there, among however many is on duty, our little mole is working his shift. I wonder what he looks like. Maybe he wears pebble-glass spectacles.

It took Timmy a year to find him, and nearly another to turn him round. But now Timmy's dead — scraped off the underground line like burnt meat. I wonder if the mole knows. I wonder what the security men screwed out of Timmy before he died. I wonder if the whole scam's been blown. But as the Big Man told Victor this morning, we have to risk it. We have to chance the only plan we had: using this shaft, on this Saturday night, dropping in quietly between twelve-thirty and one. The Big Man has spoken to the mole. The mole says it will be OK.

I am standing on the inspection platform. It's two square yards of reinforced concrete stuck out from the wall of the shaft, poised about a metre above the fan. The blades grind round slowly enough for me to make out each one as it spins.

Three tugs on the cord tell Victor I've arrived.

He lets out more rope, and I coil it at my feet. When there's plenty to reach the floor I signal up, and he stops. Then I sit on the concrete platform and wait while he climbs down.

I brood about Timmy while I wait. Here's two more of us, I think, burying ourselves a hundred feet beneath the Wiltshire earth. Maybe we're climbing into our own grave. The routine never changes, the mole said, and tonight between twelve-thirty and one the video camera at the foot of this shaft will not be on. He'll arrange that. That's what he says. In that graveyard hour, he says, no one will come along this particular stretch. No one will stir in the dead man's shift. The place will be empty. Of people.

That's what he says. That's what the Big Man says he says.

I can hear Victor's boots slithering on the iron rungs.

When he gets his breath back we both stand up. "Time's getting on," he says. I reach behind us on the inspection platform and press the red button. The noise cuts and the giant blades begin to slow. We watch them turn enough times that anyone caught in them would become slices of red salami. Only when they're absolutely still do I drop between them onto the final metal grille. My ribs shiver.

This time there isn't a padlock. I pull up the iron hatch and peer out below. Victor drops onto the grille behind me, making me jump, and as I pull back inside I hit my head on the edge.

He grins as if it was funny. I scowl, and stick my head back out through the hatch to squint along the tunnel. It is lit with gloomy neon. To my right, the tunnel wanders about a hundred yards before fading out round a bend. To my left, the corner is only twenty yards away. I don't like that. The floor is concrete, with a thin set of train rails set in the middle. Either side of the floor, boxes are stacked along the walls. Some are on racks, some just piled on the concrete. Some stuff isn't in boxes at all.

I lie there for a minute with my head out, looking for movement. Everything is still. Fifty yards to my right a solitary video camera hangs black like a bat from the ceiling. The mole said it wouldn't be working.

If he's wrong then it has already seen me. Even now the red lights will be glowing, and men will be jumping from their beds, grabbing their rifles and running soft and urgent down concrete corridors. It's too late now.

So I snake out the last few metres of rope, down through the hatch to coil onto the floor. It piles into a small heap, like a conspicuous cowpat. Then I grab hold of it where it passes me, yank it for luck, and climb quickly down the last ten feet.

Standing alone in the silent tunnel is like I'm auditioning on stage. Cold unseen eyes could be watching me. I glance up, and I hope it ain't a screen test.

Victor swings down on the rope with an empty canvas sack slung over his shoulder, grinning like he's Father Christmas. He shows no sign of stage fright. As soon as he hits the floor he ignores what's around him and tilts his head in the way we're to go. He pads off along the tunnel like he's just popped on his slippers to go for a midnight pee.

I breathe in some air before following him. Here we are at last, a hundred feet below ground in the British Army's biggest ammunition dump. That's what the mole says, and he should know. These tunnels stretch for miles — and I mean literally miles — from Wiltshire back into Hampshire, and they're stacked up the walls with firepower: guns, bullets, rockets and bombs. I could drool around here all day, like a keen student in a museum. Except that this is no museum, it's for real. To me it's like an art gallery.

While I'm thinking this, Victor is disappearing up the tunnel. He always was a philistine. No respect.

There's one of these shafts set about every half mile. Each one is topped by some kind of fake building: a cottage, a barn, a disused hangar . . . an old tower, shaped like a castle. Most are on military land, difficult to get to, harmless-looking in an aerial photograph. Just a few are like this: remote but accessible, protected only by their innocent disguise. But it ain't good enough, General. Your sophisticated radar may detect a missile twitching in its silo, but it's no defence against men like me. We're the kind drove the Yanks from Vietnam.

I walk on.

We know that the boxes we're looking for should be beyond the hanging camera, but I'm interested in the other stuff standing by the walls. You've been round a few warehouses, I guess, so you'll know how ordinary things look, stacked in boxes, not on display. I'll say this for the capitalist society: they certainly know how to pretty things up, to add desirability, to make it seem the stuff is more than just stuff.

But down here, it's like the back storeroom where the customer never sees. Bombs and bullets wait in boxes with names and partnumbers stencilled crudely outside. The shells are like seashells mouldering in an old cardboard box, forgotten in the dark after the holiday has faded. I read the stencilled names, mouthing the words silently like a religious litany. TOW, Swingfire, Milan. Dragons, like stovepipes on the floor. Weapons with numbers instead of names: British LAW80s, dull against the left-hand wall, a consignment of American M72s, even a couple of French AC300s.

I remember that one: one of the few portable anti-tank weapons you can use in house-to-house fighting. Most of the others give out such a backblast that if you shoot from indoors they stun everyone in the room. But the AC300 — you can stand in a front parlour and fire it out the window. It beats shooting grouse for lunch.

Yeah, there's many old friends, and other numbers I don't recognize, huddled together in crates like this was a huge cash-and-carry supermarket a hundred metres underground. Some of the crates are open-topped. I can reach out and touch the shells.

We're passing beneath the video camera when I hear another noise above the continual low hum. A rumble. I freeze. The trundling, rattling noise is coming closer, fast. It's the sound of something driving down the rails towards us.

We don't even glance at each other as we melt into the sides, between the boxes by the walls. I try to become part of the shadows. Before I stop moving altogether I reach inside my jerkin for the small reassurance of my Smith & Wesson 38.

I am pressed hard against the boxes as the train arrives. Three low flat-beds, shaking and screeching down the centre of the tunnel at a steady ten miles an hour. Two of the trucks are loaded, and the back one is empty. There's no driver, no guard; it's just a small working pick-up, moving stores. At this time of night it's the ghost train, still running after the fair has closed.

You'd think there would be somebody: not left dead and unattended, like a kid's toy in the cellar. They must think there is only the one line, no other trains, no cows on the track — so why should they need guards?

But there ought to have been someone. One young soldier, sitting tired on the back. One young some-mother's-son, wondering why the hell he is wasting his youth riding a train-set in the stores underground. But nobody. Just the ghost train, rumbling into the distance round the curve.

We both wait in the shadows for the silence to return. I reset the safety catch and put my gun away. I never wanted to shoot innocent young soldiers. Not any more. Anyway, opening fire down here would be a final lashing out, beating desperately against the doors of our own tomb.

As the silence seeps back, I realize I am standing between crates of stun grenades. The crates have no lids. The grenades lie like pears in the greengrocers, and I smile. I move my hand to take one, then I stop. Am I a shoplifter? We didn't come to steal grenades, we have work to do. But I'd like a souvenir.

Now we edge out into the centre, back into the light, Victor pulls a face, then turns to walk the last few metres to where they should be. Passing under that camera was like we crossed a border. Along the right-hand walls, instead of piles of boxes we now have uncartonned artillery, leaning loosely against the wall. Long thin rockets stacked into wigwam shapes like giant biros in a jar.

These are not familiar to me. The ammunition I know is the small human stuff: rifles and handguns, bayonets and knives. Stuff you can lug about with you. Stuff you can use. I never fired the big field-guns. They're the kind of thing the other side has, out of sight in the distance, bringing sudden massive destruction out of the sky.

But some I do recognize. Victor stops just beyond a stack of AIM9 Sidewinders — exploding cigars, we called them. There's a twenty-metre run of these Sidewinders, followed by a stretch of what the stencils say are AIM7s. Those are anti-radar missiles. What does Victor want with them?

But it's the crates opposite that he's interested in. Crude wooden boxes from America — roughly made, when you think what's inside. A touch of the cowboy about them, like the ammo boxes the cavalry had in old black-and-white Westerns, handed out the back of the covered wagon when Indians appeared on surrounding hills.

So everything is according to instructions. Just where he said they would be.

"Here we are, darling," says Victor. "How many shall we take?"

"We'll soon see," I say, and I heave up a crate to feel its weight. It's heavy. "We'll not manage more than one."

"Seems hardly worth coming."

"You feel the weight. We gotta haul this back up the shaft and down through that briar jungle. And for every crate of shells we'll need another crate of carriers."

He sees my point — especially since we'll be carrying our ropes and gear too. Anyway, one crate will be enough. Quite enough.

The shells we've come to get are special — they're W79s. American made, but sold to the British, French and who knows who else in NATO. Maybe you haven't heard too much about these beauties, because most governments deny they exist. Then if you point them out on the pages of world armoury manuals they agree that, yes, they do exist, but they haven't got any. Governments get sensitive because, of course, W79s are not ordinary weapons, they're nuclear. Which is why governments deny they exist.

And is why we're here.

But you will know this already. You'll know that the W79 is a battlefield nuclear weapon. And you'll know that that means it is big. Makes a hole like the Grand Canyon. And a cloud like the bubonic plague. It is fired from a portable launcher, just like any other anti-tank gun, by an ordinary soldier out with his platoon. But instead of blowing up a tank, he can eliminate a village. Or a couple of regiments. With one shell. Which ain't bad.

The missile comes in two parts. There's the W79 itself — that's the small nuclear warhead — and there's its carrier, the AFAP (Artillery Fired Atom Projectile), which allows you to fire it from a gun. Now, as with any weapon having this kind of massive strike power, you don't want to get too close to your target. You wouldn't want to pull the trigger singing "We'll All Go Together When We Go". So it's comforting to know that this baby has a range of eighteen miles, which is far enough away to let you sit back and watch the show. See the mushroom grow. Wait to hear the bang. Maybe.

It's accurate too.

Picture the scene. You're a small country in an insignificant corner of the world, fighting a long expensive war against an enemy that's bigger and stronger and gradually wearing you down. You kill their soldiers, and they kill yours. But every hundred killed on each side leaves your country that much weaker than it leaves theirs. Time crawls on.

The money in the exchequer falls as the number of bereaved

families rises. Your citizens are angry with defeat. Your enemy consolidates his gains. Your allies look the other way. What you need now is a shot in the arm, something to turn the tide. You need something that can blast your enemy off your soil. Something to blow them away.

You know what I mean?

Victor and me, we come from a country that's waited long enough. Our fair country has been trampled into the ground. It lies on its belly with its mouth full of sand, while the horde of alien soldiers grind it, rape it and bugger it deeper in the dirt. Either we give in to the pain and desolation, or we wait for a lull between one thug rolling off us and the next slumping on, and we pull ourself round to face him and grab him by the balls.

I place my hands on the rough wooden crate of nuclear W79s and heave it up waist high. Victor lifts the top crate of AFAPs. "This will do nicely," I say.

Jesus, when you think how this stuff flies through the air you'd never believe how heavy it lies on the ground. We make it back to the ventilator shaft in one go, but by the time we get there I can feel every inch of the tendon that starts in my wrists and stretches like shrinking cord round a rusty pulley in my elbow, up again through aching biceps into protesting anchors at my shoulders. Another two cables of pain stab down my back. My stomach is knotted and my hands are losing their grip.

We clunk the boxes down on the concrete floor, and stare wild-eyed like we just had a goal scored against us in injury time. The boxes are too heavy to just hand up through the hatch, so Victor nips back up the hanging rope to stand inside the grille. I truss the box of AFAPs securely, leave it on the floor below the hatch, then follow him up the rope. Together we haul the dead weight through. It lurches up through the trap like a drunk reeling home. "There has to be an easier way," I say, but we can't think of it. I drop back to the floor and make another parcel from the crate of W79s. I know it's a box of dinky nuclear warheads, but it could be a box of gravel for all I care. I maul it about like I was working part-time at the abattoir. Then it's up the rope again, into the dark hatch.

Hauling a dead weight up ten feet through a small hatchway may sound like child's play to you, but let me tell you it is agony. You get the crate half-way up, suspended in the air, and every muscle is straining so hard you think they want to burst out through your skin. But we force it through the hole onto the safety of the black metal grille.

Then I lower the iron trap and we're able to rest. "Take five," pants Victor, and we do. We sit on the metal platform with the two boxes before us. Through the square hole of the grille we can see the tunnel's concrete floor. Above stretches the black hole of the ventilator shaft. The extractor fan blades stand motionless, and the blackness disappears behind.

In our secret hideaway above the army's tunnel we sit without a word: Victor and me, a box of W79s, and a case of AFAPs to carry them on their way. Outside of the sound of our breathing the peace reassembles, trying to convince us that nothing has changed. The tunnel looks the same. Neat stacks of weaponry stand quietly by the walls.

I reckon you could have timed exactly three hundred seconds on your stopwatch while we rest. Then without a word Victor stands up and grips the iron ladder dangling down the shaft. Methodically he begins his climb, while I sit on the grille watching him disappear into the darkness. I am left alone on the hard platform with just the rope quivering at my feet.

The AFAPs have been winched up the shaft, the W79s are repeating their journey, and I'm wondering who has the easiest job: Victor on the pulley or me on the platform. The W79s have faded into the blackness. I picture Victor perched on top of the fake tower in the starlight, hauling on the block and tackle. I wonder if it's raining.

Suddenly I hear voices and the sound of studded boots crunching on the concrete floor below. I squat very still on the perforated platform. My view is restricted. I hear the soldiers long before I see them. As they come into view beneath me, one is boasting to the other of the girl he pulled last night. The other guy is sceptical: "But what's she doing *tonight*? This is Saturday — right?"

"So?"

"You know what these birds are like on Saturdays. They do it with anyone."

"Not after what I gave her last night."

"She fancies soldiers, does she?"

"Not specially. She just fancied me."

"Anything in khaki. She'll be on her back this minute."

"Will she fuck."

"Too right she will."

"Get stuffed."

"Wish I could."

They mooch along beneath me, towards where we stole the W79s. I try to remember any reason why they should give it a glance. Then there's a sudden clatter, like the first coin in a blind man's bucket, and a small clod of dirt drops onto the grille beside me. I don't move a muscle. The soldiers don't seem to have heard. They are still talking about Wiltshire girls. I wonder how young soldiers like spending Saturday night a hundred feet underground. I wonder how they really make out with Wiltshire girls.

Their voices fade into the distance along the tunnel. Then there's a movement beside me as the end of the rope snakes back onto the platform. I grab hold, and flick a whip-curve back to the top. Victor stops letting out the length, and the long nylon cord hangs trembling in the darkness. I get to my feet.

I climb the five metres through the motionless fan blades, onto the small observation platform above. I coil the dangling end of rope into a knotted tangle, so nothing extends beneath the blades. Then I press the red button.

The whole shaft seems to flinch as the huge fan shakes into motion, circulating two or three times slowly, gathering speed, then settling into a steady whirr. Stale air from the tunnel wafts past my face. I pull twice on the rope, stand on the bottom rung of the iron ladder, then begin to climb up towards fresh air.

It takes two treks to get the stuff down the hillside. The boxes alone force two journeys, since there's no way we can each fight our way through the brambles in the dark, staggering under the dead weight of those loaded crates. So we take each journey with

189

one crate between us, carrying the ropes and climbing tackle in our outside hands. By the time we finish our second journey I never want to see another wood by moonlight. I would be content to stay in concrete Deptford the rest of my days. But, piling the booty into the back of the van, I know I won't see Deptford ever again. Victor and I are back to the rootless travelling. I could be inhaling English night-time air for the last time in my life. When I slump into the passenger seat of the van I feel a familiar kind of loss.

The engine fires, and Victor reverses across night-cold grass in a slow arc. I look up into the wooded hillock and imagine I can see the chessboard castle deceptive on the top. I think back to the moment on the parapet when we closed the outside grille into place, when I sat above the hundred metre shaft and imagined dropping the stun grenade I'd stolen back down the chute, to explode among the racks and boxes in the silent miles of corridors. Suppose I'd taken a hand grenade: could that one small bomb set off all the others lurking there below?

If it did, and several more went off with a bigger bang, the chain reaction would zip along the miles of volatile corridors till half of southern England erupted in the greatest firework show since the volcanic island of Krakatoa exploded in 1883. Soot from that explosion fell all over the world — even on the pleasant fields of faraway England. Its dust-clouds dimmed the sun and plunged the southern hemisphere into unbroken night for three long days. The blast was felt over three thousand miles away, in Hiroshima. Thirty thousand people died. It happened less than six hundred miles off Australia, yet the world forgot within a few short years.

We could live without you too, England.

19

"You're brooding, darling."

We are driving back through the night on the empty motorway. I hesitate a touch too long before saying I'm just tired. "I know you better than that," he says. "You're thinking about Rachel."

"I'm just watching the road."

"Will you miss her?"

"I miss them all."

He has started me thinking now. He has brought her back to my thoughts. She will be sleeping in the Earls Court boarding house, lonely and cold in an unfriendly hotel. She'll have gone to sleep crying, wondering where the hell I am.

I hope no one who saw us there will recognize my face from the scratchy TV photo. I don't want anyone asking her about me: she has enough questions of her own. I feel a sudden need to hold her close against me. Knowing I've left her causes me to stare desolate through the windscreen into the night. Weariness seeps into my bones. It isn't the late hour, it's the old hunter yearning for a place to settle down.

Victor is talking again. He probably wants to keep himself awake. He has forgotten Rachel, and is reviewing our project and the time we have spent in England. "I believe we did it just in time. These last few days, they've been closing in."

"The police? Or their secret service?"

"Some kind of administrators. Counter-espionage, slowly piecing things together, working through odd loose ends. We've been here too long. The Big Man did us no favours."

"We kept our heads down."

"Until the end. But think of Timmy: he stuck his above the wall, and someone saw him."

"Who?"

"You know the British, darling. They have M15, M16, MOD police, the anti-terrorist Branch, SAS — so many separate units they spend more time fighting each other than chasing us. Always assuming it *was* the British, of course."

"Who else?"

"Somebody else after W79s. We're not the only ones, you know."

"I suppose not."

"No, we're small fry, really. We're just lucky to have made the contact. Clever Timmy. There are others who'd give a small fortune for what we have in the back."

"Yeah. So would the British."

"Far too mean, darling. No, there are others. We could be talking very big money — enough to retire from all this. Other side of the world, new identity . . . it's a thought."

"I didn't do this for money."

"Of course not, darling. Who did? But don't you ever get tired — slogging away in a war that will never end?"

"We all get tired."

"No place to call home? Always at their beck and call?"

"I was settling in nicely here. I liked it in Deptford, strange as it sounds."

"But we can't put roots down. They won't let us retire."

"Too much to do."

"The war is unending."

The old litany. Tired phrases, regurgitated like childhood verses — words stumbling half-awake off the tongue, like the cursory prayers of a lapsed priest. Some day we'll give it all up. Some day we'll live a decent life. Some day.

We drive on in silence. Deptford, Jancey, my flat, Rachel: already they're memories blurred in the dark, part of the night, part of last night when I began to confess. Rachel — she must have had something. It was the first time I ever cracked, to anyone. I've stayed clean as a whistle all my time in England. Clean in Germany, clean everywhere. A clean civilian, easily identified: ordinary, a bit sharp, half streetwise, one of the crowd. She must have had something, to make me open up like that. I didn't say a lot. But even so.

192

Four in the morning, of course. The worst time. And straight after the dream: the dark cupboard, my mother, my poor sister, the lizard. Yeah, the worst time. Rachel held the key to the secret cabinet — woman's strongest weapon since Delilah, since Eve: soft feminine concern. Soothe the brow. Hug to her bosom. Blow warm whispers gently in your ear: "Talk to me. Tell me. Let it all out."

I nearly did.

I've had months of boredom, wearing me down. Suddenly I find another mob is onto us. Timmy is killed for Casey. Casey dies for Deptford. Deptford explodes — Christ, what's been happening? What did I do to deserve this? No wonder Rachel found me a soft touch.

Well, it's all behind me now. No more of that. All we have to do is get this stuff out of here, and get out ourselves. It's time to forget the clean civilian, lost in the crowd. It's time to be travelling again.

Seven o'clock on a Sunday morning, and the Elephant is nearly as quiet as the Wiltshire fields. We stop the van at the end of Victor's street and I ask how long he needs to pick up his things. He says about an hour. "Come in for some coffee," he says. "I'll be as quick as I can."

"Why hurry? The pick-up's not till eleven."

"So there's plenty of time. Come and have some coffee. It'll keep you awake."

"I got something to do."

He turns to face me in the cab, his elbow leaning on the steering wheel. "What have you got to do?"

"I want to say goodbye."

He just looks at me. His voice is tired. "It's too dangerous. You're a wanted man. They show your face on the television news."

"I'll be careful."

"We can't risk this."

"It's my life."

His breath as he slowly exhales forms a cloud of mist on the windscreen. "You can't go charging around London with a crate of W79s rattling around in the back of a van."

"Who would be interested?"

For a few cold seconds he looks me in the eyes, reading the stubbornness that lies behind. Then he shrugs, turns away, and opens the van door. "As you say, it's your life." He gets out, shuts the door quietly, then raises one arm half-way in a gesture of tired dismissal as he walks away.

I slide across to his still-warm seat and chuckle to myself. He'd make a great mother. When I start up the engine I see him reach into his jacket for a small cigar. On the journey back he kept the cabin clean, but now he's out in the fresh air he needs something to take away the taste. I watch him in my mirror as I pull away. He lights up as he's walking, and tosses the match in an arc as he crosses the street.

This is the first time I've sat behind a steering wheel for several weeks. I coax the gears through their channels, and use the mirror as often as a teenage girl before a new date. Which is why I notice the green Sierra.

It's hanging back, fifty yards behind me. It's an insignificant car, and is not drawing attention to itself. Maybe I wouldn't give it a second thought, if it wasn't seven o'clock on a Sunday morning. I mooch down Borough High Street at forty miles an hour. It tucks in behind. There are two guys in it.

The simplest way to check out a car behind you is to stop dead at the side of the road. What'll he do then? Either he pulls over too, and gives himself away, or he glides by and leaves you. Now, this is all very well if you're checking out some car that's following you to see where you go, and it doesn't want you to know it. But if that car is following you because someone in there wants to get his hands on you, then you gotta have balls. Because if he does stop, the chips are down. He ain't gonna park a polite distance behind. He's gonna park across your front. Then either you produce a shooter and use it through the window, or you accelerate away in reverse. And what do you think he'll be doing all this time? Like I say, you gotta have balls.

I could head down the side streets, but the alleys off here are narrow and winding and half of them don't go nowhere. You could speed round two corners and find yourself facing a row of bollards. You'd look in your mirror and see him cruising up behind.

So I'm safer on the main road. I'd be better on my own patch, in Deptford. But it's too far away. When I turn back along Union Street we're still the only two cars on the road. Just empty dirty Union Street, a Sierra and my van.

I drift nice and easy, because he just might be coming home from a late-night party, waiting to overtake and get along home. But he doesn't.

I'm coming back due west along The Cut. The lights are with us at the Old Vic corner, and we both cruise across Waterloo Road like we were old friends. As we drift into Lower Marsh I slip into second, hit the accelerator and turn sharp right into the yard behind Waterloo station. I wouldn't exactly say the van spurts forward, but it does try its best. I roar up the concrete ramp, scream round the hundred and eighty degree curve, and hurtle into the huddle of black taxis sleeping peacefully on the upper level. The ramp has such high walls I don't know if the Sierra is still behind me. I weave swiftly through the taxis, and keep my foot down while I disappear into the tangle of cut-throughs and linkways cluttering up the front of the station.

Three months after I arrived in this country I took a night-time job mini-cabbing. No one asked questions, I needed fast money, and it was the right kind of job to meet the wrong sort of people. Most of the drivers were desperate, one way or another. Maybe they'd been in jail and now couldn't get work. Maybe they were moonlighting on a day-time job. Maybe they just needed the money. Anyway, among other things, it gave me a grounding in the intricate geography of back-street London. I came through this bird's nest round Waterloo station several times each shift, so by the time I now emerge and slip into Sandell Street opposite, I am not surprised to find I do not have a green Sierra on my tail.

I head on towards Bermondsey singing some kind of shanty under my breath. This ain't a happy occasion because I've come to say goodbye, but I'm pleased as Punch that I've shaken off that car. Assuming of course that it was following me. When I think about it, it hardly seems likely. When I think about it, it couldn't have been. So I don't think about it.

Even so, when I arrive in Bermondsey I slip off the main road, slide round a quiet block, and bring the van to a halt in the shadow of an unlit alley. I turn off the engine, and sit listening to the quiet.

Silence is relative in London. Dawn was an hour ago, and erratic flurries of Sunday morning traffic raise dust in the streets. A bus trundles by with four passengers lit up in orange inside. They all wear overcoats. When the bus has gone, it leaves the square empty and quiet again. The square is built for the weekday bustle. Now it's like a pub when the last customer's gone home.

I watch all this through the windscreen for about twenty minutes before a car stops across the square, lets three people out, and moves on. They stand chatting on the pavement. After two more minutes another car arrives. It sets down two women dressed in heavy wool suits, and two little girls wearing Sunday best. They are still saying hello when an old couple come walking round one corner at the same time a dapper guy in his mid-twenties and a crisp blue suit pops round the other. They all start shaking hands and clapping each other on the arm, as another big car pulls up and spoils my view.

By the time another two minutes has slipped away the pavement is swarming with black churchgoers. Kids have started chasing each other up and down the steps. Someone opens the wooden door in the gaunt brick frontage, but everyone stays out front greeting each other and laughing, more like they'd just flowed out from a wedding than they were waiting to go inside. Then the preacher appears in the doorway, and I expect him to clap his hands and get some order, but he is grabbed by two huge matrons and bundled down the steps. He stands in a swarm of brightly-coloured woollen suits and huge white dresses like he was Jesus handing fish sandwiches to the crowd.

I slide out of the van and slip quietly round two sides of the square, staying unobtrusive on the pavement by the wall. For half a minute I wait just off the edge of the crowd, trying to catch her eye. But of course it's the brighter eyes of little Darius that spy me first. He starts to run toward me, but remembers his dignity, and saunters the last few paces like he had nowhere particular to go. "How are things, man?" he asks me. "You OK?"

"Sure. What's new?"

"Well. The place is still buzzing some. Police getting their nerve back. Journalists and photographers show up now and then, if they nothing else to do. You know."

"Deptford is still news, right?"

"Not for much longer, I reckon. Tomorrow morning you see big notices in shop windows: Positively Last Day — Last Chance — Tomorrow Back To Normal."

I grin at him, and he adds, "They still looking for you, though. Still in your flat. Real drag having the filth next door, man."

"I'm sorry, Darius. I really am."

I sense Jancey arrive before she speaks, and I look up with the beginning of a smile. But she is bearing down on me like an angry mother. She seems to grow in size like either she's attacking me or she's sheltering me from view. "What you doing here, man, are you mad or what? What you thinking — you invisible now?"

I try something disarming, but it's strangled at birth.

"You is the most dumb-headed man I heard of. What they give you instead of a brain? Did someone take out your old one and fill your head with mango? Don't you know they all looking for you? That filth is crawling all over Deptford. They been in my bedroom twice."

"That's more than I ever was."

"Don't you talk smart-face with me. You just a liability — an idiot. You get mixed up with bad people, you turn up with some fancy woman, you saunter into here like you just anyone, you — "

She has a tear in her eye and her voice is breaking. Darius is pulling at her jacket and people nearby are turning round to see. I step forward and hug her quivering, resisting body, and I

197

use my thumb to dry beneath her eye. "Hush now, Jancey, everything you say is true. But I've come here to say goodbye." I let the words sink in.

She throws back her head and sniffs, but she doesn't step out of my arms. Blinking, she asks, "Where you going?"

"I can't tell you that, can I? I just have to get out, but I had to see you once more first. That's why I'm here."

Darius interrupts: "Why you don't take us with you?"

He is glaring up at me with such concentration that his normal instinct doesn't save him. He gets a thunderous cuff round the head from Jancey as she tells him, "You mind your sweet business, you child you." Then she spins back to face me and finds herself speechless, and I smile sorta helpless without meeting her gaze, and I kiss her gently and say, "Goodbye, Jancey. Remember me kindly." Then I let go of her arms, and pause another painful moment before turning away.

Darius plants himself in front of me. I shake my head. "You know I can't stay. You look after your mother, and —" I don't know what to say. I push past him, and he lets me go.

"I know you didn't do those things!" he calls after me. But I don't reply. He wants to think me some kind of hero, and I ain't the kind of real hero that would tell him I'm a rotten example, and he's got to grow up straight.

I walk back across the square feeling that everybody's eyes are following me, and when I turn at the van I see that I'm right. Most of these people will know who I am — hell, I recognize them, and they ain't been on television — but none of these people are gonna give me away.

Maybe this is because they give no one away to the enemy. Or maybe it's because they know I've come to say goodbye, and they respect Jancey too much to interfere with that. Or maybe they've just got some kind of instinctive decent morality that a loner like me will never understand. Something to do with community and loyalty. Something I lost when my home burnt down. I don't know. Thinking and philosophizing is not what I'm paid for.

I start up the van and drive into the square, go round two sides, and slip out an exit. The whole scene is like a stage tableau, all the people and the church are just cardboard cut-outs, and my old hired van is the only moving piece.

20

I am driving on autopilot, hardly aware of the streets I'm passing through. So it's not surprising I don't use the mirror. And I can't tell how long it is that the green Sierra has been sitting on my tail.

It's the same car. Half an hour has passed, and there are more cars on the street now. One green Sierra could go unnoticed. But not to me. So where has he come from? Did he track me to the square, or was he hanging around the area and got lucky? Anyway, he's there now — snug in the centre of my rear-view mirror. The same two guys looking squarely to the front.

I point the van towards Deptford, and wonder how I'm gonna shake them off. There's no doubt this time: two pros in a fast car, against me in a van. I wonder if they know what I've got in the back. I wonder if they fancy a tyre-busting car chase, with just three yards between them and a rattling crate of nuclear warheads. Wake up London, it's your early call.

I cruise up Jamaica Road towards the Rotherhithe tunnel, then put my foot down. We cling together for half a mile. At the tunnel entrance, Jamaica Road's dual carriageway ends at a big roundabout. You can go down the tunnel or turn right to Deptford. I glide straight round the roundabout and accelerate away, back down the other side of Jamaica Road the way I came.

The Sierra does the same.

As I hammer down the empty tarmac away from Rotherhithe, my mind is working faster than the van. I've got two heavies in a fast Sierra, and I'm in a hired heap that will need all the miles from here to Catford to reach top speed. Even if I take to the back streets I won't be exactly nippy round the corners. They'll sit snug on my tail. At some quiet spot, maybe beneath dark railway arches, the guy driving the Sierra will push his accelerator and come alongside.

He'll leave me for dead, as the saying goes.

Jamaica Road doesn't last forever, and the next thing you know I've cut round on myself and we're roaring back up the other side heading for Rotherhithe again. We can't keep this up all morning. But I don't fancy dropping down the tunnel. What I need on this big safe main road is the right kind of vehicle to create some kind of diversion. Something to even the odds between a Sierra and a van.

But it's as empty as a graveyard.

I slew back round the Rotherhithe roundabout and take the right, headed for Deptford. Jamming my foot flat on the floor is a waste of time. Any speed I could force out of this rattling van the Sierra could cruise in second gear. So I motor steadily down Lower Road keeping my eyes peeled. The Sierra sits behind. The two heavies stare out, and their faces look bored. They could have been hired from Tussauds.

Since no one's pulled a gun, and they haven't tried to pass me, I guess they're either waiting for friends or they're hoping to wear me down. All they gotta do is let me run out of fuel or do something stupid, or wait to meet their friends.

Well, I got plenty of fuel, and I wouldn't like their friends, so that only leaves something stupid. Which you may have gathered by now is something that normally I find easy, except that just now I'm out of ideas.

But if I keep driving long enough, something's gotta happen. I mean, you can't play poker all night without getting at least one crooked flush.

And what did I tell you?

Where the brass god of sinners fished this one out of I don't know. But there in the middle of Evelyn Street ahead of me, all alone and damn near empty, is a great big warm red trembling trundling, sensuously swaying London double-decker bus. A Sunday bus, for Christ's sake, an almost extinct species. Picking its way through the litter like a fastidious Victorian spinster lifting the hem of her skirts in the slums. Baby, I love you!

I pull out to overtake her, then slow to hold my position steady alongside, like I ran out of puff. The Sierra waits hard behind. The bus driver is giving me an earful, but I ain't listening. I'm watching the road ahead.

I see a nice little alley coming up on the left and I ease slightly ahead. There's no gap between the bus and my tail. Then I drop into third, command the brass god of sinners to stay with me, and I ram my right foot to the floor.

The van tries. It ain't acceleration, but compared to the bus it's enough. We surge a full five miles an hour faster, we pull across the bus's bow, and we slide cockeyed and tilting, bump across the corner of the pavement, and slither into the lane. I hear rusty brakes screeching, screams of furious horror as the poor shocked bus jolts its few passengers back to the land of bad dreams.

But the green Sierra couldn't follow me round. He'll have accelerated past the bus in the outside lane, seen where I've gone, braked, waited till the bus crawled past inside, then reversed back to get down my alley.

By which time I've disappeared. I mean, this is Deptford, almost. These alleys are home. I could slew round a couple more corners, get back onto Evelyn Street, nip across, and disappear back towards Bermondsey in the small side roads. He'd never catch me. Unless he was lucky. Or unless he just waited on Evelyn Street.

But I vanish up a narrow cutting, kill the engine and lights, and I wait in the gloom. I can hear the Sierra snarling and lurching as it checks at each corner to see where I've gone. They'll expect me to cut back to the main road. They should slip back there to wait. That's what I would have done. But they decide to be thorough. They'll do every corner.

Gears crashing at the top of my cutting tell me they've spotted the van. They reverse a couple of yards to get room to turn, and they glide in behind.

As they jump out of the car they realize their mistake. They've each pulled a shooter, but in the glare from their own headlights they see I'm not in the van. Or maybe they don't. Maybe they can't see round to the front. Because they fade to a wall either side of the van and they inch forward. Their guns are up on a level with their chins. If a cat scratches, they'll blast it into Kattomeat.

But I'm back behind them, pressed into a dark doorway, with my little Smith & Wesson rising up into the light. I take the difficult target first — the suit half hidden on the far side of the van. When I squeeze the trigger the blast crashes off the alley walls and he slumps against the brickwork. My second shot thumps into the other guy's back. He falls like a carcase from a Smithfield meat lorry, with reverberations of gunfire rolling like surf on the shore. How long do they linger in a dead man's ear?

I have to step over his body to get back to the van. As I open the door I hear someone push up a window and call out. I switch the van on, crunch into first gear and stagger away. At the next corner I automatically check the mirror. The Sierra stands with both lights blazing. A crumpled heap lies at the foot of each wall.

21

By the time I've got across the river and through the grey City I'm as bleak as the river in the Sunday morning light. The green Sierra first picked me up just after I left Victor. So they were waiting. So someone else would have been waiting for Victor. He won't have had a chance. They either shot him down or took him away.

I've been saying it for days. We stayed in this damn country too long. Last week we were anonymous. These last few days they've all been closing in.

Maybe they've been crawling gradually nearer for months. Maybe they had us under surveillance all along — even since we landed. But it was Timmy. Either he got too confident or his mole got too careless, and counter-espionage closed like a trap. Now they're cleaning us up like a Hoover gobbling fluff.

Knowing Victor is in their hands turns my stomach to cold mud. They killed Timmy in revenge for Casey. So now I've dropped two more Caseys what'll they do? You read books about this game that say it's like playing chess: cunning, cautious, carefully thought out. Yeah, that's the fiction. In real life it's vicious and immediate. I kill one of theirs, so they do one of mine. I shoot two more, so they kill Victor. On the scoreboard, I'm one ahead. Some chess.

Victor always said I had the wrong kind of brain for chess. I never stop and think. I just slide a couple of pawns out the way and send the big guns charging up the field. The only fun in the game is to get your queen and her knights behind enemy lines, lashing out in all directions. I can imagine those knights rearing up on their horses among lines of tents, tearing down the canvas with their hooves. Frightened soldiers running everywhere, noise and confusion — and right in the middle, the most fearsome warrior they've seen mows them down like drowsy flies.

Victor says that isn't the point.

*

I use the *A to Z* for the last two hundred yards, and approach the house obliquely, without driving past in front. In a quiet suburban side road across the way I park the van and sit with the engine off, for the first time looking at the place with the Woodside Park phone number.

It's quiet enough. A plain brick house in a dusty old garden, partly shaded by sad mature trees. You wouldn't give it a second glance. There are thousands like it: three bedrooms and bathroom upstairs, two other rooms and a kitchen below. Maybe a small cellar. Maybe a loft conversion or kitchen extension. Individuality expressed through the shape of the lawn, or colour of the garage door.

I suppose this is the place. It looks as sinister as a tub of butter, but I have to act on what I have. Two hours have passed since I dropped Victor and saw him walk away in Elephant and Castle. So about two hours ago they got him. Either they killed him there and then, in which case nothing I do will make any difference, or they have kept him alive for questioning. They won't have done that in his Elephant flat.

Maybe — though I doubt it — they are pukka police and they rolled him into a local nick. Or maybe they took him somewhere quiet. The only place I know is here.

On the credit side: this is where they own a phone, it could be the only place they've got, and it's somewhere I'm not supposed to know. On the debit side: what am I going to do about it?

I switch on the engine and engage reverse gear. One thing I do know is that if they're bringing Victor here they'll have done so already. I hung around Bermondsey, and then trundled up here in a van. They should be well under way by now.

As I negotiate my way round the side streets in a kind of wide half circle I am worried by the lack of any sign of life round the front of the house. I hope I ain't setting up an elaborate mistake.

The trouble with the *A to Z* is the scale ain't big enough to show you how to get into people's back gardens. It just marks the streets, and leaves you to sort the detail for yourself.

But I park the van again in a crescent of newer houses, and stroll about looking for a convenient footpath round the back. There's nothing. But the house next door also shows no sign of life. The bottom of its garden touches a piece of scrub between the crescent and the main road. I have to hang about till I get a chance to hop between an overgrown privet hedge and the remains of some fencing into the garden. A few yards up is an old shed, and I nip up to stand behind it while I think what to do next.

The garden seems fairly secluded. Being the end house it's hardly overlooked. It's untidy, and the fences are high. For a while I peer out from behind the shed making sure no one is moving inside the end house, and no one can see me from anywhere else.

Anyone looking out of a back window would see me if I moved. From next door — which is where I want to get to — they could see me only if they were watching from upstairs. All the other houses are too far away. Most of the crescent is lost behind trees.

Standing there behind the shed I can hear Sunday morning sounds from around the neighbourhood. Someone is banging nails in, a mother is yelling, and a distant car engine seems to have gone on test. Up the road, men are digging their gardens. Somewhere or other, bacon is frying. A faint drizzle is starting. It'll keep them indoors.

I'm satisfied no one is at home in this end house. It could have been empty a while. Next door looks much the same. Nothing moved at the front, and now I can see the upstairs back, nothing is moving there either. None of the curtains are closed. So if they do have Victor in there, they are not in any room at the front — which is not surprising — but they are also not anywhere upstairs. Which leaves the downstairs back — the dining room, I guess, or maybe the cellar. But in these houses, if they do have a cellar it's usually small: fine for a dungeon, but too cramped for interrogation.

The house does have a garage, of course. But garages tend to be more flimsy — the sound carries. Out of a poor bunch, it begins to look like it's gonna be the cellar.

I drift carefully up this end garden, keeping close to the inside fence so no one can see me from next door. When I get near the houses I pass a section of open fencework, and I take a peek through.

There's a light in the kitchen.

I continue up to a converted coal-house, and stand there concealed while I take stock. The house in this garden looks temporarily unoccupied. The place next door is not. There is someone downstairs.

Conventional methods work best, I find. So I shin up onto the coal-house, and across onto the roof of the heavy mob's garage. From here I may be able to enter the house by the recommended route — the upstairs back-bedroom window. Straight out of the field manual. When anyone guards a house from indoors, this is the point they usually leave unprotected. They mount a strong guard on the front, and maybe put one guy on the back, downstairs. So upstairs back is where you want to come in. It places you on high ground with surprise on your side. The first they know of being under attack is when you're inside the house, clearing out the first floor. Then you take a position at the head of the stairs, and they are pinned in the downstairs rooms: they step out and you shoot them. When you're ready, you can slip down those stairs and sweep a room at a time.

I crouch on their garage roof and squint up at the nearest window. They are seldom easy, and this one is no exception. It'll be a stretch, without a ladder.

Before making my next move I lean over and look down into the kitchen to see what I'm dropping into. In the back of my mind remains the suspicion that I've picked an innocent house, that the Big Man screwed up his telephone-number research. I have to snatch several quick glances to see anything worthwhile, because the angle from on top of this garage is not ideal. The first time I see nothing inside at all. Next time someone walks across. Then I gaze at a man's back. Then I inch to the rear of the garage roof to get a better view. I have sweat in my skin creases. I feel as exposed up here in daylight as a butterfly on a pin.

I keep watching the upstairs windows. The curtains are open and nothing is moving. Downstairs stays quiet, and the only action is in that kitchen. I've seen men, but no women, no kids. It ain't a family breakfast. Then a guy who's been leaning against the kitchen sink blocking half the view, moves. I see inside the room. They've got Victor.

I snap back out of sight and plan my next move. According to what I remember from the field manual I should now enter through that upstairs back-bedroom window. I would, if I was ten feet tall. But I'm not. I need a ladder to bridge the gap. And there is no one up there anyway. The whole shooting party is in the same room.

Where the garage meets the side of the house is an iron drainpipe. It's rusty, but it looks strong enough to help me down. I check one last time that nothing's rattling in my pockets, and I drop over the edge. I hit the concrete path with no more noise than an acorn falling from a tree.

Flattened against their back wall, I edge towards the kitchen window. When I get there I pause to listen to what they're saying inside. I pull the pistol out of my pocket and ease the safety catch off. From inside my jacket I take that useful little toy I picked up last night a hundred feet underground, and I prime it for use.

I count to two, and lash out with my left arm. The pistol smashes the window, and through the jagged hole I toss the stun grenade. I whip back, and flatten against the outside wall. There's a shout, another, and a bang that is deafening. Instantly I spin back and aim through the window.

Reeling among broken crockery and overturned chairs are four men — one of them Victor. In the few seconds I have before their senses return, I pull the trigger three times. Then I open the shattered window and call Victor's name. He is groping on the floor, and I call again: "Hurry, Victor, it's me. We got to get out of here."

He looks drunk as he staggers to the window. I stow the gun and haul him through. He's in a terrible state: bemused, disorientated, shocked. His eyes are staring and his breath rasps, as if he'd just been saved from drowning. Somehow I heave him through the gap, pull him to his feet, and try to make him run with me, away from the house.

208

Now I can hear voices calling from nearby houses. I ignore them, and stagger with Victor till we reach the section of open fencework. We crash it down, and totter the length of the overgrown garden to where I came in.

When we emerge in the crescent you'd think Victor was blind and delirious. Some guy in a cardigan appears in front of me, blocking my way, asking what happened. I push him aside. There's no time for glib lines — let them think what they like. Maybe they'll think I'm helping a victim. Maybe they'll think they should stop me. Whatever they think I know they'll do nothing.

We get in the van and I drive it away.

By the time I pull into a small deserted industrial estate, Victor has recovered. He doesn't say a lot. I drive behind a warehouse where it's quiet, switch off, and turn to face him. "So what happened?"

He shrugs. "When I got to my flat they were waiting."

"And?"

"They surprised me, they took me to their place, they started questioning."

"What did you tell them?"

"Nothing. I tried to work out what they knew, and played for time. They beat me about a bit."

I consider this. "How come they didn't kill you?"

"I hadn't told them anything. They were waiting."

"How come you weren't tied up or anything?"

"I don't know. Perhaps they felt there was no need. They had guns: there was nothing I could do."

"Victor," I say, as I let him see the pistol I'm holding, "I was listening outside the window."

He registers the pistol, but does not react. "And what did you hear?"

"You were all pretty friendly."

He nods slowly. "Yes, they were very polite."

I ask him gently to tell me why he was working for them. He gives me his impassive look, he blinks a few times, and he frowns like he didn't quite hear.

"When did you switch?" I ask him. "In the last few days, or before we even landed? Have you been with them all along?"

He sighs. "We're all fighting the same war, darling. It's a different political party, that's all. The aims are the same."

"Everyone's aims are the same. The difference is who you kill to achieve them. They killed Timmy, for example."

"They were trying to convert him. He only died because you killed Casey. It was unnecessary."

"Yeah. He was a good friend — remember?"

"I was upset too, darling. How about you and I? We've been good friends."

I smile sadly, and shake my head. "You already betrayed me, Victor. When Casey came to kill me, it was because you told them where I lived."

"They've known where you live for months. Casey didn't come to kill you. He and Patterson came to bring you over."

"Like hell."

"It's true. They expected to have to lean on you, but they thought you could be swung. We're only mercenaries, after all — that's what they thought. I told them it was hopeless."

"What else did you tell them, Victor — he's too stupid to recognize the opportunity? He's too dumb to spot the winning side?"

"I said you were too loyal, darling, too committed. They were wasting their time." His eyes have the wet look of a faithful puppy. You could believe he means this stuff.

"Yeah, so what was the plan? I lead you to the stockpile, we lift the weapons, then your friends intercept and . . . I get a bullet for thanks."

"Not the last bit. Once we had the W79s I thought I might be able to convince you — I would lay it on the line, as they say."

"But you needed me to take you there?"

"You were the only one who knew."

"Timmy knew."

He doesn't reply at first. We both know now that Timmy never told. He stayed stumm till he died. He left his secret to me.

Victor starts speaking again, quietly, without emphasis. "The cause is still the same: the same enemy, the same mission. The precise shade of political party is different — so what? They are still our countrymen. The name of the regiment doesn't matter. It's of no more importance to the real fight than the colour of a general's hat."

"It's the colour of his hat that shows whose side he's on."

For maybe ten seconds neither of us says anything. Then, still in that low flat voice, he asks, "What happens now? Are you going to use that gun?"

I hear myself reply like I was listening to a tape. "You betrayed the cause. You betrayed Timmy. Once I'd led you to the weapons, you betrayed me. You left me to be killed by your new friends. You couldn't do it yourself."

He looks tired, and he speaks bitterly. "Why should we need to kill you? And you must surely know by now that I would never let anything happen to you?"

"Crap, Victor, you're playing for time."

"It's the truth, darling."

He gives a small resigned shrug and looks me straight in the eye. Any moment now he's gonna remind me what comrades we've been, he's gonna tell me I'm the only real friend he has, he's gonna ask me to let him live. And because he knows me so well, what he can see in my face is that those are exactly the reasons I came to Woodside Park; that when I crept up to the back of that house I was either gonna bring him out or die in the attempt; but that when I smashed the glass with my gun I knew I was completely alone.

I know he reads this in my eyes. We've known each other a long time. He flashes the disarming smile I know is so dangerous and I tense, watching to see what he'll do. When his hand drops softly to his pocket I am like a rabbit before a snake, mesmerized by the smooth movement. My fingers are rigid round the gun. I won't be able to pull the trigger. He cocks an eyebrow as his hand disappears and he smiles, and the whiteness of his hand reappears from his pocket and he bends an elbow, lifts his arm, and I see something glint and I fire — once — jerking my gun. In the crash of the shot he flinches back, and thumps against the van door. Then he crumples, blinking at me. His hand twitches open, and a pack of cheap cigars tumbles into his lap. He shows his

211

brown teeth in one last grimace — or maybe it's a smile — and I stare at the dark stain spreading across his chest, and when I glance up at his face I see his eyes are dead.

22

I drive through the empty City of London like a zombie in a trance. The streets fade by without meaning. Twice I find myself sitting at traffic lights on green, and I don't know how long I've been there. Once I hang onto the tail of some car and follow unthinking like a dog for several streets, before I realize I am drifting off my route. I pull myself together, and drive with the exaggerated care of a drunk cautiously driving home.

I have left Victor in the dust and litter behind the warehouse. Maybe I should have driven his body somewhere safer. Maybe I should have kept him in the van. But I couldn't drive with him slumped there beside me. When I pulled his body out of the van I may have had some idea of stowing him in the back with the warheads, but I left him in the dirt. I tried to pretend he didn't exist.

I come east out of the City and head into the deserted remains of London's docklands. Half this place has been smartened up and turned into fancy offices for financiers, but they're all out in their suburbs on Sunday. The rest of the place is still a dump. It's as empty as a graveyard, and I'm the guy in black who drives the hearse. On the seat beside me where Victor sat, the *A to Z* lies open. The pages are beginning to curl. For these last few hundred yards of my journey the guide is vague and unhelpful, and I crawl between empty sheds and crumbling walls, trying to find my way.

But I get there. I bring the van to a halt, and stay with the engine running on the specified patch of flaking concrete. I look at the gaunt buildings, dark and empty on the cold waterfront. The only thing moving is a gull, dirty as a pigeon, scrabbling in the dust and tugging at something between its claws. My stomach jolts because I think I see the gull lift a kicking lizard from the ground and shake it in the air. But it's some piece of dead fish.

The lizard is an illusion out of my recurring dream. And I know that when I have that dream again I will see Victor's face. He will never leave me. When I stab the soldier as he defiles my dead sister he will turn towards me with Victor's anguished face.

My instructions are to wait in the van, and I sit trembling at the wheel. The throb of the idling engine echoes off the walls. Somewhere in one of these sheds the Big Man will be waiting. He will be watching the van, checking it looks OK, wondering why there's only one of us in the front.

He'll know it's me. He will know who I am. We never have met, and will do so now only because I am leaving. Otherwise we keep our lines of contact short.

And now they are very short indeed: just the two of us left in our British cell. The last two, about to meet for the first time. I look around the empty docks as expectantly as if I'd come from the lonely hearts bureau to clutch a red carnation beneath the station clock.

He gives me a good look at him. Out of an old iron door that looks like it's rusted to the wall wanders an untidy gangling man, dressed like a middle-aged hiker. His greying hair is thin and wiry. So is his body, come to that. He has the spare build of a long-distance runner, and he must measure six feet four. I watch him amble up to the van.

"*Teie olete üksi*?" he asks.

I tell him, yes. I'm alone.

"*Kus on karp*?"

"In the back."

Now that we're introduced, I switch off the engine and step down from the van. "I have some bad news," I say.

He pauses by the back doors and looks down at me. His eyes have gone cold. I tell him about Victor in one short paragraph. The narrative is so terse you could have carved it in stone. He peers at the roof of the van like he was inspecting it for dust. "No one picked you up later?"

"No. The streets are empty. Shall we unload the stuff?"

It doesn't take long. Inside the closed boat-house the Big Man opens the crates and purrs over the contents. He lifts out a rocket

214

launcher and two shells and lays them on the floor. "I'll keep one back," he says. "The rest can go on the ship."

"You thinking of using that in London?"

He grins wistfully, like I'd suggested he walk off with the ship's wages. "Oh, I don't think so. They won't ask me to do that." His smile falters. He's not so sure. Then he takes his W79 over to an old Fiat in the corner. He pulls out a blanket and uses it to wrap the gun. Then he bundles it all into the back of the car and shuts the door. "I have a nice hidey-hole. Don't worry," he says.

I'm just glad I'm heading out on a ship. The sight of him handling that weapon like it was a new electric hedge-trimmer makes me impatient to get out on the green slimy sea.

We refasten my crates and haul them over to the waterside where the dinghy is tethered. I check the inside is dry before stowing the crates away under a sheet of tarpaulin. It doesn't look much to die for, but what does?

"That's it," the Big Man says. He steps into the dinghy, making it rock in the water. "I'll take you out to the ship."

"You're not coming?"

"I'm just the ferryman. They're not onto me yet."

"You think it's safe to stay?"

"I'll keep my head down."

"That's what I said."

I look at the dinghy bobbing in the flotsam, and breathe in the familiar metallic smell of the Thames. Across the river, the shoreline of south-east London is like any urban river bank in Europe. Behind those buildings lies a place I've learnt to call home, but I can't recognize it from here. It could be anywhere. I sniff, spit in the river, and follow him into the boat. "You can't stay," I tell him. "Victor said they knew all about us."

"They only know what he told them." The Big Man pulls on a short rope, and the outboard motor jerks into life. He manoeuvres us away from the wall, out into the muddy water. "Don't worry about me," he says. "All I have to do is move to another temporary address, just in case, and they'll never find me. I'll be OK."

We're well out into the middle of the Thames, heading east

with the flow towards the sea. The river is widening, and already the land seems little more than a receding coastline. The Big Man smiles contentedly. "I have to stay here to prepare the ground for the next cell," he says. "I am the revolutionary farmer. I keep the ground fertile and nurture it. I plant seeds and water them. I watch those seeds sprout, and I help spread their roots securely in good soil."

I laugh at him, and lean back in the dinghy watching London's buildings drift away. Anyone noticing us on the river would see two men taking out their dinghy on a grey Sunday morning. They wouldn't think twice. But me, every time I hear the water lap against the side, I peer at the tarpaulin to make sure it's still dry. Those crates have cost three years of my life, biding my time in an English ghetto. But what's that, when eight men have died? I had it easy.

I glance back to the distant river banks. Nothing but buildings. Very few people. But I can hear cars, the constant background to city life. So people are there all right, away from the water, their faces fixed towards another concrete day. Me and the river are passing them by. All those teeming hidden people, intent on routine lives. When they walk in their crowded streets they look aside as they pass each other by. They think everybody must be just like them, living to the same rules. They won't accept that some of us sharing their streets live to very different rules, in alien cultures below the surface of their regular world.

Just occasionally someone lifts a stone and catches sight of us, scurrying to the safety of darkness. Just occasionally one of us bursts through into the world above. Just occasionally the ground shakes.